THE
REMNANT
BOOK 2 OF THE RARE

DIANE ANTHONY

AUTHORS 4 AUTHORS PUBLISHING
Marysville, WA, USA

Second Edition

Published by Authors 4 Authors Publishing
1214 6th St
Marysville, WA 98270
www.authors4authorspublishing.com

Library of Congress Control Number: 2020947831

E-book ISBN: 978-1-64477-142-6
Paperback ISBN: 978-1-64477-143-3
Audiobook ISBN: 978-1-64477-144-0

Edited by Rebecca Mikkelson
Copyedited by Renee Frey

Cover design ©2022 Practically Perfect Covers. All rights reserved.
Interior design by Brandi Spencer

Authors 4 Authors Publishing branding is set in Bavire. Title and headings are set in Pirulen. Author name and chapter numbers are set in Perfect Thoughts. Correspondence text is set in Segoe Print and Permanent Marker. All other text is set in Garamond.

THE
REMNANT

DIANE ANTHONY

Authors 4 Authors Content Rating

This title has been rated 17+, appropriate for older teens and adults, and contains:

- moderate language
- intense violence
- intense implied sexual violence
- negative mild illicit drug use
- discussions of mental illness, suicide, and sexual abuse
- governmental conspiracy

Please, keep the following in mind when using our rating system:

1. A content rating is not a measure of quality.

Great stories can be found for every audience. One book with many content warnings and another with none at all may be of equal depth and sophistication. Our ratings can work both ways: to avoid content or to find it.

2. Ratings are merely a tool.

For our young adult (YA) and children's titles, age ratings are generalized suggestions. For parents, our descriptive ratings can help you make informed decisions, but at the end of the day, only you know what kinds of content are appropriate for your individual child. This is why we provide details in addition to the general age rating.

For more information on our rating system, please, visit our Content Guide at: www.authors4authorspublishing.com/books/ratings

DEDICATION

To Sage and my Three Kings

WORKS BY
DIANE ANTHONY

Supernova

The Rare Trilogy

The Rare
The Remnant
The Return (July 2022)

TABLE OF CONTENTS

TABLE OF CONTENTS

1

As I lie in the hospital bed, my mind races to figure out what just happened to me. The last thing I remember, I was fighting for my life and the life of my friends and family out in the wilderness. I think they knocked us out with some kind of gas, but how did I get here?

Where is "here," anyway?

Nothing looks familiar, but then again, my eyes are blurry from having just opened them. I try to rub the gunk away, but my hand stops only inches off the bed.

Not this again.

I blink, trying to get my eyes to adjust, but they won't. Panic starts to rise in my chest, and I squeeze my eyes shut. Taking a deep breath, I open them again and squint around the room, trying hard to recognize anything that will give me a clue as to where I am. I start to tear up at the thought of needing to wear my glasses again. What's happening to me?

It's hard to tell, but the counters over by the wall reflect the fluorescent lights like they're metal. I don't remember ever being in a hospital room that had metal counters. Am I in some sort of laboratory?

Voices start coming from the hallway. I slow my breathing so I can listen. They are standing outside the door, and I can just barely hear what they're saying.

"She should be awake by now. Do you want to be the first person she sees?" a low male voice asks.

"Yes, thank you."

That voice was my mom's. What's going on? Does she know I'm strapped down to the bed? Why would she allow this to happen?

I have only seconds to decide how I want her to find me. Maybe I should pretend to be asleep. Or maybe I should give her a glare that lets her know I'm pissed. Before I make my choice, she swings the door open and catches me before I close my eyes.

"Oh, good. You're awake."

"Where am I? And why am I strapped down to this bed?" I ask as calmly as my rage will allow me to.

"Nope. You'll be answering my questions this time."

"No, I won't!" I yell.

1

"Your cooperation is what stands between you and your release."

"No, you are what stands between me and my release. Unstrap me!" I scream, flailing my arms around, rattling my restraints.

"No. Now calm down, or I'm leaving!"

"Good! Get out!"

She huffs, pushes open the door, and a nurse steps in, holding a syringe.

"Olivia, calm yourself down now, or we'll give you something to knock you out."

I close my eyes, calculating my options in this situation. I should cooperate. It would make things go more smoothly, and it might mean my release. I don't know where my friends are. They could be strapped down to beds here as well. If I get released, maybe they will too. I look at the cold expression on my mom's face as she waits for me to give her an answer.

"Screw you!" I scream, thrashing around.

My mom nods to the nurse and leaves the room. The nurse steps forward, grabs my IV line to inject the syringe into it, and leaves as I continue to scream swear words at my mother. My head is pounding from the exertion, but I don't care. How dare she do this to me! I feel my muscles weaken and go slack as my head falls to the pillow and everything goes dark.

■■■■■

My mother returns the next day just as I'm waking up. At least, I assume it's the next day since she's wearing a different outfit than she was before. I have no way to tell time in here.

"Water," I manage to croak out of my tight throat.

"Not until you answer some of my questions," she says, retrieving a cup from the sink and filling it up with water. She sets it down on the table next to me, taunting me with it. "Where were you going, Olivia?"

"Why should I tell you?"

"I need to know where you were going," she presses.

"Why?"

She glares at me for a moment. "Where's Matthias?" She grabs the cup of water and takes a sip.

My mouth drops open slightly at the audacity of her drinking my water. Wait, if she's asking me where Matthias is, then maybe everyone in camp wasn't taken. Unless she's just screwing with my head. "Why do you want to know that?" I mutter, my throat so dry, I can barely swallow.

"You need to answer my questions!" she yells, slamming the cup down on the table, splashing it everywhere.

"This is a fun little game we're playing, Mom, but I'm not telling you anything," I say as calmly as I can. My desperation for a drink of water is making it hard to keep my secrets.

"Damn it, Olivia! I am your mother. You need to obey me and answer my questions. If you don't answer me, we're going to have to take other measures to get the information out of you. I don't want it to come to that," she says, pinching the bridge of her nose. "Where is Matthias?"

"Why do you want to know? What difference does it make where Matthias is? Why didn't the soldiers take him when they took me?"

"Their orders were to find you and bring you back. Once you were brought back, President Turk decided he wants the rest of them brought in for being traitors of the Coalition."

"Oh. Well, why didn't you say that? In that case...go to hell!" I scream, injuring my throat in the process.

"Nurse!" my mom yells, slamming open the door and storming away.

The same nurse as before steps into the room and injects the sleeping drug once again.

■■■■■

A tapping noise wakes me up, but I don't open my eyes right away. My head aches, my throat is raw, and my lungs are on fire. I feel like garbage.

"I know you're awake," I hear a deep voice say as the tapping stops.

I lie still but open my eyes to see who's speaking. There's a blurry form sitting on a chair in the corner of the room. He stands up and walks toward me, his shoes clacking on the hard floor. As he gets closer, I see he's a tall man, with muscles bulging under his fitted dark blue three-piece suit.

"It's in your best interest to cooperate and tell us what we want to know."

"And if I don't?" I ask, my voice cracking from disuse.

"I've been given permission to make you talk."

I swallow hard but keep my eyes locked on his. "And how exactly are you going to make me talk?" I cough at the end to cover up the quiver in my voice.

"I have my ways. Don't worry. I'll start small and work my way up until I have the information I need from you," he says, putting blue latex gloves on his slender hands.

3

I turn my head to the side and see my glasses sitting on a little table next to me. "Can I please have my glasses?"

He reaches next to me for my glasses and slides them on my face gently. His cologne lingers in the air for a moment, making me wonder who he's trying to impress. Does he always dress nice and wear cologne for the people he's about to interrogate?

Once my glasses are in place, I look at him closer and see that he's quite attractive for someone in their mid-thirties: brown hair styled into a fauxhawk, sharp jawline, straight nose, groomed beard, full lips, and stormy blue eyes. Then I glance around the room. My heart sinks as I realize I can see perfectly with my glasses again. What happened to my Rare abilities? Where did my amazing eyesight go?

"All right, Olivia. Let's start."

Sitting next to him is a small tray of syringes. He picks one up, flicks it with the tip of his finger, and squirts out a little liquid to remove any trapped air.

"What is that?" I ask, unable to look away from the syringe.

"This is a little cocktail I came up with. Once I inject this into your IV, you will start to feel a stinging sensation throughout your body that will grow until you feel like every nerve in your body is on fire. I'll start with a small dose. I think that's all I'll need before you tell me what I want to know."

I try to say something, but my throat has closed off, and all that comes out is a squeak.

"Unless, of course, you want to cooperate with me now. You can save yourself a lot of pain if you choose to be forthcoming."

I glare at him as I weigh my options. Of course, I don't want him to inject me with that stuff, but I'm also not telling him a thing about the camp. I wish there was some way I could get my hands free and give him a taste of his own medicine.

"No comment?" he asks, grabbing my IV line. "Fine. Let's begin, then."

I start breathing heavily as he slides the needle in and pushes down the plunger about halfway. He steps back, drops the syringe on the metal tray, and watches me. I refuse to make eye contact, so I stare at the ceiling, waiting for the pain.

The liquid feels cold as it flows into my veins. A tingling sensation begins in my fingers, slowly creeping upwards until it spreads throughout my chest and down my legs. It almost feels like the same sort of pins and needles feeling you get when your foot falls asleep and starts to wake up again. Maybe this won't be so bad.

Suddenly, the tingling turns to a burning so intense, I start to scream at the top of my lungs. It feels like lava is flowing through my veins and melting my insides. Every nerve in my body is firing off in pain.

My voice gives out from the screaming, so I silently sob as the pain rips through my body. I thought I had felt pain before, but this is a new kind of horror. I'm having a hard time catching my breath, and I start to hyperventilate.

"It should be wearing off anytime now, Olivia. Take a deep breath."

My muscles are shaking uncontrollably, but I feel the pain starting to fade away back to the pins and needles sensation. I take a deep breath to try to slow my heart down and get oxygen back in my lungs.

I'm internally panicking as I realize that I won't be able to withstand that torture again. That was only a half dose? What happens when he gives me a full dose?

"I imagine you're feeling pretty terrible right about now," the man says with a stony face. "I'll give you a moment to gather your strength before answering my questions."

I squeeze my eyes shut and swallow the lump that's lodged in my throat. I know David wouldn't be mad at me if I give in and tell them what they wanted to know. He understands pain and the need for it to stop.

Suddenly, Markos's face flashes through my mind. I didn't know him for very long, but he gave his life trying to protect everyone in camp. It was my fault that the guard had found the camp in the first place, resulting in Markos's death. If I tell these people what they want to know and they capture my family and friends, then I'll be a traitor who deserves exactly what I'm getting.

No, I have to be brave. I have to endure this for them. They deserve their freedom. They don't deserve to be caught just because I was too weak to face the pain and ratted them out.

I take a shuddering breath and resolve myself. I'm going to do what needs to be done, even if it kills me. At least I'll die with honor, just like Markos did.

I open my eyes and see that the guy is still watching me.

"Ready to answer my questions now, Olivia?"

I respond by staring back at him tight-lipped.

He lifts an eyebrow at me. "Where were you headed?"

"The north pole. I wanted to see if Santa would give me my present early."

"Very funny," he says as his expression hardens.

"I'm not answering your questions. How about you let me go, and we can forget this ever happened?"

"Nice try. Where were you and your group headed, Olivia?"

"An alien landing site. We wanted to know if their world is better than this one."

"Cut the crap, and answer my questions properly. If you don't, I'll inject you with more pain."

I swallow hard and glance at the syringe on the tray.

"Where were you and your group headed?" he asks with a sharp edge to his voice.

I make a big dramatic sigh. "Fine. I really shouldn't tell you this. We were on our way to an Entmoot."

"What is an 'Entmoot'?"

"I can't be sure. I was told it's where the wisest come together to discuss things. They say it takes a really long time for anything to be resolved."

He furrows his eyebrows for a moment. "Where is this Entmoot happening?"

"Fangorn Forest," I say, holding in a laugh. He can't possibly be buying this.

"Why does that sound familiar?" he mutters to himself as he stands up and walks to the door. "You better not be lying to me, or you're in for a world of hurt."

After he steps out of the room, I burst into a fit of giggles.

I stop when I hear raised voices from outside my room.

"You idiot! She's pulling your leg. She's referring to some old books or the movies," a different male voice says.

"What?"

"Ents are tree creatures that live in Fangorn Forest, and when they get together to discuss things, it's called an 'Entmoot.' She's making fun of you. Get back in there, and get some real answers!"

The door slams open, and fauxhawk stomps back in, his face red from either anger or embarrassment. Maybe both. He doesn't say a word as he grabs my IV line and injects the remainder of the contents into it. Then he grabs another syringe, and before I can get a word out, he injects the entirety of that syringe as well.

2

"Olivia? Olivia! Can you hear me?" my mom's voice calls out.

As I wake up, it feels like I'm being sucked out of a dark tunnel. All my senses start slowly working again. I hear a heart monitor beeping and the whiny hum of the fluorescent light. I can smell a strange metallic scent that seems familiar, but I can't quite figure out what it is. And unfortunately, I feel every part of my body aching. The worst pain is in my chest. It feels like I was kicked by a mule.

I open my eyes but can't see a thing. It's all just colorful blurs.

"Mom? Where are you?" I ask in a strained voice.

"Oh, thank God!" my mother cries out. "Eva, you're a miracle worker."

"Thank you, ma'am," a gentle female voice responds.

"Mom?" I say again, my voice still weak.

"You better get out of here before we get caught," my mom says quietly, but I don't think she's talking to me.

I hear footsteps and then the door opening and shutting. Then my mom is at my side, sliding my glasses onto my face. As soon as they're in place, I take a good look at her and see that she has blood splattered on her face and down her shirt.

"Mom? What's going on?" I squeak.

"Shh! Take it easy," she says, unstrapping the velcro bonds that are holding down my wrists.

I sit up, look at the floor, and see fauxhawk guy lying in a pool of blood. That must be the metallic scent I couldn't quite place.

"What happened?"

"He killed you, Olivia. He gave you too much of that stuff, and your heart stopped. And when I came in here to save you, he pushed me away, saying you got what you deserved. So I shot him."

I slide off the bed and try to stand, but my knees buckle, and I fall. My mom catches me before I land on the floor and helps me sit back down on the bed. Fatigue is setting in, but I have to stay awake long enough to talk some sense into her. "We need to get out of here, Mom. You're going to be in big trouble! They probably heard the gunshot and are on their way now!"

"I used my silencer, but I'm sure someone still heard it. You need to leave quickly."

"What about the guy in the hallway?" I ask, remembering the guy who told fauxhawk what an Entmoot was.

"I don't know who you're referring to. Nobody was out there when I got here. Now, hurry up!"

I have mixed emotions running through me as I look at my mother. All the anger at her keeping me tied up here fades away as I think about how much trouble she's going to be in once they find out she killed someone. She is still my mother, and I love her.

"Come with me, Mom. Help me escape, and we can go find Matthias and my group. We can be a family again."

My mother locks eyes with me as she takes my face into her hands. "I can't. I have to face the consequences of what I've done."

"No, Mom. You can't do that. They'll lock you up in jail. You have to come with me. Please!"

She ignores me as she walks to the door and peeks her head out, looking both ways. "The coast is clear. Do you think you can walk?"

I push myself up off the bed and sway a little, trying to get my balance. I glance at the pool of blood surrounding the man who tried to murder me, and my sight starts swimming as the blood drains from my head, and I flop back onto the bed.

"Come on, Olivia!" My mother's voice sounds distant. She starts patting me on the cheek, slapping me a little harder than I think she means to. The stinging on my cheek pulls me from my stupor, and her face snaps into focus. Her eyes are shining with tears as she looks back and forth from me to the door. "Olivia! You need to get out of here. I'll take care of everything, but you need to leave. Now!"

I blink slowly, feeling the weight of what has happened to me turn my limbs to stone. I can't believe I died. And now she wants me to escape alone? I don't feel like I can even lift my head off the bed.

She pulls on my arms, lifting me up to a sitting position. As she's struggling to help me up, I see the door open. I want to scream, to tell mom to turn around, but I can't. I can hardly keep my eyes open long enough to see who's coming in. My breath catches in my chest when I see who it is.

Matthias. Followed closely by David. They're both dressed head to toe in soldier uniforms, but I can see their faces through their masks.

My mother notices I'm looking toward the door. She lets go of my arms, and I flop back on the bed, unable to keep myself upright. Before she turns all the way around, Matthias shoots her with a stun gun, shocking her until she goes stiff and falls over backward. He then drops to his knees and shoves something small in her mouth. I'm about to ask what it was, but David rushes past him.

"David!" I cry out as he runs to me and gives me a hug.

"Are you all right? What happened here?" David looks at the body lying in a pool of blood and then back at me, worry etching his brow.

"Never mind the small talk. We need to get out of here," Matthias says gruffly. He stalks to the bed and grabs my upper arm tightly as he tugs me to my feet. David takes the cue and wraps my other arm around his shoulder.

"How did you guys find me? How did you get in here without getting caught?" I ask as they help me walk toward the door.

Neither of them is answering me.

I look down at my mom. "We need to take Mom with us!" I say, locking my knees and digging my heels in the ground so they stop.

"No," Matthias grunts as he struggles to get me moving again.

"Come on, Matthias! She's going to be in a lot of trouble when someone finds out what she did. She was just trying to protect me, and now she's going to go to jail...or worse! You have to take her with us!" I plead as I thrash around.

Matthias stops moving and faces me; a tendon in his neck spasms. "I don't have to do nothin'! I came to rescue ya, and that's what I'm doing. Now ya better start walking, or I'll knock ya out and drag ya back to the woods!"

"David! Please! Help me here! We need to take Mom, or she's going to be in a lot of trouble."

"Keep your voice down, Olivia!" Matthias spits out and re-tightens his grip as he starts pulling me toward the door again.

I can feel my energy draining as I struggle to stop them from moving, and I just can't keep it up any longer. I go limp, and David almost drops me. We're at the door, and I realize this is my last chance to get Matthias to take my mom. I know it's risky, and we might get caught, but I can't think of anything else other than what's going to happen to her when someone finds out she killed this guy.

I fill my lungs with air and start screaming. Matthias lets go of my arm and puts me in a chokehold, squeezing both sides of my neck with his arm. I stop screaming as everything fades and I pass out.

3

I can feel my feet dragging behind me as I come back to consciousness. I'm being pulled along by two people who have my arms wrapped around their shoulders; their sweaty palms are gripping tightly on my arms so they don't drop me. They reek of dirt and sweat, and I wish I could walk on my own so I wouldn't have to smell them anymore.

I groggily open my eyes, and the light causes a wave of nausea so strong, I just about throw up. All I want to do is lie down and go back to the sweet oblivion of unconsciousness, where there were no pain or worries.

I suddenly remember why I'm in this situation and snap back awake.

Mom!

I tense up, getting ready to fight with Matthias again. I lift my head and see him in front of me, carrying my mom's limp body on his shoulders. Her head is bobbing with each step Matthias takes.

If Matthias is ahead of me, who's carrying me, then? I look over and smile when I see my brother's face. "Hi, Henry."

"Hey, Olivia," Henry answers. "Pop, Olivia's awake. Mind if we take a rest?"

"Not until we get back into the woods."

"Hang on. Stop for a second, guys. I can walk on my own," I say.

David and Henry stop walking, and I plant my feet on the ground. As they let go of my arms, I lurch a little as my vision swims. My head throbs with pain, and my thoughts feel fuzzy. What did Matthias do to me?

David wraps his arm around my shoulder and props me up again. "Steady, Liv. You okay?"

The pain abates some as I take a deep breath. My airways are tight, and I find myself wishing I had an inhaler. "Yeah. I'm okay. Just stay close to me so I can grab your arm if I feel like I'm going to fall."

"You got it."

Matthias didn't stop when we did, so now we have to try and catch up to him. As we hurry after Matthias, I take a look around and can see piles of rubble and war-torn buildings through the fog. We are at the edge of the city, outside the fence. I was unconscious for that long?

I have so many questions running through my head, I'm not sure what to ask first. They just start spilling out. "How did you find me? How long was I gone? How did you get soldier uniforms? What happened to everyone else at the camp? Is everyone okay?"

"Whoa! Slow down." David smiles. "One question at a time."

We've almost caught back up to Matthias as we make our way over brick-scattered roads. My legs are like lead, but I don't want to be dragged along anymore, so I push myself to keep up. I can feel my every footstep throb in my head.

"How did you find me?"

"The soldiers who came to our camp were looking for you, so Matthias knew it had to be your mom's doing. He then figured that you wouldn't be taken back to your apartment since your mother used government forces to search for you, so they probably took you to her government facility. He assumed you would be questioned about your motives for escaping the city."

"That's some good guesswork," I say.

"Not guesswork. I know your mother. I know how Turk operates. If he catches wind that someone might be a traitor, he either has that person killed or, in your case, tries to use ya to gather as many traitors as possible," Matthias says as he keeps walking.

At that moment, Matthias stumbles over a brick and almost drops Mom. He starts swearing loudly as he repositions her back over his shoulders.

"Pop, do you need me to take her for a while?" Henry offers.

"No. I got 'er." Matthias gives me a glare before turning around.

We continue trudging on. Soon the bricks and fallen-down buildings are replaced by moss-covered trees and wet decaying leaves. I already start to feel at home.

"How long was I gone?" I ask David.

"It's been about eleven days since the attack."

"Eleven days?" I ask, trying to decide whether I feel as though the attack happened just yesterday as memories of the event flood my mind or whether I feel like I was being held prisoner for more than eleven days because that also feels true. "Was anyone injured?"

David and Henry exchange a grim look.

"David, was anyone injured?"

"Suzanne didn't make it," David answers, his voice barely louder than a whisper.

"What? What happened?"

"She hit her head on a rock. We're not sure if it happened when we all got knocked out from the gas or if it happened during the fight."

"She had a little girl, right?" I ask, trying hard to remember.

"Yeah—Sonya. The other moms are taking care of her. She's too young to really understand what's going on, but she cries for her mom at night," Henry answers somberly.

"Was anyone else hurt?"

"Not really. Tim's mind might need some healing. He's blaming himself for the attack and Suzanne's death because he fell asleep on his watch. I tried to say something encouraging before I left to come get you, but he wouldn't listen. He looked pretty down," David says.

"As he should be," Matthias growls.

I look up, surprised.

Matthias continues walking forward, eyes trained on whatever is in front of him.

I glare at the back of his head. "How can you be so mean?" I spit out.

"He asked to take a watch. He wanted to prove that he could do what the adults do, and he failed."

"He made a mistake, and he feels terrible about it. Maybe you should try a little compassion," I say in disgust.

I know how Tim's feeling. I still blame myself for Markos's death. I would hate for Tim to fall into the pit of self-loathing that I often find myself in.

Matthias stops suddenly and turns around to face me, my mom's head swinging back and forth from his quick movements. His face is red, and his eyes are narrowed to slits. Henry is at his side in moments, with his hand resting on Matthias's shoulder, concern etched across his face.

Matthias glances at Henry and takes a deep breath before talking. "I ain't gonna coddle someone who made a mistake that cost someone their life. I'm in charge. It's my responsibility to keep people safe. Tim's lucky I didn't kick him out into the woods."

"As someone who also made a mistake that got somebody killed, I can tell you that it doesn't do any good to make him feel worse. The guilt is enough punishment on its own. You have no idea how badly I wanted to be the one who died instead of Markos. I would trade places with him in a heartbeat," I choke out as I start to cry.

"No. You're right. He shouldn't spend time feeling bad," Matthias says.

I breathe a small sigh of relief.

Then he continues, "He should stop acting like a damn baby and learn from his mistakes, like a man."

My sadness turns back to rage, and I want nothing more than to punch Matthias in the nose. My heart pounds in my chest, causing my head to throb so severely that my vision pulses red around the edges with each heartbeat. I take a step toward Matthias, but before I'm able to take another step, I pass out.

■■■■■

I wake up to the sensation that I'm drooling, but before I get too embarrassed, I realize that there's something pressed against my lip. I open my eyes slightly and see David's concerned face hovering over mine. He has my head resting on his lap, and he's trying to give me a drink of water.

"Come on, Liv," he says with a slight quiver in his voice.

I open my eyes all the way and make eye contact. A grin spreads across his face, and for a moment, I hardly recognize him. The David I once knew is gone. All the little changes I noticed when we first went out to the wilderness suddenly hit me as I gaze up at him. His skin is smooth and completely clear of acne, his teeth are still slightly crooked, but they're white now. His eyes are a rich golden color with flecks of green instead of muddy brown, and his black hair looks thick and healthy. And since when did his lips get so full and soft?

"Liv, are you okay?" he asks, concern creeping back into his voice.

My cheeks blush as I realize I was staring at his lips a little too long. He helps me sit up, and I rest my head in my hands, waiting for the dizziness from changing positions to go away. "Yeah, I'm fine, I think."

I go to stand up, but I hear Henry say, "Stay sitting. Jeez, Olivia. You scared us!"

I look around to find Matthias, but I don't see him anywhere. "Where's Matthias?"

"After he tied up your mom, he left to scout the area, make sure it's safe for us to stay here for the night," David answers.

"Sorry I made us have to stop," I say sheepishly.

"Nah. Pop was getting exhausted. He's just too stubborn to admit it." Henry smirks.

I gaze around and see my mom leaning against a tree with her hands tied behind her back and her ankles tied together. Her head is lolled back, and I'm starting to get a kink in my neck just from looking at her. "Any idea how far away from the city we are?"

"Too close for comfort. We're all going to have to take turns keeping watch tonight, just in case someone comes looking for you and your mom," Henry answers.

"Our mom," I respond, watching him to see how he reacts.

He gives a quick dip of his chin, and his eyes flit to where Mom is tied up, but he turns his back to her and scans the area, deliberately looking anywhere else.

"Here, drink this." David offers me some water.

I know that I should conserve our water, but as soon as I swallow the first drink, I find that I can't stop myself, and empty the entire bottle. "Sorry," I say, trying to catch my breath. "So, how did you guys get the uniforms and get inside the government building to rescue me?"

"Well, let's just say that Pop is a man who likes to live inside the gray areas of life, sometimes stepping over the line into the black," Henry answers.

"What does that mean?"

David looks at the ground and won't meet my eyes.

"David?"

"He took them off some soldiers who died."

"How did they die?" I ask, unsure I want to hear the answer.

"I broke their necks to save yours," Matthias says, startling us all. "Now, stop your yapping, and everyone get some sleep. I wanna start moving before the sun comes up."

4

I can't sleep. I know I should be getting rest so I can regain some of my strength, but I can't stop thinking about how both of my parents murdered people to save me. Should I be grateful that I'm no longer strapped down to a bed, being tortured, when my freedom cost other people their lives? Should I feel happy that my parents care about me enough that they would do anything to ensure my safety?

I look at David, who's sitting with his back to us, keeping watch. Does he agree with what Matthias did? He shot a guard to help us escape the city. How do we know that guard didn't die? Am I the only one here who believes murder is wrong?

I roll onto my back and look up at the sky, glad that I still have my glasses on. Between the blackness of branches and leaves, I spot a star in the inky sky. I continue to stare at it until it's the only thing I see, and I let my mind wander.

Maybe this is what life is: you'll always be surrounded by darkness in one way or another, but you have to keep your eyes trained on the light—the good in this world—or better yet, be the light in this dark world. I may allow myself to get angry. I've punched people and even squeezed the breath out of Alexandrine when sparring, but I will never kill someone. Matthias can train me in combat all he wants, but I will not kill. I will not allow him to turn me into a murderer.

Then my mind turns to Markos again and how I was part of causing his death. Who am I kidding? My hands are not as clean as I would like them to be. I led that guard right to our camp, and Markos was killed because of my mistake. Matthias is right. I was only thinking about my hurt feelings.

I can feel the darkness closing in around me. My chest suddenly feels heavy, as though the depression has manifested itself into a tangible entity that can hurt me physically. A tear trails across my cheek onto my ear, and a sob escapes my lips.

"Liv? You okay?" David whispers.

"Y-yeah. I'm fine," I lie.

"No, you're not. Come over here."

I stand up and quietly make my way to sit by David.

"What's going on?"

I don't answer him at first, embarrassed that he caught me crying. He puts his arm around me and gives me a gentle squeeze, reminding me that this is David I'm talking to. I can tell him anything.

"I was just staring up at a star, resolving myself to focus on the small points of light in this dark world, but then my mind went directly to Markos, and the darkness overtook me again, and I fell." I sniff.

He understands what I'm referring to. I've used the imagery of me standing on the ledge of a pit, and when depression takes me, it's like I'm falling into the abyss of darkness, emptiness, and sadness. He always jokes that he'll carry around a rope so he can help me back out, and he seems to know just the right things to say to make me feel better. I don't know what I would do without him.

"Liv, you can't keep blaming yourself for Markos. Everyone else has forgiven you. You need to forgive yourself and let it go, or you'll drive yourself crazy."

"I don't think Matthias has forgiven me," I say, being stubborn.

"Matthias can be a prick, but I'm pretty sure he's forgiven you too."

I pull my knees up to my chest, wrap my arms around them, and bury my face as I try to hide from the world.

"C'mon, Liv," David tries again, rubbing my shoulder gently. "Remember that time when we were in second grade, I kicked the soccer ball too hard, and it hit you in the nose? I thought for sure I had broken it. You bled so much."

I nod, remembering how the pain caused starbursts in my vision, and my mom was angry that my new dress got blood all over it.

"Remember how I wouldn't let it go? I was so afraid that you were never going to talk to me again that I kept apologizing to you over and over for days until you finally yelled at me to stop?"

"Yeah. I was angrier with you for repeatedly apologizing and bringing it up than I was that you hit me with the ball in the first place."

"Think of this as me yelling at you," he says gently. "Everyone has forgiven you and wants to move on. Not that they want to forget Markos, but they want to mourn him or remember him in their own way. But if you keep sulking around, wallowing in your guilt, it's like bringing up what happened over and over again."

"You're right, I guess." I sigh, letting his words sink in.

"Of course, I am," David says with a sly smile. "Now, you need to get some sleep. I think we only have a couple more hours before Matthias will want to head out."

"What about you? Have you gotten any sleep?"

"I'll be fine," David says, and I hear some shuffling around. "Here, take my hoodie. It's a little chilly out tonight."

I grab the hoodie and pull it on. It smells like campfire smoke and David's deodorant. I find the scent comforting. "Thank you, David," I say, pouring as much meaning behind my words as possible.

Then I crawl back to my spot and lie down. I pull my hands inside the sleeves and tuck them under my chin. His words roll around inside my head, and I feel the darkness ebb away. As I start to fall asleep, I realize David is my light. I need to be more like him.

■■■■■

Matthias wakes me with a hard shake. I open my eyes and see that it's still dark out, and I wonder how long I actually slept.

"I want to head out in five. Eat quick, and let's go," Matthias says gruffly, handing me an apple and a strip of dried meat as I slip my glasses on.

I sit up and stretch out my stiff back. My body still aches from yesterday, but my head feels clearer. My eyes turn to Henry when he flips on a flashlight momentarily to search for something in his bag, and I sigh when I realize I can't see with my glasses again. I really didn't like being unable to see with or without my glasses the last time. Hopefully, I'll get my vision back faster since I wasn't in the city for too long.

"How're you feeling?" David asks as he stuffs a few things back into his bag.

"Better. Thank you for last night."

When David says, "Anytime," I know he means it.

I had barely finished eating when Matthias began moving. It's going to be tough trying to keep up since it's dark and I can hardly see. After tripping over a stick and almost face-planting on a fallen tree, I hurry to catch up to David so I can follow him like last time. "I can't see. My eyesight is changing again, and everything is blurry," I say to David in a slightly panicked voice as I stumble over another branch.

"I got you," David says, reaching out and grabbing my hand.

At one time, I would have been repulsed to be holding hands with him, but his touch is comforting, and I thread my fingers with his so my hand won't slip as he leads me through the woods.

We march on, putting as much distance between ourselves and the city as possible. The forest around us comes to life as the sun begins to rise.

Birds sing out their cheerful songs as they search for their breakfasts, and squirrels scamper through the dead leaves, chasing one another around the trees. I inhale a deep breath and smell the pleasant scent of dirt and leaves. My chest still hurts from the nurse restarting my heart yesterday, but my lungs have opened up again, and I can breathe freely.

My hand's getting sweaty, and I let go of David before he gets grossed out. Instead, I hold onto a strap on his bag and follow behind him. I peer around David and spot Henry just up ahead, scanning the area with his bow out and an arrow nocked, ready to fight off any Havoc or people that might get in our way. Farther past him, I can see what must be Matthias carrying my mom on his shoulders again.

"David? Is my mom still unconscious?"

"Yeah."

"How?"

"He's been giving her something to keep her asleep."

When I scoff, he quickly adds, "Just until we get back to camp."

"I hope it was the right choice, bringing her along. I pushed him into it, but now I'm starting to wonder what's going to happen when she wakes up."

We stop to eat lunch by a little stream. Matthias props my mom up against a tree and disappears into the woods without a word. I look at Henry questioningly, and he just shrugs. After eating a couple of carrots and a handful of sunflower seeds, I check on Mom to see if she has any injuries. There's a small cut on the back of her head from when she hit the floor after being stunned, so I grab a water bottle, fill it in the stream, and carefully wash away the dried blood.

I sit next to her and look at her closely. This woman raised me, provided for me, worried over me, and now killed to save me, and yet, I can't help but feel like I don't really know her. She tries so hard to keep her distance, to keep her secrets. And we fight so often, I feel like she's more of an older sister than a mom. A mom is supposed to be warm and loving like David's mom, not harsh and argumentative.

The sound of footsteps behind me pulls me from my thoughts. I whirl around and catch Henry standing a short distance away, watching me with her.

"So, this is the woman who abandoned me?" Henry asks coolly.

"I guess you could argue that Matthias abandoned her...and me," I shoot back, his accusation rubbing me the wrong way.

18

"Matthias wanted to leave the city and the tyrannical government that was holding people prisoner. He was trying to protect us. She," Henry says, jabbing his fingers toward her, "refused to come. I had to grow up without a mother because she was too stubborn to leave."

"She might not have been the greatest mother in the world, Henry, but she's a better parent than Matthias."

"You have no idea what you're talking about! Pop has worked hard to raise me with very little help. He provided for all my needs and taught me how to survive."

I start to speak, but he interrupts, "How about you? She did such a great job of raising you that you wanted to kill yourself!"

His words cut deep, and I can feel my cheeks grow hot from embarrassment.

Just as I'm about to lay into him, Matthias returns with a bundle of wood in his arms. "Knock it off! Ya two want to get us caught?"

"Sorry, Pop."

"What are ya fightin' about, anyway?" he asks, as he builds a fire ring from some rocks by the stream.

"You and Mom and who was a better parent," I say with a glare.

"We both suck. There. Argument over. Now Henry, fetch the pot outta my bag, and let's get some drinking water made up so we can move on."

We trudge on as day turns to dusk. I move on autopilot, stepping in rhythm to David's footsteps as I replay the argument with Henry over and over in my head, feeling guilty that I raised my voice at him. It was unfair of me to accuse Matthias of being a bad parent. I've hardly known him. I don't know what made me defend my mom so hard. In all honesty, she's not great either. But she's all I've had.

We find a thick patch of trees and settle in for the night. The air is starting to get cooler as we head into early fall. David lets me borrow his hoodie again, which I'm grateful for.

I'm told to take a watch tonight so the others can get some sleep too. I choose to take the first watch, that way I can get it over with quicker. It seems silly that I should be keeping "watch" when I can't really see that well, but my hearing is just fine. Before he lies down, Matthias hands me his gun. I try to protest, but he says he doesn't have any swords with him, so I'm going to have to make do. I stick it inside the pocket of the hoodie and try to forget it's there.

I keep watch while standing up, bouncing back and forth to try to stay warm. The woods always seem a little eerie at night, and tonight is no exception. The steady sounds of breathing from everyone sleeping makes me feel lonely. They're all right here, but they might as well be miles away.

An owl hoots in the distance, setting my nerves on edge. I don't like to think about what kind of creatures are out at night. After a while, my legs grow weary from being on them all day, so I sit down with my back against a tree. It's not long before my eyelids grow heavy, and I struggle to keep myself awake. I don't blame Tim for falling asleep the night I got caught. It's not easy being the only one awake.

My eyes snap open when I hear some leaves rustling a short distance from behind the tree I'm leaning against. I carefully peek my head around the tree and see a dark shape walking on all fours.

Oh, crap! Not another Havoc!

5

"Matthias!" I whisper-shout. "Matthias, wake up!"

He doesn't stir. I want to slap him awake, but I'm afraid to move away from my hiding spot. Last time I came face to face with a Havoc, the skunk stench saved me. I don't have that to save me now. I'm going to have to face it.

I slowly stand up, careful to not make any noise. Leaning against the tree, I peek my head around until I can spot it again. The creature is darker than the nighttime, making it just visible. Now that I'm standing up, I realize it's smaller than I was expecting. Maybe it's a baby Havoc? In that case, where's its mother? I scan the trees but don't spot anything.

This creature's making a lot more noise than I remember Havoc making. It's shuffling the leaves around and making snorting sounds. I jump when I hear a twig snap farther away in the woods. Crap! Maybe if I shoot at it, it'll run away, and its mom will too. I pull the gun out of my pocket and flip the safety off. I can hardly see, but I don't need to kill it. Just the sound should scare it away. I hope.

I point the gun up toward the sky above where the creature is standing, and right before I pull the trigger, I shout, "Matthias, wake up!"

Bang!

The men are on their feet in an instant, drawing their knives, ready to fight. Henry and David have their flashlights out and are shining them all over the woods, looking for the attacker. I breathe again when I hear the creature running away from us.

"What the hell was that?" Matthias yells.

"There was a black creature making its way toward us. I thought it was a Havoc, so I shot at it to scare it away."

"Well, ya coulda gave us a warning!"

We both stop talking immediately when we hear footsteps approaching.

"You idiot! You scared away our food," a cranky voice accuses.

I already know who it is before I see her.

Alexandrine.

"What are ya doin' way out here?" Matthias questions, sliding his knife back into its sheath.

Henry and David relax and do the same.

21

"Hunting. And we're only about a mile away from camp," she says, pulling something off her head. "Aww. Did the mighty Matthias forget where camp is now and get lost?"

"I was following the stream. I knew we were gettin' close," he answers defensively.

"Why were you hunting in the dark?" I ask.

"One of the soldiers dropped a pair of night vision goggles during the attack. It's the only good thing that's ever come from you being here."

I give her the finger, and she sneers at me.

"What were you hunting? Was it a Havoc?" Henry asks.

"No. Wild boar. They live around this area, but they're nocturnal, so we never see them. I was on watch tonight when I just happened to spot one way out in the woods. I woke someone else up to take my place so I could hunt it. I needed to get away from the incessant sniveling anyway. I swear the kid never sleeps."

"If you're referring to Tim, it's because he feels guilty and needs time to heal," David interjects.

"He needs to man up and move on," Alexandrine says.

"You are such a—" I start to spit out.

"Enough," Matthias interrupts. "Since we're close to camp, let's get moving so we can get some proper protection and sleep tonight."

Everyone but the people on watch are sleeping when we get to the camp. While Matthias figures out a place to tie Mom up, David spots Tim curled up in the fetal position about twenty feet away from everyone else. We quietly make our way over to him and lie down. David shuts off his flashlight, leaving me squinting in the dark. Before I close my eyes, I let out a happy sigh, knowing that I'm home again.

■■■■■

I wake up to the sound of quiet muttering. It takes me a moment to remember where I am. I open my eyes, sit up to stretch, and am relieved when I can see everything clearly again without my glasses. I look to my right and see David sitting next to Tim, facing away from the camp. They're talking low enough that I can't hear what they're saying. I look to my left and see a head of bushy hair.

"Cass!" I call out involuntarily. I'm so happy to see her.

She spins around, and her face lights up when she sees me. "Olivia!" she squeals, coming over to give me a hug. "I thought I was never going to see you again. You have no idea how hard it was to let you sleep. As soon as I saw you, I almost screamed!"

We both giggle, and I look over at Tim, who's still facing away. "How's Tim?" I whisper soberly.

"Not good. I've tried talking to him, but he just ignores me. So I make sure I stay close to him in case he needs anything. Maybe you could talk to him sometime."

"I could try."

"All right, gang, listen up," Matthias calls out. "Now that everyone's awake, I thought it'd be a good time to fill y'all in. First off, we found Olivia and were able to bring her back."

A few people clap, while others look at me indifferently.

"We also brought her mother with us," Matthias says, pointing to my mom, who's still tied up and asleep.

"What?" a few people proclaim.

"Why would you do that? She works for the government! They're gonna send soldiers out to find her, and we're gonna lose more people!" Rebecca shouts.

"Fool!" Alexandrine pipes in. She already knew that Mom was with us. I think she just wanted to call Matthias a name.

"I know! Shut up, and listen!" Matthias yells. "This woman was in trouble. She killed a soldier to save Olivia, and Olivia didn't want her mother to die. I have control of the situation. Y'all need to trust me."

Some people nod, while others shake their heads.

"Now, another thing. While I was in the city, I got to talkin' to a guy. He gave me more information on the Haven."

A few loud groans echo through the camp. I wish they would stop. I want to hear what he's talking about.

"Give it a rest, Matthias!" Alexandrine growls. "The Haven doesn't exist!

"Ya don't know that! I've heard enough rumors goin' 'round that I think it's true. We know it's out west somewhere, but this guy told me that there's someone the next city over who can get us there, who has connections."

"Great. Another wild goose chase," Alexandrine scoffs.

"Let the man talk!" Frederick scolds.

"No, forget it. I'm done talkin'. Get to work."

Everyone starts chatting amongst themselves as they get up to do chores.

"Alexandrine, I want a word with you," Matthias snarls and stalks off.

Alexandrine groans and turns to follow.

"What's 'The Haven'?" I ask Cass as I stand up and brush off my pants.

"Oh. It's supposedly a city where a bunch of Rares live in secret. He's talked about it before, but everybody's skeptical."

"What about you? Do you think it exists?"

"I think it would be great if it did. But I've learned long ago to not get my hopes up. It seems a little far-fetched that a place like that would exist undetected."

I don't know Matthias that well, but I don't take him for a liar either. Maybe there's something to this. I just shrug as we head out to help with chores.

As I'm walking back to camp with an armful of wood, I hear Matthias's raised voice. I step around a tree and see him squatting down in front of my mother, who's now awake. She has tears streaming down her face as she looks at him. I quickly hide behind the tree to eavesdrop.

"Bull! I did not abandon ya, Jan. Ya refused to do the right thing!"

"It wasn't like that! You were asking me to leave the safety of the city while pregnant so we could go live out in the woods. What was I supposed to do?"

"Listen to reason, for one thing! Ya've always been so damn stubborn. Can't ya see what the government's doin'? They're lockin' people inside the city and tellin' them that they're safe. It's not safety, it's imprisonment! People should be allowed to leave if they want."

I hear my mom sob out, "I loved you, Matthias. You left me to raise Olivia alone. You took *my* son away. I wanted to find you. I wanted to send soldiers after you to bring you back, but I was scared. I was scared they were going to kill you!"

They both go silent, and I start to wonder if Matthias left. I'm about to peek around the tree when I hear Mom ask in a whisper, "How is he?"

"What?" Matthias grunts.

Mom clears her throat and asks a little louder, "Henry. How is he?"

"He's fine. He's a smart young man. Strong. He's got a good head on his shoulders."

"I'm sorry..." she starts to say, but her voice cracks. And then she starts crying again.

I hear Matthias mumbling as he stomps off, "I don't have time for this."

I come out from my hiding spot and carry the wood to the firepit. I turn toward my mother, and she's sitting against a tree, with her face buried in her hands. It looks like Matthias cut her hands free but bound her ankles and legs with zip ties. I grab a cup and fill it in the pot of clean drinking water to take to her.

"Here, Mom," I say gently, offering her the cup.

She wipes her eyes with the heels of her hands, spreading mascara across her cheeks. She takes the cup and drains it, her bloodshot eyes never leaving mine. "What are you doing, Olivia?" she asks, handing me back the cup.

"What do you mean?"

"You should never have had Matthias take me. I would have been fine."

"You would have been killed or thrown in jail!"

She shakes her head. "Is this really better than being in jail?" she asks, holding up her raw wrists. "You've only made things worse. I told you I had it under control. I told you to leave, but once again, you didn't listen to me."

I stare at her with my mouth hanging open in disbelief.

She sighs dramatically. "But I guess you did it with good intentions, so I should say, 'thank you.'"

I stand waiting for her to say, "thank you," but when she doesn't, I realize she's too proud to actually say the words. "Mom, I was afraid of what they would do to you. I thought you would be better off leaving the mess you made behind and coming out here with me, to be with your family."

I grow angry as she stares at the ground and doesn't respond to me.

"You know, maybe this is your chance to prove that you don't value yourself and your secrets over the wellbeing of your children. This is your chance to redeem yourself from being a terrible mother. I suggest you take it."

I storm away before she has a chance to talk. I can't help but feel like this was a bad idea.

6

I spend the next few hours circling around the camp to pick up any fallen branches or dead logs I can find for firewood. It hasn't been decided whether this is the new permanent camp location, but for now, we are trying to make it as livable as possible. Everyone has chores to do to get supper prepared for tonight. David got put on hunting duties since he's such a great shot. I wish he could have come with me. I'm bored without him.

I venture out a little farther from camp on my fifth trip out into the woods. As I bend down to pick up a large stick, I hear a primal yell coming from farther out. I drop the branches I'm holding and run toward the direction of the yell. I hope nobody is injured. I'm bad with injuries. Maybe I should have run back to camp to get Rebecca, but it's too late now.

I continue running until I hear someone wailing loudly up ahead. I take a few more steps and see Tim on his knees, curled over, holding his face in his hands. His body shakes violently as he sobs. I stand there for a moment, unsure of what to do. Should I give him his privacy or try to say something to help? Before I've made my decision, he turns his head and looks at me. He quickly wipes his eyes and nose, trying to hide the fact that he was crying.

"Tim? Are you okay?" I ask tentatively.

"I'm sorry you saw that," he says, embarrassed.

"Don't be. It's okay. Do you wanna talk about it?" I make my way over to where he is and sit down beside him.

"Not really," he sniffs, avoiding eye contact.

"You know, sometimes it helps to talk about it, especially to someone who understands."

He picks up a stick and starts breaking it into pieces. I sit quietly next to him and wait. I grab a stick and break it into little pieces too, tossing them at a hollowed-out stump. He notices what I'm doing and joins in. We make it through about six sticks each before he finally starts talking again.

"I just can't stop thinking about what I did," he says, voice quivering. "It was my responsibility to keep everyone safe, and Suzanne died. It should have been me."

"I get it. I really do, Tim. I led a guard to our camp, and Markos died because of me."

Tim shakes his head and is silent for a moment. "How do you make it stop?"

I think I know what he's talking about, but I ask anyway, "Make what stop?"

"The guilt. The pain. The feelings of worthlessness that seep from your brain down into your chest and fill you with an ache so powerful, it feels like it's suffocating you. It feels like you're dying, but you're not. And then, after a while, you find that you wish you were."

"I don't have the greatest track record to be giving you advice on not wanting to die, but I can tell you that things will get better. I'm glad that I didn't succeed in my attempts now. I never would have found you, this camp, or my Rare abilities had I died," I say, starting to tear up. "I can also tell you that there are a lot of people who would miss you if you died."

"Yeah, right. Like who? Matthias gives me an accusing look every time I'm near him. The women seem to busy themselves whenever I'm nearby so they don't have to look at me. Little Sonya cries for her mom at night. She's going to learn what I did and hate me too."

"No, she won't. It was an accident. You're going to have to learn to forgive yourself, or you will drive yourself crazy. Remember what you once told me? 'We all make mistakes.' Well, you made a mistake. But you didn't make Suzanne hit her head. It just happened," I say, paraphrasing what David said to me when he tried to make me feel better.

He shakes his head, and I start to get frustrated. He's completely unwilling to listen. Maybe this is how David feels when I won't listen to him. I start to feel guilty about that but force myself to stop. I do not need to be pulled down into the pit with Tim.

I stand up and brush myself off, then offer my hand to Tim to help him up. "We should really be getting back, Tim. Will you walk with me? I need to bring another load of wood back to camp, and I could use the company."

He grabs my hand, and I pull him to his feet. I keep pace with his slow shuffle as we silently make our way back to camp, picking up any pieces of wood we can find.

The people at camp have started a fire by the time we arrive. We drop the wood on the pile, and Tim disappears back to where he slept last night, turning his back to everyone. I miss the Tim I got to know, the bubbly, overenthusiastic Tim. But I will never say that to him. That would break him even further. I know that the best thing to do is exactly what Cass said she's doing: to just be there for him when he needs us and to check in with him from time to time.

As I'm trying to decide where I can help out, David comes trooping back with the other hunters, who are pulling along a deer, two turkeys, and a couple of squirrels. He gives me a proud smile. I'm glad to see him being able to contribute to the camp.

While David and the others prepare the meat for cooking, I take Mom another cup of water. They have her set against a tree close to the fire so they can keep an eye on her. She rubs absentmindedly at her wrists as she silently watches what everyone is doing.

"Are your wrists okay?" I ask as I hand her the cup of water.

"I'll live." She takes the cup and drinks. "So, this is what you all do every day? Just gather wood and hunt so you can have a meal? Then what? You do the same thing all over again? Doesn't seem like a good way to live life. At least in the city, you can have access to all the food and comforts you need."

"Sure. You can have all the comforts you want—for the price of your freedom."

She begins laughing.

"I don't see what's so funny."

"You sound just like him. The government is not imprisoning people, Olivia! They are protecting people. Your father is just a paranoid conspiracy theorist hellbent on fighting against the government for no reason. There are no enemies."

"If there are no enemies, then why do they need a fence?"

"The fence is to keep predators out. And traitors like your father who can't be trusted!" she shouts as Matthias walks closer.

"I'm not the one around here who can't be trusted," Matthias growls.

"Why did you bring me here, Matthias? Huh? Am I your prisoner?" Mom asks, pulling on her the zip ties to try to get her legs free.

"I brought ya because Olivia was worried about ya. If it were left up to me, I would have been more than happy to see ya get what ya deserve!"

She scowls. "And what exactly would that be?"

Matthias looks like he's about to go over and smack her, but then he glances around and notices everyone is silently watching them. Instead, he heads over to his bag and pulls out a length of rope and a strip of cloth. He marches over to Mom and forces her arms behind her back.

As he's tying her wrists together, she yells, "If I'm not your prisoner, then release me! You have no right to imprison me like this! Let me go, Matthias!"

He finishes binding her wrists together and then gags her mouth with the cloth. She continues yelling even though it only comes out as a muffled grunting sound.

"This was a mistake, Matthias!" Alexandrine shouts out at Matthias as he storms away. "You need to fix this fast, or I will."

Matthias just continues walking, heading out into the woods. Alexandrine turns and gives me an evil glare. She spits on the ground, right next to my mom's feet, and then disappears into the woods, opposite the direction Matthias went. Everyone in camp seems to have snapped out of their trance and goes back to what they were previously doing.

I had no idea bringing her out here was going to be such a train wreck.

7

"Why are you acting like this, Mom? Can't you be happy just being here with me?"

She stops yelling and looks at me, deadpan.

"Please, Mom," I plead. "Please cooperate. I love you."

She closes her eyes and leans her head back against the tree.

I feel like I'm about to cry, but then I see Henry walking past, keeping out of Mom's sight, and I have an idea. I get up and catch him before he disappears into the woods.

"Hey, Henry," I whisper. "I need you to help me with Mom. She's angry with me because I didn't listen to her and let her stay in the city. She won't cooperate with Matthias and keeps being a pain in the butt. Will you please come talk some sense into her? I want her to choose to stay here with us. It would mean a lot to me."

"I don't know, Olivia..." He shifts his weight back and forth while scratching at his head.

"Please?" I ask, giving him big pathetic puppy dog eyes. "C'mon, big brother. Pretty please?"

He smirks a little and then gestures with his hand for me to lead the way. I have a seat in front of her, and she opens her eyes to glare at me. Her stony expression melts off her face as Henry steps around the tree she's tied up to. He kneels beside me and reaches over to remove Mom's gag.

"Henry?" she whispers.

"Yeah. It's me."

"Look at you! I never thought I would see you again." She sobs.

Henry takes a seat next to me on the ground facing our mother. His blue eyes are cold and calculating as he looks at her. I nudge him a little with my elbow, worried that he's not going to get her to stay by glaring at her.

"I'm so sorry, Henry. I'm so sorry for not trying harder for you."

"I managed. Pop took good care of me."

"I see that. Oh, Son! I can't believe I'm looking at you. You've turned out to be so handsome," she gushes. She makes a motion with her arm as though she wants to reach out and touch him, forgetting momentarily that she's tied up.

30

Henry scratches at his head awkwardly. "Look, this is uncomfortable for me. I don't know you. Clearly, you're happy to see me, but from where I stand, you abandoned me, and now you're nothing but a stranger."

Mom cringes as though he just slapped her with his words. I feel a slight sense of contentment knowing he just hurt her a little.

"We can get to know each other now," Mom offers. "I'm sorry you feel like I abandoned you, Henry. Not a day went by that I didn't think about you."

"If you want to get to know me, then you're going to have to get along with Pop. I know you two have a bad history, but we need everyone to live peaceably for survival."

"I will do whatever it takes. But you're going to have to tell him that."

My mom continues to stare at Henry in awe. I start to feel a little jealous. I don't think she's ever looked at me with that much love in her eyes.

"Okay, then. I guess I'm going to go help get supper going. I'll talk to Pop about having you released," Henry says, looking at me with a raised eyebrow as though questioning whether he's done enough.

"Thanks, Henry," I whisper.

He nods at me, then gets up to leave.

I look at Mom, and she's still smiling as she watches Henry walk away. "You were right. He's handsome, just like your father was at that age. I can't believe that's my little boy," she says quietly, still wonderstruck. "Did you know his very first word was 'Mama'?"

"Yeah...that's great," I say, a little annoyed. "Henry's right, you know. About you getting along with Matthias. If we cut you loose, you have to behave yourself."

"I get it," she snips. "Who was that woman who tried to spit on my shoe?"

"Oh, that's Alexandrine. You'll want to stay away from her."

"Why?"

"Because she hates you."

"She doesn't even know me!"

"You work for the government. Around here, that's enough reason to hate you."

She scowls. "Great. Am I going to have to watch my back every second of every day?"

"It depends. If you pitch in and help around here, I'm sure you can be adopted into the group eventually."

She looks around camp, scrutinizing everyone, and gasps.

"What?" I ask.

"Saul?" she calls out.

I look behind me and see Saul sitting against a tree on the outskirts of camp. He looks up from his whittling when he hears his name called. His eyes narrow; then he goes back to whittling.

"Hmm. He must not recognize me. I can't believe he's here. I honestly thought he had died. I'm glad to see he's doing okay," she says, but for some reason, I don't believe her.

"I should probably go see if there's anything for me to do. Are you going to be okay here?"

"I'd be better if you cut me loose."

"I can't do that. I have to okay it with Matthias first."

"Of course," she mumbles and rests her head against the tree again.

I sure hope Matthias lets her loose. If he doesn't do it soon, I think I might just so we can start working on getting along.

Before I go check in with the camp ladies to see if there is any food prep for me to do, I make my way over to Saul. He's carving the same symbols as he always does. He hears me as I step closer to him, and he looks up at me with a twinkle in his eye.

"Hey, Saul. How're you doing?"

He smiles at me and nods. I interpret that to mean "good."

"Did you see that my mom is here with us?" I ask, wondering how he will react.

His smile falters a little when he glances her way, but then he looks at me, and his smile returns as he nods.

"She's agreed to cooperate. She wants to get to know Henry, so she's decided to stop fighting with Matthias. We might actually get to be a family again."

He puts down his stick and pats me on the cheek with his soft hand. His eyes have a look of pity as he pulls his hand away.

"You don't think it's ever going to happen, do you?" I ask, deflating.

When he sees that I'm sad, he grabs my hand and places the stick he was whittling on my palm.

I look down at it and run my thumb over the carvings in the wood. "Thank you," I say, putting it in my hoodie pocket.

Saul leans over and grabs a different stick to start working on. I take that as my cue that he's done with our little conversation, and I turn to find where I'm needed. I scan the camp and realize that Tim is gone.

Something about his absence puts me on edge. I check with David first, in case Tim decided to help them. "Hey, have you seen Tim?"

"No, sorry. We've been busy with this," David answers, tossing a chunk of meat into a bucket. "Do you want me to come help you find him?"

I take a look at his bloody hands and shake my head. "You can finish with what you're doing. I'll go see if Cass knows where he is. I don't think we should let him out of sight for too long," I whisper quietly so the other men can't hear me. I don't know why I'm being secretive, but this feels like a personal matter.

I go to the spot that Tim usually sits and scan the woods to see if I can find him. Nothing. I try to tell myself that maybe he went out because "nature called," but something is needling me in the back of my mind. I know the terrible place Tim is in mentally, which means I need to find him before it's too late. I can't find Cass in camp, so I decide to search for him myself. I head toward the stream and see Tim leaning over the water, washing his hands and arms.

My hand goes to my chest as I blow out the nervous breath I was holding. "Hey, Tim."

He whips his head around to look at me, and his eyes widen a bit, but he gives me a little smile as he finishes up and rolls his sleeves down. "Hey, Olivia."

"I didn't see you in camp, so I got a little worried. You okay?"

"Yeah. I'm fine. I thought about what you said earlier, about working on forgiving myself and how people will miss me if I...you know," he says, looking down at his feet. "I think it'll take some time, but I'm not ready to give up on life yet."

"I'm so glad to hear that, Tim. If you ever need to talk to someone, I'm here for you. Anytime," I say, patting him on the shoulder.

We walk together back toward camp, and as I step out of the tree line, I see Matthias cutting the zip ties that are holding my mom's legs together. Henry is standing next to them, and my mom is smiling up at him. Tim heads off toward David, and I go to see what's going on.

"You're on a very short leash, Jan. The only reason I'm cuttin' ya loose is because Henry asked. Any funny business, and I'm tyin' ya back up," Matthias threatens, pointing the knife toward her face. "Got it?"

"I wouldn't expect anything less from you," she says through a fake smile.

Matthias slams his knife back in the sheath and turns to leave.

As he's walking past me, I mouth, "Thanks."

He nods curtly and heads over toward Saul.

Henry offers a hand to Mom to help her up.

She takes it with a smile, genuine this time, and he pulls her up. "Thank you, Son."

"You're welcome. Now, my help is needed elsewhere. Olivia, you wanna keep her company?"

"Sure. And thanks, Henry."

I take her over to where I have my stuff and help her find something she can wear. We didn't have time to bring a bag of clothes or blankets for her, so she'll have to borrow some. I pull out a pair of athletic pants and a T-shirt, and I keep watch while she hides behind some trees to change. While she's changing, I put my hands in my hoodie pocket and find the stick Saul gave me. I slip it into my bag so I won't lose it. I really want to go ask Matthias for the pendant, but he just did a favor for me by letting Mom go. I better not push it.

We walk down to the stream to wash her clothes out, and I find that I'm feeling cautiously optimistic. I can't believe I have my whole family in one place. A small flicker of hope blossoms in my chest. It'll take some time, but maybe I can start to think of Matthias as a dad, and Henry can finally have a mom.

"I'm glad you're here, Mom."

"I never thought I would say this, but I am too. I'm looking forward to spending time with Henry."

"And me."

"Of course," she says, her voice a little too high.

As I'm stepping up to the stream, I stop short when I see a large rock with drips of blood on it. How did that get there?

8

For the next week, my mom upholds her end of the deal by helping wherever she can. I've never seen her put forth so much effort to make anyone else happy. It's kind of surreal. Anytime she can assist Henry, she does, even if it means getting her hands dirty. The other camp members are still uneasy around her, but she doesn't seem to notice. She only has eyes for Henry.

He's been warming up to her a bit. He's even included her in some of our combat training. We watch in awe as she performs a perfect roundhouse kick and knocks the volleyball out of the air. Henry and I both clap for her, and she beams brightly as she does a playful curtsy. I wish I could've had these sorts of moments my entire life.

Tim seems to be doing better. I caught him whistling the other day, and it made Cass and I look at each other and smile. She's relaxing a bit now that his mood is shifting, and we've been hanging out a little more.

I want to hang out with David, but he's always dragged away to do some type of chore, and I only ever see him at mealtimes. At lunch today, Matthias sits by the fire with David, Henry, Mom, and me, which is a rare occasion. We eat in awkward silence until Henry starts telling Matthias about earlier.

"You should have seen it, Pop," Henry says, swallowing a bite of venison. "Jan just did a roundhouse kick and knocked the volleyball right out of the air. It was pretty cool."

"Huh. Ya've come a long way since I last knew ya. This is the woman who couldn't even walk and chew gum at the same time when we were together."

"Oh, shut it, Matthias," she says around a mouthful of food.

My muscles tense as I feel a fight coming on.

But then she swallows and chuckles a bit as she says, "That was one time. I stumbled over a patch of grass, and the gum fell out of my mouth."

Matthias smirks a little.

"My coordination has improved a lot over the years. One of the many things I've had to work on for my career."

"Don't mention working for the government, Mom!" I whisper-yell.

She swallows a bite of food and side-eyes me. "Every employee is subjected to target practice and martial arts training."

"Is that so?" Matthias grunts. "You and your government buddies get to practice with the very weapons they stole from civilians. Sounds about right."

"Oh, get over yourself, Matthias! Not everything is some evil conspiracy or plot. The government is put into place to protect the people. And that's what we're doing."

David and I exchange a worried look that this is about to go south.

"Oh, is that what they were doin'? Stealing our weapons and then protectin' us? I don't need some pencil pusher who takes a few target practice lessons to protect me! I can protect myself!"

"Prove it! I bet I could outshoot you any day!"

"Don't make me laugh! All right. Let's have a little competition. If ya outshoot me, I'll allow ya to ask me any question ya want, and I'll answer it truthfully. And vice versa," Matthias offers.

I look at mom as she thinks this over. She loves her secrets, so these are pretty high stakes.

"Deal!"

Matthias raises an eyebrow at her. "Okay. We'll get things set up after lunch."

Word travels fast through camp, and soon everyone crowds around as Matthias sets up the cans. Excited whispers come from the crowd. They all want to see Matthias put a government worker in her place.

Matthias finishes and shoos people back to give my mother and him room. My mom is stretching her arms out, and Matthias chuckles a little at her. I stand between Henry and David, watching with butterflies in my stomach.

Alexandrine stomps up to Matthias and says in a not-so-quiet voice, "Do you really trust her with a gun? What are you going to do if she turns the gun on you, Matthias? This is idiotic!"

"Ya don't know her like I do—"

"Did."

Matthias huffs, "She was one of the most competitive women I've ever known. She never backed out of a challenge. I trust that she'll follow the rules for this. Now ya need to trust me."

Alexandrine scowls but turns around and stands next to Frederick to watch.

"Ya ready?"

"Yes, I'm ready to win," she smirks.

If I didn't know any better, I would think she's flirting with him. This is so weird to watch. I'm feeling nervous, so I reach over and grab David's hand to keep me grounded. From the corner of my eye, I see him glance at me, then down at our hands, and then back at my mom and Matthias as a smile spreads across his face.

"All right. Two cans, four shots total. I'll go first and show ya how it's done." Matthias gets himself set up and starts shooting. He shoots the first can, knocking it over, and then shoots it again as it's rolling away. He does the same thing with the second can. He has a smug look on his face as he turns to look at Mom.

"Not bad."

Matthias puts the safety on and then goes to set the cans up for her. He looks the cans over to see where he shot them and nods. He places them in the same spot they were in and walks back to Mom, handing her the gun. A heavy silence spreads over the camp as everyone has their eyes on her.

She gets herself in her shooting stance, turns the safety off, and aims at the cans. She shoots the first one, and it pops up into the air, and then she shoots it again before it hits the ground. She does the same with the second can.

I look at Matthias, and he's still staring at the cans, his cheeks turning red under his beard.

My mom puts on the safety and hands the gun back to Matthias. "I told you so."

"Yeah, yeah. I ain't too stubborn to admit that that was some pretty good shootin'."

My mom smiles at that. "I do believe you owe me a truthful answer to any question I ask."

"Those were the terms. Go ahead. Let's get this over with."

I look around at everyone to see how they feel about this deal. Some people look scared. Some are shaking their heads slightly in disapproval. Alexandrine looks like she wants to take the gun away from Matthias and shoot my mom.

"I'm not ready to ask one yet. I need to think about it first."

A collective sigh seems to escape the crowd. I let go of David's hand as everyone starts to disband now that there isn't anything to watch.

"That was some really good shooting, Mom. I didn't know you knew how to do that," I say.

"There's a lot you don't know about me," she mumbles as she steps past me to catch up to Henry.

I stare at her in disbelief.

"Well, what do you think, Son? Was that some good shooting?"

"Yeah. You'll have to teach me how you get the cans to pop up in the air like that."

"I'd love to. But I was thinking about something when Matthias was loading the gun. How do you guys have enough bullets for target practice?"

"Pop knows a guy."

"That's it? 'Pop knows a guy'?" she says, nudging him with her elbow. "C'mon, Henry. You can tell me."

Henry scrunches his eyebrows at her and shakes his head slightly. "Look, the bet for a secret was between you and Pop. If you want to know, ask him."

Henry walks off, leaving Mom behind looking disappointed. I want to go talk to her, but she keeps giving me the cold shoulder. She can't still be mad at me for making Matthias take her from the city. She seems so happy to be spending time with Henry. I need to know why she's treating me like this.

Just as I'm about to go talk with her, I hear Cass yell, "Tim! Tim, get back here!"

I look over to where she's yelling, and I see Tim running away from her out into the woods. I take a closer look at what Cass is holding in her hand, and my breath catches in my chest. It's a shirt I've seen Tim wear, but the sleeves are bloody.

9

I hurry over to Cass, forgetting about my questions for Mom. I'll talk to her later. David must have heard her yell, because he's right behind me.

"Cass? What's going on?" I ask.

"Everything okay?" David questions.

"No. Everything is not okay," Cass spits out in hushed tones. "I caught Tim trying to hide this shirt," —she shows us the bloody sleeves— "and when I asked him what was going on, he told me to leave him alone and took off running."

"Is he hurt?" I ask, hoping the blood is from hunting or something, although I already know that it can't be from that because he's refused to have anything to do with hunting or meat prep since I've been back.

"I don't know," Cass says, voice shaking. "You guys have to help me find him. Please?"

David and I nod, and we take off running the direction Tim ran. I want to run at full speed, but the underbrush is too thick. Sure enough, I trip over a stick, but I tuck and roll, coming back up onto my feet in one fluid motion. I love having these reflexes.

"You okay?" David asks.

"Yeah, I'm good."

We both stop for a moment so Cass can catch back up.

"Can you hear anything?" I whisper to David. His hearing is now better than mine. I can't believe he used to wear hearing aids.

"Hold on," he says, scrunching up his face and turning his head to the side. "There! I just heard some leaves rustle in that direction."

We take off to the left where David heard the leaves. It doesn't take long, and we find Tim sitting against a tree, hugging his legs, with his forehead resting on his knees.

"Tim?" David says cautiously. "What's going on, man?"

Tim lifts his head and glares at Cass. "Cass is sticking her nose in my business. That's what's going on!"

"I'm worried about you! Where did that blood come from, Tim?" Cass quavers.

Tim rocks back and forth, looking down at the ground. "It's nothing. I just tripped out in the woods and cut my arms on some sticks. I didn't want to worry you, so I was trying to hide my shirt until I had a chance to go wash it."

"Let me see your scratches, then," Cass says.

"No! Leave me alone!"

David gives me a quizzical look.

"Tim, you should probably have Rebecca look at them," I offer.

"It's not that bad. Really."

David kneels next to Tim and places his hand on his shoulder. "Look, I know you're hurting, but we all care about you," David says, gesturing to Cass and me. "What's really going on?"

Tim continues to stare at the ground, refusing to make eye contact.

David grabs Tim's arm and pulls it away from his leg. Before he's able to pull his arm free, we see fresh blood staining his clean long-sleeved shirt and his pants where his arms were resting.

"Holy crap, Tim!" Cass shrieks.

"You need to get that bandaged up," I say, biting my bottom lip.

"Look, guys. I don't really want to talk about it anymore," Tim says, getting frustrated.

"I don't care! I'm your sister, and you need to tell me what's going on. I think you're lying about tripping and scraping yourself on sticks. Now spill it!"

Tim glares at her again but then starts to cry.

I sit next to him and wrap my arm around him. Cass kneels in front of him and rubs his knee gently.

"Tim, you don't have to suffer alone. We are all here for you," I say. "I don't know about Cass, but David and I both know what it's like to be depressed. We can help you, but you have to talk to us."

"Please, Tim. Please." Cass sniffs. "I love you. What happened to your arms?"

"I don't want to tell you, because I'm ashamed," Tim says through his fingers.

"Ashamed? Of what?" Cass asks quietly.

"I found a way to cope with my guilt. I found a way to release my misery. For a little while, anyway."

The silence hangs heavy in the air as we wait for him to tell us what he's talking about.

Tears are rolling down his cheeks as he presses his lips together. Finally, he sighs and hangs his head. "When I do it, I feel lighter, more relaxed. It makes me feel in control of myself," Tim says weakly.

David gently grabs Tim's wrist and unbuttons the cuff of his shirt. This time, Tim doesn't pull away. He squeezes his eyes shut and shakes his head in shame. David carefully rolls Tim's sleeve up until his forearm is exposed. Cass gasps in horror and starts bawling.

His forearm has a number of angry red cuts from the crook of his elbow to his wrist. Some of them are scabbing over, while others are deep enough that the skin is gaping open and bleeding.

"Why would you do this to yourself?" I hug myself, rubbing my hands up and down my arms.

"I told you. When I do it, it makes me feel better. Like I'm in control. When I make a cut, it's like the guilt seeps out along with the blood."

"This isn't okay, Tim," David says firmly. "You need to figure out some other way to cope."

Tim's face screws up with anger, and he pulls his wrist out of David's grasp. "I didn't expect any of you to understand! This is why I didn't want to tell you! Just leave me alone, and let me deal with my problems how I want."

Cass stops crying when Tim raises his voice. She wipes her tears away angrily, then points a finger in his face, "No! This is insane! *You're* insane! How could you do this to yourself? How could you even *think* about doing this to yourself?"

I stand up and grab Cass's arm, dragging her away from Tim. I pull her up to her feet and walk her away so I can talk to her for a moment. "Cass, that isn't helping! I know you're concerned about your brother, but he's hurting inside, and yelling at him is only going to make it worse. We need to handle this calmly."

"I can't be calm," she says, shaking. "He's going to kill himself."

"I don't think he plans on going that far. But if he doesn't get those cuts taken care of, he could get an infection. We need to go back there and gently persuade him to get Rebecca to stitch some of those deep cuts up."

"How could I not have known this was going on? I thought he was getting better," Cass says, distressed.

"I thought so too, but we've been doing our own things or helping around camp; none of us have been paying much attention to him."

"I blame Matthias for this! He's been so hard on Tim, he's caused Tim to do this to himself!" Cass says, still shaking.

"He has been hard on Tim, I'll give you that, but this isn't anyone's fault. Tim is doing this on his own. We need to figure out a way to help him, a way for him to deal with his pain without hurting himself," I say. "Let's go get Tim to Rebecca."

We make our way back over to the boys, and I see that David has wrapped Tim's arm with some cloths to stop the bleeding.

"Where'd you find something to wrap his arms with?" I ask curiously.

David lifts his sweatshirt up, exposing his abdomen. "I used my T-shirt."

I blush slightly. I can see his training sessions have been paying off as he flexes his stomach before pulling his sweatshirt back down. He used to be so scrawny, but now he looks healthy and strong.

"C'mon, Liv. Help me with Tim."

David grabs Tim's upper arm, and I go to Tim's other side and grab the other. We help Tim up and walk him back toward camp.

"You guys can't tell Rebecca how I got these. I don't want anyone else to know."

"How are we going to hide it?" David asks. "She's going to see that they are clean lines cut with a knife."

"I don't know. Tell her we were sword fighting, and it got carried away?"

"We're not going to lie for you, Tim," Cass says. "We'll just take you to her and ask her to help. If she asks how you got them, tell her you cut yourself. If she asks you how, tell her you're an idiot."

"Very funny," Tim responds.

10

Rebecca stitches the deeper cuts and gets Tim bandaged without asking too many questions. I could tell she wanted to, but David took her to the side and whispered something to her when we got there. She looked at Tim with motherly concern but got to work.

When she's done, we all follow Tim to his sleeping spot. Cass grabs her notebook out of her bag and has a seat facing Tim.

"Let's make a list."

"Of what?" Tim asks sulkily.

"Of things you could do instead of that," she says, pointing the pen at his arms.

"I think that's a good idea," I say.

Tim just shrugs.

"You could have my notebook and start writing in it. Write about how you feel. Or why you're hurting," Cass offers.

"You could whittle on a stick like Saul does. Maybe cutting a stick would help," David suggests.

Cass writes both things down in the notebook.

"You could go for a walk," I say.

"Talk to someone when you're feeling the urge."

"Pray."

"Let your emotions out. Cry or scream."

"Ask me for a hug," Cass says sweetly.

"Skip stones in the stream."

"Okay, guys! I get that you want to help me, but you're kinda stressing me out right now. I need to think for a moment."

We all sit quietly next to him. I get distracted by the snippets of conversations I hear as people pass close to where we're sitting. A couple of people accuse us of being lazy, just sitting here making everyone else work.

Then I catch Henry's voice in the mix and focus my attention on him. "She wanted me to tell her how we have enough bullets for target practice, but I didn't tell her anything, Pop. All I said was that the bet was between you and her, and if she wanted to know, she should ask you," Henry says.

"So, you didn't mention anything about the bunker?"

"Of course not."

"Good. I'm going to have to head over there and get some more ammo soon. I don't want anyone but us to know about it."

He found a bunker with ammo? Where did that come from?

I focus my attention back to Tim and see him staring down at the ground, almost in tears. He's rubbing at his arm, and I suddenly have an idea. I stand up, run over to my bag, take out my hairbrush, and pull off a hair tie that I have twisted on the handle. I run back over to Tim, who's now watching me with a questioning look.

"Here, try this. You can wear this hair tie on your wrist, and when the emotions start overwhelming you or you start thinking about hurting yourself, you can snap this hair tie on your wrist. Maybe the sting will be enough."

"I can try," Tim says, putting it on.

"But he's still hurting himself," Cass points out. "Shouldn't we think of something that doesn't cause pain?"

"I think Liv is on the right track. I don't think Tim is going to heal overnight, but this is at least something he can do in the meantime that won't be dangerous."

We all look at Tim, and he nods as he snaps the hair tie on his wrist.

"Were you just thinking about cutting again?" Cass asks worriedly.

"No. I just wanted to see what it felt like. I think this will help. Thanks, Liv."

I give Tim a hug, and Cass and David join in, making it a group hug. We go off balance and all tip over, laughing. Even Tim. David helps me back up, letting his arm linger around my waist for a moment longer than natural. I give him a smile while nervously running my fingers through my hair.

What is happening to me? I told David we were only ever going to be friends, and I meant it. So why do I suddenly find myself so awkward and nervous around him?

"C'mon guys. We should probably go help everyone else out." Cass grabs Tim's hand to drag him over by Frederick, who's piling wood up in the fire pit to get a cooking fire going.

"We're going to go get some firewood," David calls out to no one in particular.

I follow him out of the clearing, but I turn to spot my mom before I do. I see her helping Caroline peel vegetables for our next meal. They're both laughing about something. Maybe Mom is going to be okay here after all.

David and I walk about a quarter of a mile away from camp before he starts talking. "I'm glad to finally be hanging out with you again."

"Me too. It was beginning to feel like they were keeping us apart on purpose or something."

"So, how are you, Liv?" David asks, eyebrows furrowed.

"I'm okay. Why?"

"Just all this stuff with Tim got me thinking about how important it is to be there for each other, to check in once in a while." He stops and grabs my arm, pulling me to a fallen tree to sit down.

"I'm doing a lot better now that I'm back out here."

"I've been meaning to ask, what happened in the city before we rescued you? You looked pretty rough."

I grind the toes of my shoes in the dirt before answering. I try to not think about what happened—or what could have happened if my mom wouldn't have saved me. "They tortured me to try to get answers about where Matthias was or where we were going."

"They tortured you?" David asks in disgust. "How?"

"Some guy injected me with something that made my insides feel like they were melting," I say, my voice quivering. "He told me he would do it again unless I told him what he wanted to know. I had a moment where I didn't think I could go through it again. And I thought about how you would understand if I gave in to avoid the pain."

David reaches over and wipes a tear away with his thumb.

"But then I thought about Markos and how he died protecting everyone. I wanted to do the same, so I gave him fake answers. He got pissed and injected me with three times as much as the first injection, and I guess I died," I say quietly.

David shakes his head slowly. "I almost lost you again? I am never letting you out of my sight."

I smile a little at him. "Mom shot the guy who injected me and had a nurse restart my heart. Once again, my death was thwarted."

"Thank God for that," David says softly. "I honestly don't know what I would do without you, Liv."

"You'd survive."

"No. I don't think I would."

I look up at him, and he is looking at me so intensely, I blush and look away.

"Liv, I can't help but notice some changes between us," he says, gently grabbing my hand and cupping it between his.

Crap. Here we go again. "If you're referring to when I held your hand, that was because I was nervous when my mom and Matthias were about to shoot. I needed to hold your hand to ground myself," I say defensively.

"So, nothing's changed, then? Between us?" he asks, looking at our hands instead of my eyes.

I stop and think about how to respond. He has been pursuing a relationship with me for so long, and I keep rejecting him. I hate to think that I'm causing him pain.

"I wouldn't say that, David. Some things have changed," I start to say, and I see his face light up. I need to keep going quickly so he doesn't get the wrong idea. "I care so much for you, but our situation hasn't changed. We are still out in the middle of the wilderness, trying to survive. Your friendship has been my only saving grace. You have helped me to keep going, to not want to give up on life—"

"And if you give me the chance, I could love you like you deserve to be loved, Liv. I would treat you like the warrior princess that you are, and you would never have a doubt in your mind that you are desirable or wanted," David interrupts, lifting my chin to face him. "You are the most important person in my life. Please, Liv, give us a chance."

A wave of emotions comes crashing over me: anger that he keeps doing this to me, that he keeps trying to be more than friends; frustration that he can't just leave good enough alone; sadness that I am about to hurt him once again; flattery that he cares about me enough to want to be in a relationship; confusion that a little part of me is curious to see how it would go. "David...I—"

He stops what I'm saying with a gentle kiss on my lips. I'm about to pull away, but this is the first kiss I've ever had, so I allow myself to go with it. His lips are soft and warm against mine, and I find that I actually enjoy it.

He pulls away and rests his forehead against mine. "I love you, Liv."

I jerk my head back and look at him to see if he's serious.

Love? What does he know about love? How does anyone know if they love someone? I suddenly feel sick to my stomach. I pull away from him and scoot over a little to put some space between us. I can feel his eyes on me, but I can't look at him, so I just stare at a leaf on the ground as those words keep rolling around in my head.

He loves me? What is there to love?

"Liv? C'mon. Say something."

I finally get up the nerve to look at him. My heart drums in my chest as I stare into his golden-brown eyes. "I love you too, David," I say slowly, shaking my head. "But I'm not *in* love with you."

I watch as his entire demeanor shifts. His loving gaze turns stony after I say those words. He stands up abruptly, back straight and chin held high. "Fine. I get it."

"David, please, I—"

"I should get back to camp."

"No, David, please!" I stand up and grab his arm. "Don't do this! I need you and our friendship!"

"I'm not going anywhere, Liv," David says with a pinched voice. "If you need me, of course, I'm still here for you. But I'm done trying to convince you that we would be perfect together. I'm done getting hurt." He pulls his arm out of my grasp. "I'll see you back at camp." He turns and walks quickly away.

I sit back down on the tree and stare out into the woods. Why do I always make such a mess of things?

1|1

I sit out in the woods until the sun starts going down, and a chill fills the air. I pull my arms into my sweatshirt and rub the goosebumps away as I walk back to camp. My mind is numb as I plod along. I should be more nervous about a Havoc or some other wild animal picking me off before I make it back, but with the way I'm feeling, it's almost a welcoming thought.

I can smell the food cooking well before I get back to camp. My mouth waters, even though I don't feel hungry. As I enter camp, I see David sitting by the fire. A part of me wants to talk to him some more, but instead, I just go back to my sleeping spot and curl up on the ground. I lie there sulking, thinking about things, about how I made David feel. I'm so deep in my wallowing that I jump about a foot off the ground when I hear a voice right behind me.

"Here, Olivia. I brought you some food."

I sit up and see my mom offering me a plate of meat and boiled veggies. She has a concerned look on her face as she passes me the food.

"Thanks."

"Are you okay?"

I take a moment to see if she really cares. She continues to look at me with concern, so I take a chance and tell her what's going on. "Well, actually, no. I just hurt David's feelings, and I feel terrible about it."

"What did you do?" she asks, sitting down next to me.

This is weird. She's trying to be nice. Why is she trying to be nice? "He kissed me and then told me that he loves me."

"Well, that sounds wonderful! What did you do?"

"I told him that I love him but I'm not in love with him."

"Ouch."

"I keep telling him that I need him to be my friend. What happens if we try to do the relationship thing, but it doesn't work out? Then I'll have nobody. Why can't he just leave good enough alone and keep our friendship the way it is?" I ask, getting angry.

"I get it. Commitment issues run in the family," she says, nodding knowingly.

"Really?"

"Before I met and married your father, I was in love with someone else. I was afraid to be in a relationship at the time, so I kept him at a distance. It stems from my upbringing."

"What happened to you when you were a kid?" I ask, knowing I'm pushing my limits.

She looks up at the trees as tears brim her eyes. "My father was verbally abusive. On particularly bad days, my mom would turn around and take it out on me. She'd tell me it was all my fault. That he wasn't like this before I came along." She stops talking and takes a moment to collect herself.

I wipe away the tears that are forming in my eyes as well.

"I don't have any memories of my parents ever telling me they loved me. Sure, they gave me what I needed to survive—food, shelter, clothes—but that was it. It took me a long time to believe I was worthwhile. So, when a boy started showing interest in me, I thought it was a trick, that he was going to treat me just like my father treated me."

"So, what happened?" I'm shaking slightly from nerves at my mom actually opening up to me and telling me about her past. I don't know what she's playing at, but I'm going to see how long I can keep her talking and relish this moment. I've always wanted my mom to have heart-to-heart talks with me. I wonder what's changed?

"We hung out, spent time together, flirted, even kissed a few times. Eventually, he told me he loved me, and he wanted to be with me forever. I told him I wasn't ready to be in a relationship for what felt like the hundredth time, and he finally gave up. I was crushed. Looking back at it, it was foolish for me to think he would wait forever. Teenage me was smitten with him but too afraid of getting hurt. In the end, I hurt us both."

"What was his name?"

She chews on her bottom lip for a moment as though deciding whether she should tell me or not. This must be hard for her. She's never told me anything about her past life. Or current life, for that matter. "We all called him Arty."

"Arty? Was he good at painting or something?"

"No." She chuckles a bit. "His initials were RT, so people called him Arty."

"Ah. That makes sense."

We're both quiet for a moment. I grab the plate of food I had set down, stab a chunk of carrot, and pop it in my mouth.

"I'm sorry I haven't always been there for you, Olivia."

I turn and look at her with furrowed eyebrows. I swallow and ask, "Where is all of this coming from? Don't get me wrong, I'm really enjoying talking to you, but this is strange. You've never wanted to open up and talk about feelings."

She shrugs and tucks her hair behind her ear, looking self-conscious. "I know," she whispers. "I was talking to Caroline, who, by the way, has been the only one that's even talked to me like a normal person since I got here."

"Sorry about that, but you are a government worker in a camp of anti-government people. Give it time. I think they'll come around."

She gives me a skeptical look but continues on, "Anyway, she was giving me some parenting advice. I guess I've always been so focused on my work, I never stopped to try to be the mom I never had and always wanted. I honestly didn't know how to be a loving mom, and so I just threw myself into my work and told myself that I was providing for you, and that should be enough. Now that I'm out here, I realized that I missed so much. I never got a chance to know Henry, and I never tried to get to know you."

"You've been kind of cold to me since you got out here."

"I'm sorry about that," she says.

We sit in comfortable silence while I eat the rest of my food. I mull over what my mom told me about her childhood. If what she told me is true, I can understand why she struggled so much to show me love. It's a foreign concept to her. I look over at her and see her watching the birds in the trees, and my heart breaks a little for her. Our relationship is not even close to perfect, but she's never made me feel completely worthless. I've felt that all on my own.

When I'm done eating, she takes my plate to wash up, saying she volunteered to be on dish duty.

Now that I'm alone again, a part of me wants to continue sulking over here away from everyone, but I look over by the fire and see that almost the whole camp is sitting together, Tim included, and I suddenly feel lonely. I can hear the children playing a game of keep away, and their giggles send a wave of longing through me.

I want to be happy. I want this ever-lingering darkness to go away. I want to feel hope and contentment. I'm the healthiest I have ever been in my life. I can see better, hear better, breathe better. I even have amazing reflexes with my Rare abilities, and yet there is a darkness in my mind that just won't let go, won't allow me any peace. Maybe I'm broken and will never be free.

I can't stand being alone with my thoughts anymore, so I make my way over to the group and see David sitting between Tim and Alexandrine. Tim's nervously fidgeting with the hair tie on his wrist like he wants to snap it but doesn't want to bring attention to himself. Alexandrine is cleaning out dirt from under her fingernails with a knife.

David looks up at me as I come closer but then looks back at the fire quickly. The pain in his eyes is heart-wrenching.

I find a spot next to Cass and sit on the ground. "What did I miss?" I whisper to Cass.

"Everyone is telling stories about things they witnessed in the city that didn't sit right or that made them wonder if there was something going on."

I sit up a little straighter and listen in.

"The rain. The rain is what got me questioning things. Has anyone actually seen the effects of the rain on a person?" Caroline asks.

I look around, and everyone is shaking their heads.

"Rebecca? You worked in the hospital. Did you actually see anyone with their flesh melted off after a rain?"

"I can't say that I did."

"See? I knew it!"

A few people around the campfire are nodding.

"I was chopping wood one day," Frederick says, "and I got it in my head to do a little target practice with the ax. I enjoyed it, so the next day, I set out to do it again, but a guard just 'happened' to be passing by and took my ax, claiming I was a danger to the neighborhood." He scoffs. "More like I was becoming a danger to the government by learning how to fight. Jokes on them, though. Markos brought his ax over, and we spent hours practicing in my basement."

A little shock of guilt runs through me when he mentions Markos's name. I glance at Frederick, and instead of the sadness I was expecting to see, I see a small smirk of amusement at the memory. That makes me feel a little better somehow.

Nobody else is talking, so I decide to say something, "I never really had any feelings of my own that something was going on until David started questioning things, and it put it in my head." I give him a little smile when he looks up at me. "There was one weird incident that happened in the psychiatric ward, though. A young girl named Charlotte told me about 'the magic within.' At the time, I just assumed she was crazy, considering where we were. But now I'm wondering if she could have known about Rare abilities."

I look around at everyone and see that Alexandrine's giving me a weird look.

Just then, my mom comes back from dish duty, and the conversation dies out. Apparently, nobody wants to continue talking about the government being shady around her. I don't blame them.

"I think I'm ready to ask my question now," Mom announces to Matthias.

Matthias shuffles around on his seat and crosses his arms over his chest. "Shoot."

"It was difficult to figure out what I wanted to ask since there are so many questions I have for you, but I think I'm most curious about where you get enough ammunition to do target practice."

Henry looks worriedly at Matthias, but he just shrugs. "Why do ya care?"

"I'm just curious."

"There's a bunker with ammunition and a few weapons hidden to the northeast of the city," Matthias answers, annoyed.

"Hmm. So, you don't know about the weapon cache on the west side of the river then?"

"No?" Matthias uncrosses his arms and leans forward.

My mom glances at Henry and smiles mischievously. "It's big enough to arm a sizable militia."

"Why are ya telling me this?" Matthias asks distrustfully.

"Because I want to help," she says, winking toward Henry.

Alexandrine stands up abruptly and storms away.

"What's her problem?" Mom asks, her smile fading.

"You. Alexandrine trusts ya about as far as she can throw ya. To be honest, I'm feelin' the same way. What's your objective here, Jan?"

Mom scoffs and shifts her weight back and forth for a moment, looking both embarrassed and angry. "You're a real piece of work, aren't you? You're the one who brought me out here, Matthias! 'What's my objective?' How about the fact that I can't go back now? The fact that you kidnapped me, brought me out here, and I haven't shown back up yet? That tells them that either I'm dead or I've become a traitor. They don't think very kindly toward government workers leaving to go hang out with rebel groups. If I waltz back in there, telling them that my estranged husband kidnapped me and I stayed because I wanted to spend time with my son, they would put a bullet in my head for misconduct. I swore an oath to my position, and now I've not only killed a fellow comrade, but I've been cavorting with their enemy." She takes a deep breath to try to calm down. "No. The only way I can go back now is if I have you in custody or I kill you all. And I'm not willing to do that."

"But why tell us about the secret weapons? What do ya have to gain?"

"Henry is my son too, Matthias! I haven't gotten to be his mom. Maybe this is my way of trying to make up for that!" she yells, crossing her arms over her chest and scowling.

Matthias puts his hands up as though surrendering. "All right, all right. I'm standin' down. Tell me what ya know, and then we'll make the decision."

"Why don't you give her some rectitude wine? Then we'll know whether she's lying or not," one of the men shouts from the crowd.

"Can't. I haven't made a new batch yet."

I shiver as I remember how it made me want to divulge all my secrets. Mom would hate that stuff.

12

"Hey, have ya seen Alexandrine around anywhere?" Matthias asks me.

"No. Why?"

"I wanted her to be a part of the discussion on the weapons cache."

"I'll let her know if I see her."

I watch as he goes back to a group of people, and they look around the camp once more before heading out into the woods. I'm so happy that my mother decided to help us all out. I'm hoping to start fixing our relationship now. It's never too late to start over.

My good mood is making me antsy. I spot the kids' volleyball, and I get an urge to play. "Hey, Cass!" I yell out. She's sitting next to a tree, writing in her notebook. "Wanna play?"

She looks up from her notebook, and when she sees me holding the volleyball, she drops the notebook and pen on the ground. She comes running over and tries to grab the ball out of my hand while giggling. "Tim! Get over here!" Cass shouts.

Tim has been sitting by the firepit, staring at the ashes, for a better part of an hour. I think this will be good for him.

He looks over his shoulder at us, and his eyes light up a bit. He makes a big show of reluctantly standing up and shuffling his way over slowly, but once he's about five feet away, he lunges at the ball in Cass's hands and knocks it out of her grip.

"Hey!" Cass laughs.

Tim picks it up and holds it over his head, well out of Cass's reach. She jumps a couple of times, but it's no use, so she starts tickling his sides. He drops the ball, laughing, telling her to stop.

As they're goofing around, I see David and skip my way over to him. "Hey, David. I know you're mad at me, but Cass, Tim, and I were about to play a game with the ball. Would you like to play?"

"I'm not mad at you, Liv," David says, exasperated. He looks over at Cass and Tim and smirks. "Sure. Let's play."

We team up to play a game of soccer, girls against boys. David's and my reflexes are so fast, Cass insists that he and I have to play against each other; otherwise, it isn't fair. It's a little awkward since we have to be so close to each other, but we just play the game as best we can. I've never been good at sports, but I find myself really enjoying this: the competitiveness,

54

the skill and coordination involved, and running around getting the blood flowing.

We attract the attention of the small children, and before we know it, they're all running around with us. Rebecca and Caroline stand off to the side, watching us with amused looks. Little Sonya pulls her hand out of Rebecca's grasp and runs over to play too. Tim's smile fades a bit when he sees her. He stops what he's doing and hands the ball to her. She gives him a big smile and takes off with the ball toward the goal we made with some sticks. We all cheer for her when she throws it and scores. She turns around and hugs Tim's leg before running off to get the ball again.

I watch Tim stand still for a moment.

"See? It's going to be okay, Tim," I say.

He nods, and we go back to the game. We play until the adults come back from having their discussion.

"So, what did you decide?" I ask Henry, a little out of breath.

"Pop's going to announce it at supper. You'll just have to wait like everyone else." He winks, and I punch his arm playfully.

I worked up a sweat while playing, so I decide to take a quick bath in the stream before we work on supper. When the weather gets cooler, we're going to have to boil water and do sponge baths or something, but today is still mild, so I'm just going to do it the quick way.

As I'm heading over to get some clean clothes, I see Mom lying down on the ground, facing away from camp. I tiptoe my way to my bag, and as I get closer, I hear her talking, but I can't quite figure out what she's saying. I try to sneak up so I can hear her, but my shoe catches on a rock and sends it clattering.

She rolls over, eyes wide.

"Who were you talking to?" I ask lightly, walking normally to my bag so it doesn't look like I was spying on her.

"Oh. I was just praying," she answers in that high-pitched voice again, fixing her hair as she sits up.

"I didn't realize you believed in God enough to pray," I say slowly.

"Of course I do."

I raise my eyebrow at her. "You never took me to church or anything."

"That was some game you guys were playing over there! Who won?" she asks, clearly trying to change the subject.

I try to let it go. She's putting forth the effort to be better; I shouldn't push her too hard. "We weren't really keeping score, but I got more goals than David did, so I'd say that Cass and I won."

"Sounds like fun," she says distractedly. She keeps playing with her hair. I've never seen her so fidgety.

"It was. Anyway, I'm going to go take a bath before we get started on supper."

"Okay, sweetheart."

Sweetheart? She's acting so strangely. I wonder what she's hiding now.

13

After my brisk bath, I bundle up and head over to where I see a group is gathered. They're standing around Matthias, so I hurry up to hear what the decision was.

"I'll need volunteers," Matthias says.

"Volunteers for what?" I whisper to David as I step over to where he's standing.

"They've decided to check out the weapon cache."

A few men raise their hands, Henry included. Before I know it, David volunteers too.

"Are you sure you want to go?"

"It's better than sitting around here day after day. Besides, they could use my help," he answers without looking at me.

"...four, five, six. Good. We'll start planning and head out in a few days. We're gonna need supplies for the trip there and back, but we'll need to pack light so we have space for bringing as much ammunition back as possible. It's gonna be heavy, so ya better be ready."

Everyone disbands, and I follow David back to his bag.

He opens the zippers and dumps his belongings out onto the ground without saying a word to me. He starts sniffing his clothes to figure out what's clean and what needs washing. "Will you watch my stuff while I'm gone?" David asks as he makes a pile of dirty clothes.

"Is it going to do a dance for me?" I ask in a lame attempt at humor.

He gives me a halfhearted smile as he continues to add clothes to the dirty pile. By the time he's done, he only has one change of clothes left. "Huh. I guess I should go do some laundry. I really miss washing machines."

"What would you know? Your mom used to wash your clothes for you," I tease.

He throws a balled-up dirty sock at me, and we both laugh.

·····

The entire camp is together having supper the night before the group leaves to get extra ammunition. That is, everyone except Alexandrine. She still hasn't shown up yet, and nobody knows where she went. Matthias seems a bit on edge with her absence, but he carries on with the planning anyway.

We're all sitting around the fire as my mom and Caroline hand out bowls of the stew they prepared. Mom walks over to Henry and me with two steaming bowls, and my stomach rumbles in anticipation. I reach out to grab one from her, but she pulls it away from me and hands it to Henry.

"This one's for Henry. I picked the peas out of it for him since I remember he hates peas." She gives a knowing smile.

"That was when I was like two. I don't mind peas now."

Mom's smile fades, so I elbow Henry, who's completely oblivious to how he just made her feel.

"Ow. What?" he says through a mouthful of food.

I jerk my head toward her and give him a look.

He swallows quickly. "I mean, thanks for thinking of me. I appreciate it. The stew's good with or without peas."

Her eyes brighten a bit as she turns back to the pot to dish up more.

After supper, everyone decides to turn in early so the group can get up with the sunrise and head out. I can't seem to slow my mind down to fall asleep, so I just lie there, listening to the deep breathing of those who are already sleeping.

I keep hearing Tim snap the hair tie on his wrist, and my soul aches for him. I can't imagine being tempted to hurt yourself like he did. I know I tried to commit suicide a couple of times, but I was trying to escape pain, not inflict it. I have spent so much of my life being in pain and miserable, I can't imagine the place you have to be in mentally to want to hurt. Before I fall asleep, I say a little prayer for Tim in hopes that if there is a God, he will be able to help Tim through it.

Morning comes, and I wake up to voices murmuring nearby.

"I need to go, Pop. You need my help," Henry says weakly.

"You're sick as a dog. Ya ain't comin', Henry. You'd only slow us down," Matthias scolds but then changes his tone. "Ya need to stay here and get better. We'll manage without ya on this one."

Just then, I hear Henry retch, and Matthias pats his back.

"Rebecca. Ya got anything that could settle his stomach down?" Matthias asks with a touch of worry in his voice.

"I'm afraid not. He's going to have to just ride it out. I'll make sure he stays hydrated."

I turn over and see that David has his bedroll all packed up, and he's sitting by the fire, ready to go.

"Well, we're down a man. Anyone else wanna come?" Matthias calls out.

I watch as Cass runs up to Matthias and whispers at him. Matthias looks toward Tim, then back at her and sighs.

"Timothy? How 'bout you?" Matthias asks.

Tim lifts his head to look at Matthias. He's silent for a moment as he fidgets with the hair tie. "Sure." He shrugs. Before the accident, Tim would have jumped at the chance to go along with the guys, but now he seems reluctant.

"Okay, grab your stuff. We're gonna head out soon."

I join David by the firepit as Tim gets his bag ready. "Stay safe out there," I say, poking the side of his leg.

"I'll try."

"Promise?" I ask nervously.

He reaches over to wrap an arm around me but stops before he touches me. A pained look crosses over him as he takes his arm away. I find myself longing for the comfort of his touch, but I'm the one who made it weird between us.

"I'm sorry about the other day. I pushed too hard," David finally says after a moment of awkward silence.

"No, I'm sorry I hurt you."

"It's my own fault. You've told me how you feel. I was asking to get hurt again. I just hope that maybe someday we can get settled enough that we could give it a try."

"Maybe. Perhaps if we ever find the Haven, we could focus more on us than on survival."

"So, you believe Matthias? That the Haven is a real place?"

"Maybe...?" I say, suddenly self-conscious.

"Look at you. It took me forever to get you to leave the city, and now you believe that there is more out there all on your own."

"Yeah, well, it's like Tim had said once, it's foolish to think we're the only ones who don't trust the government. The more I'm out here around 'rebels,' the more I realize how blind I was while I was in the city. No pun intended." I chuckle. "Sure, we had access to food and hospitals and all that, but what were they really doing for us? I think I feel safer out here in our camp than I remember feeling in the city."

"Me too. It doesn't hurt that you and I can kick some serious butt now. I would give anything to see you fight Victoria."

I laugh. "She wouldn't stand a chance! I'm glad I'll never see her stupid face again. Or Cindy's. Did you know that she wrote me letters from the looney bin?"

"Who? Cindy?"

"Yeah, she threatened to kill me if she ever got out of the hospital all because I was trying to help Joselyn. Thank God she's stuck in there! Cindy...not Joselyn."

"I knew what you meant. Poor Joselyn. Some of the people who were in there didn't seem like they deserved to be locked up. Did I ever tell you about one of the people I met when I was in there?"

"Bartholomew, your imaginary friend?"

"No. Not him." David scoffs. "There was this guy who was in there for only a little bit. He wasn't suicidal or anything, so I have no idea what his deal was. Anyway, I sat at the same table as him for lunch once. He was chatting away, keeping those around him captivated. He seemed to know things before they happened. It was weird."

"Like what?"

"While we were eating, right before the alarm started sounding, he told us it was about to start raining. Then, midsentence, he turned around and caught a fork someone accidentally dropped before it hit the floor. Also, before he finished eating, he got up and left abruptly, and just as he walked out of the room, one of the other patients had a violent meltdown and had to be restrained. It was nothing big, but it was like he was clairvoyant or something."

"Do you think he had some sort of super-level Rare reflex abilities?"

David shrugs. "How could he if he was living inside the city? Any of his abilities would have been dampened just like ours were."

"True."

"Ya ready, David?" Matthias calls from the group that gathered while we were talking.

"Yup!" he calls back, then turns to me. "Stay out of trouble, Liv."

"Of course. You know me."

"Exactly. You always manage to get into trouble while I'm not with you."

"I'll be fine."

"Good. See you soon." He straps his bag on his back.

I glance over at Henry, and he's watching them all with envy on his pale face. Mom is sitting next to him, patting his arm gently. I hope I don't catch whatever he has. He looks miserable.

I stand and wave to David as he heads off on this adventure. I'm kind of jealous, but I think this will be a great opportunity to spend some time with Mom. Tim looks nervously around camp once more, waves to Cass, and then turns to follow the men. I hope this trip helps him.

1 4

I feel like I'm slowly going crazy. Mom spends most of her time helping Rebecca nurse Henry back to health, which doesn't give us much time to do anything together. Chores seem so much more tedious, knowing that David is out there doing something adventurous without me. Cass isn't a whole lot of fun to be around, because she keeps fretting over Tim. I understand her worry, but every time I try to strike up a conversation, she only talks about whether I think Tim will struggle and start cutting while he's away. I just sigh and reassure her once again.

It's been a day and a half since the men left, and now that Henry's almost back to normal, he keeps trying to tell us he can catch up if he leaves now. He won't listen to us when we tell him he can't.

Finally, Frederick has had enough and scolds him. "Sit yourself down, Henry, and stop acting like a fool! They left yesterday morning. They're probably almost there by now."

Henry glares at Fredrick with his fists balled at his sides, but after a moment, his shoulders drop, and he relaxes. "You're right. I'm just not used to sitting around."

"Well, if you're feeling up to it, let's go get some food for supper."

Henry nods, and they take off into the woods. Finally, Mom and I have a moment together.

"I hope Henry will be okay out there," Mom worries.

"He'll be fine. You and Rebecca did a good job taking care of him."

She looks me dead in the eyes and says gravely, "I just want what's best for you and Henry. Always remember that."

A chill runs up my spine as she turns and walks toward the stream. "Where are you going?" I call after her.

"I've got something to do."

"Need any help?" I ask, confused.

She turns and looks at me. "No, I need a little time to myself to collect my thoughts. I'm tired," she says, stroking her forehead. "Why don't you go help Caroline and Rebecca with the kids? They could probably use a break." She gazes at me for a moment, then turns back toward the stream and walks away.

My mind immediately plummets into thoughts of being unwanted and unloved, but I refuse to entertain them for more than a few seconds. She just spent the last couple of days doting on Henry, and sometimes you just need to be by yourself.

After about five minutes of sitting here, I can't shake this uneasy feeling I have after that interaction with my mom. Something is niggling me in the back of my mind. I consider following her to see what she's up to, but I stay put. I decided that I would try harder to get along with her, and following her would just make her mad.

I don't feel like hanging out with little kids right now, so I head over to where Cass is sitting doodling in her notebook. I take a seat against a tree and listen to the birds sing, mulling things around in my mind.

"My mom's acting weird again," I blurt out.

"Was she ever normal?" Cass smirks as she continues drawing.

"I'm serious. Something seems wrong. I can't shake this feeling that something is about to happen."

I look over at Cass and see that I have her attention now. She puts down her pencil and sits up straighter. "Why? What do you think will happen?"

"I don't know," I mumble, shaking my head.

"Maybe you're just nervous because David went with Matthias."

"Maybe," I say skeptically, but in my gut, I know that isn't it.

"I'm sure they'll be fine. Matthias is in charge. He's too stubborn to let anyone get hurt on his watch. I'm sure that Tim will be fine too," Cass says, reassuring herself more than me. She gives me a smile and then picks her pencil back up to continue working in her notebook.

I decide to lie down and take a nap. Being temporarily unconscious sounds amazing right now. I slow my breathing down and tune out all the different noises coming from camp. I let my mind wander, feeling sleep tugging me down into its comforting embrace. My muscles relax, and it's as though I'm sinking into the ground. As I'm just about to fall asleep, a surge of adrenaline rushes through my body and pulls me awake with a painful jolt. I sit up and look around for the imminent danger.

"What's the matter?" Cass asks, looking at me with worry. "Did you have a bad dream?"

"No," I answer, breathing heavily. "Something's wrong. I need to find my mom." I frantically stand up and am heading the direction my mom went when, suddenly, a faraway boom echoes through our camp.

My heart immediately drops into my stomach.

Cass is up on her feet, looking as scared as I feel. "What was that?" she yells.

Everyone in camp has stopped what they're doing and are all looking around at each other questioningly. My entire body shakes with fear of what that explosion could have been. I need to get higher so I can see what's going on.

I run out to the woods and pick the tree that seems to be the tallest in the area. I get a running start and use one foot to kick off a nearby tree's trunk, which pushes me toward the one I want to climb. I jump back and forth, kicking off each tree as I climb higher and higher toward the branches. I give one last hard push and grab onto the bottom branch. I swing myself up and take a moment to catch my breath. I can't believe I can do things like that!

I quickly climb my way to the top of the tree, and even though it's not a clear view, I can see a thick column of black smoke swirling up from west of the river, right from the direction David was heading.

15

I find myself on the ground, but I don't remember climbing down the tree. I'm on my hands and knees, breathing fast and hard. My vision fades black around the edges as terror rips through my body. I look up as I hear footsteps crashing through the trees and see Henry and Frederick running back to camp. I push myself up and stumble my way back. I have just enough sense not to take off by myself to find David, even though I desperately want to. My head is fuzzy as I try to process what's going on. I finally make it back and see everyone in camp flocked around Henry and Frederick.

"I have no idea what that was," Henry says to Cass, who looks white as a ghost.

"It came from where David was going. West of the river," I choke out, my throat tight with emotion.

"Are you sure?" Henry asks.

"I climbed a tree and saw smoke billowing from there."

Henry lets out a frustrated yell toward the sky.

"We don't know that anything bad has happened to the group yet. We need to keep our heads. Henry, take a seat before you pass out," Frederick says.

Henry plops down on a tree stump, bracing his head in his hands.

"Did Matthias mention anything about blowing the cache up after they got the ammo?" I ask, hoping with all my might that that's the case.

"No. Why would they do that? That would announce their location and bring attention to themselves," Henry answers in a condescending tone.

"Okay. I'm sorry. I just don't want it to be the alternative."

Henry rubs at his face with both hands, letting out a frustrated groan. "Where's Janice?" he growls, standing up abruptly. "She did this. She had to have had something to do with this!"

"After you went off to hunt, she said she had something to do and wanted to be alone," I answer. "But why would she do something like this? She said she wanted to help us. Especially you."

Henry stands there thinking for a moment and then looks straight at me with his piercing blue eyes. "I don't think it was a coincidence that I got sick the night before we were supposed to leave for this. She didn't want me to go, because she knew there was going to be an explosion. That's why she insisted I get the bowl of stew you had grabbed. She poisoned it to make me sick!"

My stomach does a flip when I realize he might be right. But why would she do this?

"Let's stop standing around talking about the whys and why-nots. What are we going to do about it?" Frederick asks.

"We're going to go save whoever might still be alive," Henry replies. "Who's coming?"

Frederick and Henry look around camp to find any volunteers.

"Rebecca, we're going to need you to come with us. You're the best at this kind of thing. Bring your medical kit," Frederick says.

Rebecca nods and runs to grab her equipment.

"I want to come," I say because I need to know David is okay.

"No. You're part of the reason this happened. We just had to bring her out here because of you. You better hope to God that Pop is all right," Henry barks angrily, pointing a shaky finger at me.

I take a couple of steps back, stunned at the venom in his voice. He's right. If mom did cause the explosion and anyone died because of it, it would be my fault.

"Cool it, Henry!" Frederick yells. He gives me a sympathetic look before grabbing Henry's shoulder and dragging him off to gather supplies.

I glance around at everyone in camp, suddenly feeling vulnerable. I don't want to be standing here in front of everyone. I spot Cass, who's rocking back and forth, hugging her knees and crying. I have a seat next to her and wrap my arm around her shoulders.

She leans into me, sniffling. "Do you think anyone died?" she asks with a shudder.

"I don't know."

"Is this the bad feeling you were having? Did you know this was going to happen?"

"I had no idea about the explosion. I just felt a weird sensation that something bad was coming."

"I hope Tim is okay. I'm the one who told Matthias to take him along. If something bad happened to him, it was my fault," she blubbers.

"We need to stop blaming ourselves for everything. You didn't make Tim go. You only suggested that he did. Everything else was out of your control. I made Matthias bring my mom out here, but I didn't make her do this, and how do we even know this was her doing? Henry might be right, but he could be wrong too."

"True. But you said it yourself that your mom was acting weird."

I nod reluctantly. We sit together, watching the group of people gather up their things and get ready to head out to find the survivors. Rebecca heads over to where we're sitting.

"Please help keep an eye on my boys for me," Rebecca says as she straps her bag on her back. "Caroline already has enough on her plate with taking care of her kids and Sonya. Oh, and make sure you help Saul out too. We'll be back as soon as we can."

We watch as a group of people set out toward the explosion. I don't know what I'm going to do for the next couple of days before they get back. I wish they would let me go with them. I want to know if David is okay, and it's going to drive me crazy until I do.

"What are you going to say to your mom when she comes back?" Cass asks.

"I'm just going to ask her if she had anything to do with this. I can sometimes tell when she lies to me," I say weakly. "Do you think I should go out and try to find her?"

"No. I think you had better stay put here and help out as much as you can. Henry seems pretty angry with you. You wouldn't want to go get lost or something."

I'm so full of nervous energy that I can't just sit still anymore. I get up and start walking laps around the camp, chewing on my fingernails. Some people have suggested that we start packing up our stuff in case we need to leave as soon as they get back, but I'm not in the mood.

What am I going to do if David died? I can't imagine my life without him. I would never survive, and not just physically, because he is always there to help me out of the mental darkness. Without him, I don't stand a chance.

Cass is right. What am I going to say to Mom when she gets back? I really hope Henry is jumping to conclusions. Maybe he just got a stomach bug. It happens. She's not the greatest mom in the world, but I could never imagine her doing something like this, poisoning him to make him sick.

Maybe Matthias decided to take what he needed from the weapons cache and destroy the rest. Sure, it would have alerted people from the city, and it might mean their capture, but I can't live with the idea of the cache being rigged. That would definitely mean my mom had something to do with it.

I pace and pace, getting more agitated as I mull these things around in my head. I need to figure out a way to keep my mind occupied and away from these thoughts.

I find Caroline and have her point out where the peeler and carrots are. I might as well do something useful. I grab a bowl and start peeling carrots for supper, saving the scraps for the animals. There's something therapeutic about mindless repetition, and I suddenly understand why Saul whittles sticks. I think he's onto something.

After a while, though, my mind goes back to David, and I can't stop thinking about him. I wish I would have tried to talk him into staying here with me. If I had told him I love him and left it at that, maybe we would be here, making out or whatever it is couples do, instead of him possibly lying dead somewhere.

I look down at the carrot I'm peeling and realize I scraped it away to a nubbin. This is no use. I'm going to end up hurting myself because I'm not paying attention. I abandon the carrots and pace around the camp some more. Cass is curled up into a little ball on her bedding, shaking from her sobs. Everyone else in camp is somber as we wait to find out what happened. Even the little kids are quietly doodling in the dirt.

Saul is whittling as usual, but I can feel him watching me as I pace past him. I stop and take a seat next to him. "It seemed like you were not happy that Mom was here. Do you think she's capable of poisoning Henry so he wouldn't go with the group because she knew there was going to be a trap?"

Saul looks at me and nods.

My breath catches in my chest, and I want to be alone. "I'm going to go into the woods for a little bit," I mumble as I get up.

If anyone around here knows Mom, it would be Matthias and Saul, and now Saul just let on that my mom is capable of doing something this evil. I certainly hope she comes back soon. She and I need to have a serious talk.

16

Sleep was agonizing. I tossed and turned all night, with visions of exploded body parts raining from the sky. I'm thankful when the sun starts to come up. At least I can stop being angry that I'm not sleeping.

I sit up and look around to see if Mom came back during the night. It's still pretty dark despite the dawn light filtering in, but my enhanced eyesight allows me to see with very little light.

Once again, there's still no sign of Mom. I'm so angry at her right now. She better hope that she had nothing to do with this, or she's going to regret it. I don't care if she's my mother. She tried to hurt people I love, and she's going to pay for it.

I shiver as I crawl out of my blankets into the cool morning air. I start to wonder what I'm going to do once winter comes. I didn't pack anything heavier than a hooded sweatshirt. Maybe Matthias will go on a recon mission to get some winter gear. If he's still alive, that is.

I'm one of the first ones up, other than the two men keeping guard. I throw on an extra layer of clothes to try to stave off the chill and go over to relieve Stan of the last hour or so of his duty. He seems like a nice guy, but I haven't really gotten to know him that well. He's a middle-aged man who mostly keeps to himself. He always seems to have a sad expression on his face and hardly ever smiles. He gratefully accepts my offer and heads off to rest.

I sit with my back leaning up against the tree, staring out into the woods when I realize that Stan never handed me the guard weapon. I look around the ground to see if maybe he set it down, but there's nothing there. No gun, no sword, no knives. I just shrug it off because I won't have to keep watch for much longer.

To stop myself from thinking about David, I run songs through my mind, bopping my head along to the beat. I quit when I see movement out in the woods. I stare at the spot where I thought I saw it, but nothing else happens. Maybe it was a tree that seemed to move weird because I was bopping my head? Or a bird that flew through the trees and now is gone? I watch for a little bit longer but then go back to keeping my mind occupied with music.

There! I see something again. This time it was closer. It looked like someone's head peeking around the tree and then disappearing behind it once more. I start to panic as I remember that I don't have any weapons. I stand up, my muscles tensing in preparation for a fight. Just as I'm about to alert the camp, I watch Alexandrine step out from behind a tree with her arm around Charlotte, the girl from the hospital. And hidden behind them trails someone I can't quite make out.

"Hey, Olivia," Alexandrine calls out as they walk closer to camp.

"Alexandrine! Where have you been?"

"Finding Charlotte." She smiles. She looks like a completely different person. Her eyes are bright and cheerful as she looks down at the girl.

"Hi, Charlotte." I acknowledge the girl with a smile. Then I turn back to Alexandrine, "Is she— Is this your daughter?"

"Mmhmm! I also brought along her friend," Alexandrine says, looking back at the person trailing behind them.

When I see who it is, my heart leaps into my throat, and I instinctively put up my fists in self-defense.

"Olivia!" Joselyn squeals and runs over to give me a hug.

"Joselyn?" I ask, hugging her back.

She nods as she pulls away, smiling.

"Joselyn! I'm so happy to see you!" I half lie. "How are you? How did you get here?"

I glance over at Alexandrine, who has her arm wrapped protectively around Charlotte's shoulders as she watches Joselyn and me. She tenses a bit when I ask how they got here.

"I'm fine. Alexandrine brought me along when I asked if I could go too. After you left, Charlotte and I got to be friends, and I didn't want to be alone again. I'm feeling so much better out here. It's beautiful."

"Good," I say through a forced smile. I really need to talk to Alexandrine alone for a moment, but I know she's not going to want to be away from Charlotte for long since she just got her back. I go for the easier questions first. "How did you know where to find Charlotte?"

"It was what you said that night around the fire that made me realize where she was. A girl named Charlotte in the mental ward who said something about 'magic within.' I knew it had to be her. They took Charlotte from me because she had Rare abilities, so I knew it was possible that she would wind up in the psychiatric hospital since that's what often happens to Rare people."

I nod, even though it still seems like a stretch that she would go waltzing back into the city on so little.

"Where's Matthias?" she asks, craning her neck to try and spot him.

"Did you hear the explosion on your way back?"

"Yeah. We picked up the pace once we heard it. What was it from?" Alexandrine asks as she plays with Charlotte's hair.

Charlotte looks unsettled, like she's not sure of Alexandrine, but she doesn't pull away either. I can only imagine what she must be feeling right now. A woman who claims to be your long-lost mother finally shows up to rescue you after years of being abandoned.

"Matthias went on a mission to gather weapons and ammo from a bunker my mom told him about. But then the explosion happened. Smoke was billowing up from the location my mom said the bunker was in, so Henry gathered a crew to go rescue any survivors," I say as a fresh wave of fear crashes down on me.

Alexandrine's eyes no longer sparkle with happiness. Her chest heaves as her face grows dark. Before I know what's happening, I'm on the ground with her knife against my neck. I grab Alexandrine's wrist that's holding the knife and thrust my hips up to knock her off balance, careful not to let her cut me. I spin myself out from under her and am up on my feet in seconds, ready for her next attack.

Charlotte's hiding her face, peering between her fingers to watch. Joselyn suddenly has a twisted smile on her face and claps her hands as she watches Alexandrine come at me again. Looks like Cindy's back.

I dodge Alexandrine's swipe at my abdomen and grab onto her wrist, spinning it behind her back into an arm lock, making sure I keep the tip of the knife away from me. I make sure to lock her wrist as she bucks around to try to free herself.

"What is wrong with you?" I scream in her ear.

"We never should have let your mother into this camp! I should've put a bullet in her head the first moment I saw her!" she grunts as she struggles to get free.

I let go of her and put distance between us, holding up my hands in defense. "I'm sorry! Okay? I just wanted my mother with me like you want Charlotte with you!" I yell, tears stinging my eyes.

Alexandrine glares at me for a moment, but then the hand holding the knife toward me drops to her side, and her shoulders slump as the fight seems to leave her.

"C'mon! Kill her!" Cindy shouts to Alexandrine.

"Oh, shut up!" she snaps back.

My words seem to have had an effect on her. She slides the knife back into its sheath. As she does, I notice that it has dried blood on it and cringe at the thought of her having cut me with that thing.

"Fine. You want to be with your mom. I get it. But that doesn't mean I'm letting you off the hook if Matthias is dead," she says, walking toward me, pointing her finger at my chest. "And if your mother had something to do with this, I'm going to put a bullet in her head right here," she growls, poking me in the forehead between the eyes.

"Fair enough," I concede.

She raises an eyebrow at me in surprise.

"What? That's it?" Cindy sneers. "If you don't kill her, I will!"

Cindy starts running toward me, but Alexandrine steps in front of me and knocks Cindy to the ground.

"What is wrong with this chick?" Alexandrine asks as we watch Cindy stand back up and brush herself off.

"This girl's name is Joselyn. She's a sweet kid with DID, but one of her personalities is named Cindy, and Cindy hates me."

"Why?"

"Because she wants to get rid of me, that's why!" Cindy yells and tries to get to me once more, but Alexandrine stops her again.

"Cool it! I brought you out here because you're Charlotte's friend, but if you become a threat to this camp or anyone in it, Olivia included, I have no problem killing you. Got it?"

Cindy hesitates a moment but then nods, which appeases Alexandrine. But not me. I know she's going to try to kill me. It's just a matter of time.

17

Alexandrine and Charlotte head off to go get something to eat, leaving me with Cindy. Before she leaves, Alexandrine hands me a spare pocketknife and whispers, "Do what you have to do."

I slide the knife into my pocket and hope to God I won't need it. Cindy stands still, her pale eyes boring a hole into mine.

"I wanted us to be friends, Olivia. But you had to ruin it by trying to get rid of me."

"We've been over this, Cindy. You're just a personality trapped in a little girl's body. It's not fair to Joselyn."

"Fair? What the hell do you know about fair?" Cindy yells, gesturing to her body.

"You're right! Okay? The entire situation sucks. Now that you're out here, though, there's no medication for Joselyn to take, so I won't be trying to get rid of you or anything. Can we please just try to get along? Everyone relies on everyone else for survival out here. We need to have each other's backs."

Cindy pulls her ponytail over her shoulder and twirls it around her finger as she thinks about what I just said.

I watch awkwardly, never taking my eyes off her.

"Okay," she says, tossing her hair back over her shoulder. She thrusts her hand out in front of her. "Let's shake on it."

I furrow my eyebrows at her as I slowly reach my hand out to shake. She grabs my hand and rakes her fingernails down my wrist.

"Ow!" I scream, holding my wrist tightly. "What the hell, Cindy?"

"There. Call us even. For now, anyway." She smiles wickedly.

My hand starts going for the knife in my pocket, but I take a deep breath and remind myself that I would be hurting Joselyn. I look down at my wrist and see that she didn't draw any blood, thankfully. Just red marks.

"What do you guys eat around here?" she asks in a friendly tone as though she didn't just attack me.

"We hunt animals and gather any food we can find. We also grow our own crops."

"Hunt? So, you guys have weapons?"

I ignore her and lead her to the basket of apples. "Here. You can snack on some apples. We also have that pot of drinking water. Just grab a cup from over there if you want a drink."

As I'm watching Cindy sort through the apples to find one that appeals to her, Cass cautiously steps up behind me and whispers, "Who's that?"

"That's Joselyn. I think I might have mentioned her before. Anyway, she's a girl with DID. This is one of her personalities, Cindy. You'll wanna stay away from her. She's crazy."

"DID?"

"Dissociative Identity Disorder. She has multiple personalities."

"What? Really? That must suck."

Before I know what's happening, I reach out and catch an apple that's flying at my head.

"I know you're whispering about me," Cindy says around a mouthful of apple. "I don't like being whispered about."

"Sorry. Cass, this is Cindy. Cindy, this is Cass."

"I like your hair! Can I brush it?" Cindy gushes.

Cass looks at me quizzically.

I shake my head slightly.

"Um...no?"

Cindy shrugs and goes back to eating her apple. She twirls in a circle on her toes a few times and then starts moseying around the camp, checking things out. I follow closely behind to try to keep her out of trouble. I can't believe Alexandrine brought her out here. We make a few laps around camp. I introduce Cindy to a couple of people, but she decides to take over the introductions and bounds up to everyone with so much enthusiasm, it puts them off. They look confused as they shake her hand reluctantly.

Alexandrine and Charlotte are down by the stream, washing some laundry together. They're not talking, but they seem to be content in their silence. I'm happy for Alexandrine. Hopefully, she'll be nicer now that she has her daughter back.

We make our way over to the firepit and have a seat.

"So, Cindy? What do you think of our camp?" Cass asks, trying to make conversation.

"It's crap," she answers, picking at her teeth. "But it's better than the nut house, so there's that."

Cass seems insulted, but I put my hand on her shoulder to warn her to let it go.

We're quiet for a while as Cindy looks around at the colored leaves that still remain on the trees. She should have been here a couple days ago.

It was like the woods were on fire with all the warm-colored hues. I couldn't stop staring at them.

"I will admit that the scenery is nicer," she says, smiling at a red maple tree.

"I couldn't agree more," I say, watching her.

She closes her eyes and shakes her head like there's a bug bothering her. She stops abruptly and looks at me with a kind expression. "Oh hey, Olivia!" she says. "Who's this?" She points at Cass.

"I'm Cass..." Cass says slowly.

"I'm Joselyn. It's nice to meet you."

I hear Cass whisper, "Whoa!" quietly to herself.

"So, what is this place?" Joselyn asks.

"This is a rebel camp full of people who got tired of living in the city and following the government rules."

She nods as she looks around at everyone. "How long have you been out here? Is that why you stopped answering my letters?"

"Yeah. I'm sorry. My friend David and I escaped a while ago. I've gotten a lot better since I've been out here. It's been really wonderful."

Cass stands up and starts pacing around, worry etched on her brow. It brings the fear for David and the others back to my mind, and I start bouncing my knees up and down.

"What's the matter?" Joselyn asks, noticing our nervousness.

"We think some of our friends and family might have gotten hurt or killed in the explosion. Now we have to sit around here and wait until people come back before we can know anything." Anger bubbles up in my chest towards my mom. It's been a couple days now since she's left. At this point, I have no doubt in my mind that she must have had something to do with the explosion.

"What are their names?"

"What does it matter to you?" Cass asks. "Sorry. That came out meaner than I meant. I guess I was just wondering why you care. You wouldn't know who we're talking about anyway."

Joselyn looks down at the ground, fidgeting with her fingers. She glances up nervously at me and then looks away again.

"Joselyn? You okay?" I ask. "Is there something you want to tell us?"

"You're going to think I'm crazy," she mumbles. "I think I'm crazy."

Cass and I both hold still as we wait for her to spit it out. I'm not sure I want to know what could make her feel crazier than she already is.

"I've been told that one of the people living inside me can talk to the dead," she says, blushing with embarrassment. "I just thought that if I knew their names, maybe he would be able to know if they were...you know."

Cass takes a step back, hugging herself. She rubs her arms briskly with her hands.

"Landon?" I ask, remembering the goth guy I met during one of the group meetings.

"No," she answers, shaking her head, making her ponytail wave back and forth. "His name's Jack. He doesn't show up very often, but I've had nurses tell me that he freaked them out, talking about their loved ones who died recently. The nurses sometimes come around looking for him, saying his name at me, in case Jack has taken over."

I can't believe what I'm hearing. The nurse did mention that there were more personalities, but I thought she meant Landon. I feel even more sorry for Joselyn now.

"You think I'm a freak, don't you?" she asks, her face scrunched up with anguish.

"No. No, of course not. I just feel bad for you, is all. I never met Jack while I was in the hospital with you. To be honest, I'm kinda glad I didn't." I chuckle.

She nods knowingly.

"Girls, we need help getting supper done," Caroline says tiredly, holding Sonya on her hip. She does a double-take when she sees Joselyn looking up at her. "You know, you look a lot like someone here at camp. What's your name?"

"Joselyn, ma'am."

"Hello, Joselyn. Anyway, it looks like the woodpile could use a bit more. Cass, maybe you could help me peel some potatoes while Olivia and Joselyn go get some wood?"

We all nod and stand up.

I can't help but feel uneasy about going out into the woods alone with Joselyn. This ought to be interesting.

I lead her out into the woods along a deer path. We pick up whatever sticks we can find as we make our way farther away from camp. Farther away from safety. I toss around the idea of keeping the knife in my hand the whole time, but that would make it harder to hold the gathered wood.

No. I need to just calm down. Cindy was civil after she scratched me. Maybe things won't be so bad.

"What did she mean that I reminded her of someone?"

"Oh. Just that you have the same shade of blue eyes and black hair as someone else from camp."

"What's her name? Where is she?"

"Her name's Rebecca. She took off to go find the others after the explosion."

Joselyn stops walking and stares at the middle distance for a moment. She looks at me with a sad expression. "Could it be?" she whispers to herself.

"What?"

"Never mind." She goes back to collecting sticks

I want to ask her what she was talking about, but the poor girl has had enough difficulties for one day. I have no idea what Alexandrine was thinking, bringing her out here. So what if she said she was Charlotte's friend? Why would you break a person out of the mental hospital? Her daughter...sure. That makes sense. But some strange girl who asks to come? I'm seriously questioning Alexandrine's judgment.

We both have an armload of branches and head back to camp. I suddenly have an urge to talk to David, and my stomach turns sour as soon as I remember that he's not at camp.

That he could be dead right now.

Damn you, Henry! I really wish I was with them so I could know what happened sooner. Waiting is torture.

"Branches aren't going to cut it, girls," Stan comments when we return. He's at the firepit, trying to get a fire going. "We're going to need logs of wood. Take the hand saws, and see if you can find a fallen tree to block up."

"I've never used a saw before," I say. "Isn't there someone else who could do it?"

"No. We're down too many people. You're going to have to learn."

I turn around and see that Joselyn retrieved the saws already. I'm filled with dread as I look at her innocently holding a potentially dangerous weapon. I don't want to be alone in the woods with a girl whose alternate personality would love the chance to kill me. I involuntarily shiver at the thought of having that toothed blade run across my skin.

"You ready?" Joselyn asks.

"Yeah. Want me to carry the saws?" I ask as nonchalantly as I can.

"I've got it," she says, shrugging. "C'mon, let's go."

Before we go, I pat my pocket just to reassure that I still have a weapon to defend myself. The knife's presence is only slightly comforting.

We hike through the woods, making circles around the camp, moving farther away as we go. We want to find a tree that's close so we won't have as far to haul the wood. After going around about three times, we find a tree that's tipped over, its roots pulled up out of the ground. I think this might be the tree I sat on when David told me he loved me. The thought brings a pang of grief.

"I think we should cut off the branches first before we start trying to cut it into chunks," I say, trying to figure out what would be the best way to do this.

Joselyn nods, and we start working. "You know, this survival stuff is kind of fun. It's at least more fun than group time or the lame arts and crafts they made us do. I felt like I was going crazy in there."

I laugh.

"What?" she asks, stopping to look at me.

"You just said you felt like you were going crazy...in a psychiatric hospital."

"Oh, yeah. I guess that is kind of funny," she says, smirking a bit. She goes back to sawing while she continues talking. "You know, when I'm me, I don't feel crazy. I feel like I don't belong with all the other people who have serious problems. I don't think I'm a squirrel or that I have magical powers or have an irrational fear of spiders. I'm just me. A normal twelve-year-old girl."

"But you're not," I let slip.

She stops sawing again and looks at me, taken aback. "What?" she says, clearly offended.

I stop sawing too and look at her as I answer quickly, "I just mean that you're not a normal twelve-year-old. When you're you, you're amazing!

Sweet, kind, friendly. But your other personalities are not so nice. So even though you—Joselyn—are great, you have lived an abnormal life. You've experienced things not very many other twelve-year-olds have experienced, and that makes you different. Special," I add, hoping I defused the situation. I'm kicking myself for having even said something. If she wants to feel like she's a normal kid, then I should let her. She deserves that much.

"You're right. Who am I kidding? Even if I got rid of all the extra personalities, I would still be messed up." She starts sobbing, and now I feel like a jerk.

I take a step toward her, but she stops crying abruptly. I watch as she wipes the tears off her cheeks with her hand and looks down at them, confused.

She then looks at the saw in her hand and up at me with a malicious grin. "You made the kid cry. I thought you were friends."

"We were—are. I mean, we are."

"Tsk, tsk, tsk. Then why're there tears on our face?" she accuses, pointing the saw at me.

"I might have said something that made her cry. Why do you care?"

"I protect her. That's what I do, silly Billy. That's why I'm here," she says, spreading her arms theatrically.

"You protect her? But you told me yourself that you tried to commit suicide. How is that protecting her?"

Cindy rolls her eyes and huffs. "You wouldn't understand. It's a secret."

"I wouldn't understand, or it's a secret?" When she doesn't answer, I decide to just let it go. I would really like to know what triggers Cindy's return so I don't have to see her anymore. "Why don't you take a little break? I'll work on it for a while."

She places the handle of the saw in my hand but doesn't let go when I grab it. I tug a few times, and just when I'm about to get angry at her, she releases it with a smirk.

I put her saw on the ground and position myself so I can see her in my peripheral vision as I work on the branches. At first, she just stands around looking at the trees, but then she starts doing ballet poses. Pretty soon, she's twirling and leaping her way around the woods. I consider complimenting her on her form to be nice, but honestly, I'm sick of talking to her. I wish she would go away for good, and I worry that if I keep engaging her, it will somehow make her stick around.

I choose to ignore her and throw myself into a particularly thick branch, sawing back and forth until my arm starts to ache. Sweat droplets run down my face and into my eyes. I stop for a moment so I can wipe them away, and then pain explodes on the back of my head, and I black out.

1 9

I wake up to the sound of someone humming "Mary had a Little Lamb." I let out a groan as I try to open my eyelids, but the sunlight burns, and I squeeze them shut again. What happened to me?

I go to sit up, but as soon as I lift my head off the ground, a wave of nausea hits me hard. Saliva pools in my mouth, and before I can try to stop it, hot bile rushes up my throat, and I turn to the side as I spew it out onto the ground.

The pain in my skull is so intense, I'm certain my head is about to explode. I honestly think drilling a hole in my skull would make me feel better right now. It would at least release some of the awful pressure. I try to sit up again, and this time I can without feeling sick. I shield my eyes from as much light as possible and crack my eyelids so I can see where I am.

"Wakey, wakey, Olivia!"

I whip my head around to where I heard the voice come from. Bad idea. Another wave of nausea hits me, and I throw up again. "Cindy?" I say, wiping the drool from my mouth. "What happened to me?"

"I told you I was going to make you pay. Ka-ching, ka-ching! It was only a matter of time."

I know I should stand up and face Cindy, but another wave of agony crashes through my head, and I lie down, unable to sit up anymore. "What did you do?" I whimper.

"I found a thick stick and hit you quick, chick. Haha! I'm a poet, and I didn't even know it," she giggles to herself.

"You're insane," I groan.

"Now, now, Olivia. There's no need for name-calling," she says in a mock scolding tone.

"I'm so tired..." I say as everything fades away again.

"You can rest when you're dead! Now it's wakey-wakey time," she says chipperly.

My head throbs where she hit me, and I find myself wishing she'd leave me alone so I could either go unconscious or die. I start to dream about smoke billowing in the distance and a feeling of terror pressing down on me. Suddenly, I'm back awake, and someone's slapping my face.

"Ow! Stop hitting me," I say and crack my eyelids open. Panic rises up as I look at who's hitting me, and I can't remember who she is. She seems familiar, but the thought just won't come. "Who're you?"

"Methinks I might've hit you too hard," she says, tapping a finger on her temple. "Whoopsie!"

"You hit me? Why? Is that why my head hurts?"

She sneers. "Ugh. You're starting to get annoying."

I watch through my eyelashes as she stands up, looking in every direction around us. She licks her finger and holds it straight out in front of her. She spins around a few more times and then kneels down by my head again.

"All right, here's the thing. I mighta, sorta got turned around, and I need you to take us back to camp."

"Camp?"

"Yes. Camp. El Camperino. La Campitan."

Nothing she says makes any sense to me. I close my eyes again, desperate for the sweet oblivion of sleep.

"Wake up!" I hear Cindy say, but her voice sounds distant. "Whatever. Joselyn, it's your turn."

I'm just about asleep again. Images of a gentle kiss and how soft it felt on my lips play through my mind, but I can't tell if it's a memory or a dream. Who would have kissed me?

David!

I sit bolt upright, panic spreading through my body with a jolt. Everything around me starts spinning, but I force myself to stay sitting as I squeeze my eyes shut again until it subsides.

"Olivia! Are you okay?"

I open my eyes back up and see those pale blue eyes staring at me with concern. Looking at Joselyn, I suddenly remember who she is. "Hey, Joselyn. Where's David?"

"I'm not sure, but I think he was one of the people in the explosion..."

"Explosion?"

"What's wrong with you, Olivia? You seem confused."

I stand up slowly, grabbing onto a tree to steady myself. My ears start ringing, drowning out the sounds of the woods, which just makes me more off balance.

Joselyn wraps my arm around her shoulder to help me. "Okay, Olivia. I need to get you back to camp. Do you remember what direction camp is?"

I hold my hand up to my forehead to block the sun and look around. I slowly spin in a circle, but everything looks the same; nothing stands out. That is until I see the fallen tree and the saw still stuck in the branch where

I was cutting it. "I remember! I think camp is back that way," I say, pointing. "Grab the saws, and let's get out of here."

By the time we make it back to camp, I'm feeling nauseous again, and I beg for her to let me lie down.

"Hold on, Olivia. Not yet."

We stumble our way to where my stuff is, and she helps me sit. She then goes to find someone to have a look at me. The ringing in my ears has become a deafening roar, and I just can't take it any longer. I lay my head on my pillow and immediately start to drift off.

■■■■■

"Olivia? Liv!"

I wake with a start when I realize I recognize that voice. "David?"

"Holy crap, you had me scared to death!"

It takes me several seconds to remember where I am. David comes into focus, and I gasp when I see the state he's in. He has scratches all over his face, a white bandage soaked with blood right above his eye, and his arm is in a sling. I sit up and wrap him in a hug before I realize I shouldn't have sat up so quickly. My head pounds, and I lie back down before I throw up again.

"Whoa! Take it easy, Liv."

Suddenly, I feel the need to explain why I'm acting this way. "I was out getting wood with Joselyn, and Cindy hit me in the head with a branch."

"Cindy? Like, crazy hospital Cindy?"

"That's the one."

"Where is she now?" David brushes a lock of hair out of my eyes before looking around camp to spot her.

I stare up at him, unable to comprehend what he just asked me. Why is the ringing in my ears so loud? I can't think straight. I close my eyes again and feel the weight of sleep taking me under.

"Stay with me, Liv." I hear David say. I open my eyes when I feel him stroke my cheek with his thumb. "Why do you always get yourself in trouble when I'm not here?"

"Hey, David! Do you know what I got on my history test? Did you see my grade?"

"History test?" he says, furrowing his eyebrows while shaking his head.

"Yeah, the one were you going to help me study for," I say.

"Liv, we haven't gone to school for weeks now," David says slowly. "I think Rebecca better take a look at you. You're acting weird."

"No, don't go," I say weakly as he stands up. Before I can stop myself, I fall back to sleep.

●●●●●

I wake up to a bright light shining in my eye as someone holds my eyelid up. Then they do the same to the other one.

"She's got a concussion. By the knot on the back of her head, I'd say it's a pretty severe one."

"What can I do for her?" David's voice asks.

I groggily open my eyes and see Rebecca, David, and Cass all leaning over me.

"You shouldn't be doing anything, David. You need to get some rest and heal yourself," Rebecca answers sternly.

"Not when Liv's hurt," David responds defiantly. "I'll be fine."

A happy sigh escapes my lips. Leave it to David to put my needs before his own.

"Do you know what happened to her?" Rebecca asks Cass.

"Cindy hit me over the head with a stick," I say.

"Who?" Rebecca asks, confused. "Where is this Cindy now?"

"She started acting crazier than before and took off down by the stream," Cass answers. "She's been sitting down there talking to herself since before you guys got back. I check on her every now and then to make sure she's still there."

"Can you tell her to come up here? I'd like to talk to her," Rebecca asks tiredly.

Cass nods and heads down to the stream.

"Olivia, we're going to have you sit up for a while. Sleep is good, but you need to drink something." Rebecca has David grab my other arm, and together, they help me up and set me against a tree.

As Rebecca is tipping a cup for me to take a drink, I see Cass walk back to camp with Joselyn. Rebecca notices me staring and glances over her shoulder to see what I'm looking at. Suddenly, she drops the cup of water, soaking my pants, and gasps loudly. "Joselyn?" she whispers.

"Mama?"

A warm feeling spreads through my chest as I get ready to watch this heartfelt reunion. Joselyn deserves this.

"Stay away from me! Just stay right there!" Rebecca yells as she takes a step back.

20

I look between her and Joselyn in disbelief. Joselyn looks like Rebecca just slapped her hard across the face. Anguish washes over her, and she lets out a sob.

"Who let her in here? Who brought her here?" Rebecca is yelling, panicked.

I stand up between Rebecca and Joselyn, my head swimming in the process. I start swaying slightly as the pain pulses in my skull. David's at my side in an instant, holding my arm to steady me.

"What's going on, Rebecca? Why are you acting like this?" I ask calmly.

"You don't know what she is. I put her in that hospital for a reason. How did she get out? How did you get out?" Rebecca asks Joselyn angrily.

"I brought her out here," Alexandrine says, walking back from the stream. "What's going on?"

"She's a lunatic!"

I hear Joselyn lose it and start bawling loudly.

"David, Cass, would you guys please help with Joselyn? I need to talk to Rebecca," I say.

"Are you sure, Liv?" David asks, concerned. "You need to take it easy."

I just nod in response, and he reluctantly lets go. I make my way over to Rebecca, and the exertion causes me to see stars in my vision. I grab a hold of her upper arm to stop myself from falling headfirst. I wish I wasn't feeling so crappy.

"Would you guys mind keeping an eye on Charlotte for me too?" Alexandrine asks reluctantly. I can tell she doesn't want to be away from her.

Cass nods, and we walk a short distance away from everyone.

"What is going on?" I ask once we have a seat on some moss outside of the camp.

"She is not who you think she is," Rebecca says, her eyes flashing with fear.

"I know that she's a twelve-year-old girl who's lived a hard life, dealing with different personalities and being stuck in a mental hospital..." I start to say but stop when Rebecca shakes her head vigorously.

"She hasn't been Joselyn since...I don't even remember. I'm not a hundred percent sure she's ever been just Joselyn."

"She said Cindy took over once her dad died when she was young," I say, holding my head in my hand to try to stop the pain that's throbbing in my brain.

"She's a liar. Cindy was around a lot longer than that, Joselyn just doesn't remember because she blacks out when another person takes over. Did she happen to mention how her dad died?" Rebecca asks, her face ashen.

"No."

I look at Alexandrine, who meets my eyes for a moment, and I can feel the dread passing between us as neither of us are ready to hear what she's about to say.

"He 'fell' down the stairs," she scoffs, making air quotes. "When I came running to see what the noise was, I saw him lying at the bottom of the stairs, blood pooling on the floor and his neck at an odd angle..." She stops to let out a sob before continuing, "And there she was, standing at the top of the stairs, staring down at us. She didn't look sad or scared. In fact, she looked—I don't know—pleased? Curious? Nothing you would expect from a four-year-old."

I cannot believe what I'm hearing.

"Of course, I couldn't prove anything. I wasn't there to actually see it happen. Whenever I asked her about it, she would shrug." Rebecca stops to wipe her nose on her sleeve.

"C'mon, Becca. A four-year-old pushed a grown man down the stairs? He must have just tripped, and she was standing at the top of the stairs because she heard the commotion," Alexandrine proposes. "What makes you think she pushed him?"

"Well, as I said, there's always been something...off...about her."

"Of course there was something off about me, mommy dearest."

We all jump a little at her voice. Rebecca's eyes are wide as she scoots back away from where Joselyn is now standing. I look up at Joselyn's face and see she's got a wild look to her. Cindy.

"Sorry, ladies!" David apologizes as he comes running up to Cindy, panting. "She started going nuts and slipped away before we could catch her."

Cindy just ignores him and keeps talking. "You blame me for Dad's death, but did you ever stop to think about why I killed him?"

Rebecca looks horrified. "I knew it!"

Cindy gives a wicked smile that turns to a sneer. "I didn't show up when he died. I showed up when he started hurting Jossy."

87

Rebecca angrily shakes her head. "You're lying. Samuel wouldn't have done that."

"Guess again! Didn't you ever find it odd that he was always willing to give Joselyn a bath every night?"

"He just wanted to help. He knew I was stressed by the end of the day, and he wanted to give me a hand with her," Rebecca says desperately.

"Wrong again! He hurt her. Every. Time."

Rebecca buries her face in her hands.

"Didn't you see the signs? Didn't you hear me start yelling before he would cover my mouth with his big hand? I would take over because even though I wasn't strong enough to stop him, I was strong enough to shield her from the trauma."

She turns to me and says, "You asked me earlier about my suicide attempt. Secret's out! After a particularly bad night, I didn't think I could keep protecting her. Dying seemed like a good way to protect her from him."

"That was you? I thought she cut her wrists on the broken fence she tried to climb," Rebecca shrieks.

"I had to make it look like an accident," she scoffs as though it were obvious.

"She was only three and had to be hospitalized for a week!" Rebecca yells.

"Whoops," Cindy says with a halfhearted shrug.

I feel like I'm about to throw up.

"I finally got to the point that I knew I had to stop it from happening to her again. So, when I saw him standing at the top of the stairs, I ran and shoved him as hard as my little four-year-old body could. I wanted to hurt him. I didn't realize it would kill him. I'm not sorry it did. He couldn't hurt her—us—ever again."

Hot tears roll down my cheeks. Poor Joselyn! Crying is making my head throb, and I realize I need to stop. The pain is becoming too much.

"Liv? You okay?" I hear David ask as I tip over to the side and pass out.

2 1

Voices whisper around me as I come back from the darkness. It takes me a moment to understand what's happening. My ears stopped ringing, and the throbbing in my head is mostly gone, but a feeling of sorrow still presses down on me. I begin to cry before I remember why I'm feeling so sad. The memories of what Cindy told us trickle in, and I'm distraught all over again. I may not like Cindy, but I respect her for taking over during those bad times to shield Joselyn.

I look up and see David next to me. A shock runs through me when I realize he's back, and I have no idea what happened to him and the group. I was so out of it, I never thought to ask.

"David," I croak out, then clear my voice and try again. "David. What happened?"

"You blacked out..."

"No. I mean, the explosion. What happened?" I ask as I sit up.

A grave look crosses over him, and I'm afraid of what he's about to tell me. I'm not sure I'm ready for more sadness.

"The bunker was rigged. Jeffery, Andrew, and Ryan volunteered to go in and retrieve the ammo. Matthias insisted he go too, but Ryan told him no, that if anything happened, the camp needed to have their leader. It was like he knew something was going to go wrong," David says, rubbing his hand over his face.

"Or maybe he didn't trust my mom," I say darkly. I'm embarrassed that I vouched for her. She hasn't shown back up yet, which just proves that she had something to do with the explosion. I should have followed her when I had the chance.

"That too. Anyway, Tim, Matthias, and I were positioned in the tree lines around the building to keep an eye out for soldiers. I heard one of the men inside yell 'Run!' just before the explosion happened," David says, stopping to look up at the trees as he clenches his jaw a few times.

I lay my hand on his bicep. "What happened then?"

"This is where it gets a little weird. Don't judge," he says, rubbing the back of his neck awkwardly. "Do you remember Bartholomew?"

"Your imaginary friend?" When he gives me a glare, I put my hands up. "Sorry. I mean your guardian angel..." I say, keeping my tone in check.

"Well, just as I heard them yell, 'Run,' Bartholomew materialized in front of me and shoved me as hard as he could. I was already on the ground when the explosion happened. And a good thing too, because when I finally came to my senses, I stood up and saw a piece of the steel wall from the building lodged in a tree right where my head would have been. Bartholomew saved my life."

"Thank you, Bartholomew," I say, playing along.

"Anyway, I realized we needed to get out of there, quick. I found Matthias with blood running down his face from his eye, but he didn't seem to care too much as he was cinching his belt around the remaining part of Tim's arm."

"What?" I whisper. "Tim lost his arm?"

"Yeah. We were in rough shape. I was the luckiest one. I only came away with some cuts that needed stitches and a broken wrist."

"A broken wrist still sucks, though."

"It does, but at least I'm alive and I still have my arm."

I nod, which was a bad idea as everything starts spinning uncontrollably. I hold still and close my eyes until the vertigo passes.

"We did a quick check to see if any of the men survived the blast, even though we knew they didn't. There's no way they could have. The building was completely destroyed. But we had to check...you know, just in case," he adds weakly.

"Well, where's Tim and Matthias now? Did they make it back to camp?"

"They made it because of Rebecca. It was a miracle when she showed up. She's a badass, by the way. I know we just found out some terrible stuff about her with Joselyn and all that, but I'm glad she's a part of this camp."

I'm not so sure. How could she have not known what was going on with Joselyn? You would think her motherly instincts would have kicked in or something when Joselyn started acting weird.

"She didn't have the right stuff to handle a missing arm, so she did something she had seen on an old tv show once. She had Matthias pull open some bullets and dump out the gunpowder onto Tim's bloody stump. Then she lit the powder on fire, cauterizing the wound."

"That actually worked?" I ask incredulously.

"Yeah, for the most part. It at least stopped the heavy bleeding. I didn't really understand why she had asked me to find a stick and remove the bark until I saw her stick it between Tim's jaws just before they lit the gunpowder on fire. I thought he was unconscious and would be fine, but as soon as the gunpowder ignited, his eyes bulged open, and he clamped down on the stick hard while screaming. I felt so bad for him."

"How about Matthias's eye? Was Rebecca able to save it?"

"No. His eye's gone. He's walking around with an eyepatch now, which just makes him look even tougher. Missing an eye has made him pretty cranky, though. Understandably."

"Crankier than he's already been? I can't even imagine."

David smirks at me, then sighs.

"So, all this happened, and yet you came to my side to help me feel better from my concussion?"

"What do you expect? You were hurt. Of course I'm going to worry about you." He leans over and kisses the side of my head, then pulls back quickly and apologizes.

"I'm so glad you made it back to camp." I ignore the kiss and the apology about it.

"Me too."

"Oh, good. You're awake," Henry stops to say as he's passing by. "Start packing your things up. We're heading out soon."

"What's going on?" I ask, realizing everyone around us has been bustling about getting things packed.

"Pop decided that we have to leave. For good. We gave as much time as we could for healing, but we can't afford to wait around any longer."

"Where are we going?"

"To the next city over. It's going to be slow, so we need to get started."

David stands and helps me up off the ground. A wave of pain spreads through my skull. I thought I was doing better, but standing up just made me realize that it will take a while to heal from this.

"David, what if my mom comes back here to explain what happened? If we leave, she's not going to be able to find us."

"It's probably better that way. I have a feeling that if she ever shows her face again, it's not going to end well for her," David says darkly.

I nod. "I know I'd like to give her a piece of my mind. What she did..." I stop as the emotions form a lump in my throat.

David pats my shoulder. "Let's get packed and get out of here."

I follow behind him to where my stuff is piled. I check my bag to make sure I have everything packed up. I tie my pillow back on and go to see if Caroline needs any help with the kids. As I'm walking back toward her, I overhear Alexandrine talking with Matthias. I stop to listen, pretending to tie my shoe.

"Where are we headed?"

"We're headin' west to the next city over."

Alexandrine huffs. "You really think that's a good idea? Winter is imminent, and moving away from the ocean is going to make the temperatures colder."

"We don't have a lot of options. We've survived the winter before. We can do it again."

"But not like this," she says, gesturing to Matthias's eye and then over to Tim.

"We need to get movin' before the troops get out here. Ya know as well as I do that that explosion means they're comin' to see who set it off. We don't have the manpower to fight 'em. Our time here is done," Matthias says gruffly.

"Okay," Alexandrine concedes.

"Okay? Ya ain't gonna fight me more on this?"

"My priorities have changed." She looks over at Charlotte, who's getting her hair braided by Joselyn.

"Huh. We should've rescued your daughter a long time ago. You're a lot more agreeable."

"Oh, shut up, Patches," she says with a smirk playing at the corners of her mouth.

"Don't," Matthias warns.

"What? Too soon?"

He answers by turning around and storming away from her. I watch her snicker to herself for a moment before heading over toward Charlotte.

■■■■■

Rebecca gives me a tablet of painkiller for my head before we take off. She says she would have given me two, but we have to ration them. I feel bad for even taking one when Matthias, Tim, and David need them more than I do.

I look around camp one last time, but I don't feel as much attachment here since we haven't stayed as long. I'm nervous about leaving, though. The days are getting shorter and a lot cooler. I've always had a nice warm apartment to live in during the winter months. I don't know how I'm going to survive this.

I follow behind David as we all take off in a line through the woods. I'm beginning to grow accustomed to the back of David's head and his backpack. It's almost a comforting sight at this point. I feel safe when I'm with him.

"Hey, Olivia?" I hear Tim's voice say over my shoulder.

"Yeah?"

"I'm sorry I lost your hair tie."

I turn and look back at him, confused.

He motions his head at his missing arm.

"Are you serious? You lost your freaking arm, and you're apologizing for my hair tie being on it?"

His eyes twinkle a bit with humor before turning serious again.

"How are you doing?" I ask.

"Okay, I guess. I mean, this sucks pretty bad. It hurts, and I find myself missing my arm. But I feel like I've paid up a debt. I know it might not make sense, but I feel at peace about it. I'll have to live the rest of my life without my arm, and that seems like a just punishment for what I did."

I stop walking and face him so he knows I mean what I'm about to say. "Tim, you didn't owe anything. It wasn't your fault," I say, looking into his eyes seriously. "But I'm glad you've found some peace."

He nods, and I pat his good arm before turning around and hurrying to catch back up with David.

The day started off mostly sunny, but as we walk, dark clouds roll in and bring an uncomfortable chill to the air. When we stop for a water break, I pull out a couple extra T-shirts to throw on under my hoodie. It's not much, but it's all I have.

We continue walking until it grows too dark for Matthias to see, and we stop for the night. Finding a comfortable spot to sleep is near impossible. Rocks poke into me wherever I try to lie. We finally get everyone settled in, but by the shuffling noises and heavy sighing, it sounds like nobody is sleeping well.

By morning, everyone is awake and cranky. I stretch out my sore muscles and look around to see what's being decided for breakfast. We missed supper last night, and now my stomach is growling loudly. A pot of water is heating over a fire to make it safe for drinking, but nothing is cooking from what I can tell.

"What's for breakfast?" I ask nobody in particular.

Everyone looks around at everyone else, waiting for someone to have the answers. Eyes turn toward Matthias, who's glowering at the fire. He doesn't give us any indication that he heard us. He just keeps staring at the fire as though he wants to kill something or someone.

Finally, someone suggests that we eat the chickens so we have less to carry. We take a vote, and all the adults agree to it, but the kids are sad.

"I don't want to eat Henny Penny!" Caroline's little girl whines.

"I know, baby, but they're starting to get old, and we can always get new chickens once we find a different place to live."

Emily starts wailing loudly, which sets off Sonya. The noise echoes through the woods, and everyone looks around at each other nervously.

"Shut them up!" Cindy growls, holding her hands over her ears.

"You can't just make a kid stop crying automatically," Caroline says, exasperated as she hugs the girls.

"There was a song her mom used to sing to help Sonya stop crying, but I can't remember what it is," Rebecca adds, picking a red-faced Sonya up off the ground.

Caroline shrugs in frustration.

This commotion can probably be heard for miles. If there were any soldiers following us, this is going to tell them exactly where we are. I hear someone whisper that maybe now's not the time to eat the chickens. Minutes tick by, and the noise is starting to give me a headache.

"I don't know that one." I hear Cindy say in a deep voice with an English accent. I turn my head in surprise and see her looking up at something, but I don't know what she's looking at. "Okay. I'll try, but go slow."

We all watch as Cindy stands up, walks over to Sonya, and begins singing in that oddly deep voice, *"Hush little one, with a face so sweet."* She pauses, turning her head to the side, then nods and continues singing, *"A precious little girl, I was blessed to meet."*

I glance over at Rebecca and Caroline, and they are both staring at Cindy in shock. Sonya has stopped crying loudly and is watching Cindy with big tears on her cheeks.

"Ten perfect fingers and ten tiny toes," Cindy sings, pausing as she looks over her shoulder and nods again. Her low voice is soothing as she continues, awkwardly touching the parts she's singing about. *"Brown curly hair and a cute button nose."*

The entire camp is silent as we watch what's going on. Sonya smiles and reaches out for Cindy to hold her. Cindy takes her in her arms uncertainly but smiles when Sonya lays her little head on her shoulder.

"Mommy's little angel sent from heaven up above. A perfect, joyful life because it's you I get to love," Cindy finishes.

She stops singing, and the camp is silent.

"How did you..." Rebecca starts to ask, but Cindy holds up a finger to stop her from talking.

She closes her eyes as though listening to something, then turns toward Tim. With the same deep, accented voice, she says, "It wasn't your fault. You need to stop blaming yourself for what happened. It's time to heal and come back to the Tim we all love. Your enthusiasm helps everyone to stay positive. You are important to these people."

Tim's eyes are wide with shock at her words, and his mouth hangs open slightly. He drops to his knees as what she says sinks in. He covers his eyes with his hand as he rocks back and forth on the ground, overtaken with emotion. Cass goes to him and pats him on his back, hushing him. I get goosebumps up my arms that aren't from the cold.

Cindy's eyes grow wide, and she spins toward Matthias. "You need to leave. They're coming."

2'2'

I watch as Joselyn staggers backward, holding her hands to her head. Everyone is on their feet and all speaking at once.

Matthias claps his hands loudly to get their attention. "What do ya mean 'they'? Soldiers? Havoc? What?" Matthias asks her.

She looks at him, confused. "I don't know what you're talking about," she says with a tremble in her voice. She cowers away from Matthias's stern look.

"Stop playin' around! You just said they're comin'!" Matthias barks out, pointing a finger in her face.

"Leave her alone," Alexandrine says, stepping up to Joselyn. "She's confused. Let's just pack up and leave now. We were going to be leaving soon anyway."

Matthias looks between her and Joselyn with a look of annoyance. "Fine. Everyone get yourselves ready."

"What about breakfast?" Noah asks him timidly.

"Grab an apple to eat as we walk. Let's move!" Matthias answers for her.

Matthias heads over to Saul to help him get ready. I shove my blanket into my bag and strap my pillow back on. My stomach growls as I grab an apple. I know this isn't going to be enough, but I take what I can get. The drinking water is still boiling hot, but we try to fill up our bottles and cups as much as we can. Water is water, whether it's hot or cold. Frederick takes the pot down to the pond to cool the metal before packing it up.

Matthias sends Henry and David to the back of the line with guns to keep watch. Luckily for everyone, it wasn't David's shooting wrist that got broken. I'm sad that I don't get to be by him, but now's not the time to be picky. We walk at a faster pace than we usually do. I can't see ahead of me to know how Matthias gets Saul to walk this fast, but I'm grateful to be moving quickly.

Joselyn is just ahead of me, and I can't help myself from asking her about what happened. "How did you do that?"

"Do what?"

"Sing that song? How could you have possibly known the words to a song that Suzanne made up for her daughter?"

"I have no idea what you're talking about. I sang a song?"

"Oh, right. It wasn't you. But I still don't know how Cindy would have known that song."

"This Suzanne person wouldn't happen to be...you know...dead, would she?" Joselyn asks hesitantly.

"Yeah, she died not too long ago."

"Then it must have been Jack. Remember? I told you about him. Jack can talk to the dead."

"Oh, yeah. I remember you mentioning him." I shiver at the thought of being able to talk to dead people. I didn't believe her when she told us about Jack, but I don't know how else she could have known that song.

We finally stop for a break, but Matthias insists it needs to be a short one.

"I'm sorry, Pop. We need to keep going." I hear Matthias say to Saul.

Saul looks worn out, and I start to worry about him. Is he going to be able to survive the journey?

"David? Did ya hear anything followin' behind us?" Matthias asks.

"No, sir. My ears are still ringing from the explosion, but I don't think I heard anything."

"Good. Let's hope it stays that way."

All this walking makes my skull ache. I want to hold out from taking painkillers, but I don't think I will be able to handle it much longer. I get some from Rebecca, who I noticed is staying as far away from Joselyn as possible.

"You know, it's not her fault she has DID," I say gently. "She doesn't like it any more than you do."

"I just can't live with what she did to Sam," Rebecca replies.

"You heard Cindy. He was hurting Joselyn."

"I don't believe her," Rebecca says stubbornly. "That's not the Sam I knew."

"We all have demons we deal with, Rebecca, secrets we keep hidden away. Do you really think Sam would tell you he's the kind of guy who wanted to do those things to your little girl? Maybe you should try believing your daughter," I say as anger bubbles up to the surface.

"Cindy is not my daughter," she says, pointing in my face.

"But Joselyn is! And right now, she has different personalities living inside of her that she can't control! She's scared, lonely, and believes she's a freak. She could use her mother. Aren't you a nurse for Pete's sake? Shouldn't you know about mental illnesses?"

Rebecca stares at the ground, shaking her head.

"What's goin' on over here? We need to get movin'," Matthias says, but I don't acknowledge him. I'm so angry right now.

"What if Cindy was telling the truth? Your little girl was being hurt by a man she should have been able to trust, and now her mother won't believe her or support her? In my mind, that makes you just as bad as he was," I spit out before turning and storming away while everyone in the vicinity watches.

I head straight over to Joselyn and give her a big hug. I don't care if she's Joselyn or Cindy or any of the others. She deserves some support. She gives me a confused look and a small smile.

"I believe you," I whisper. I glance back at Rebecca, and she's glaring at me with her hands on her hips.

I look around and see that everyone is on their feet, ready to leave, so I hurry over to my bag. I make sure I'm as far away from Rebecca as possible, staying close to the back by David. I don't think I'll be getting any more painkillers from her.

It's a good thing Matthias has a compass. The clouds are so thick that there's no way to tell the direction from the sun's positioning. I hate days like today because I'd rather take a nap than do anything else when it's so dreary. It reminds me of being in the city with the fog that blocked out the sun. I shudder at the memory.

A strange rumbling sound snaps me out of my stupor, and I look around to figure out where it's coming from. I see that David is looking around the woods too, but nobody else around us seems to be bothered. It must be something only we heard.

"Did you hear something?" I whisper to David.

"I did," he says, looking up at the sky that can be seen between the branches. "It could be thunder. Maybe a storm's moving in."

"Should we tell Matthias?"

"It sounded far away. Let's just keep walking, and if we hear it again, we can tell him."

David and I never hear the sound again. I decide that it must have just been a passing storm cloud.

Day turns to dusk, and my stomach feels like it's digesting itself from hunger. I also ran out of water about two hours ago, and I'm really feeling it. Everyone is tired as we start to set up camp. There is barely enough energy to go around to prepare supper, but the thought of food gives people a second wind. Much to Emily's displeasure, we decide it's time to eat the chickens tonight. There's just enough for everyone to have some but not enough to fill anyone up. We top it off with some rice and boiled carrots.

Frederick heads off to get some water for everyone. Henry volunteers to go along, taking David's flashlight and a gun.

No one talks as we all huddle together by the fire to stay warm. Rebecca refuses to look at Joselyn or me. I don't care if she's mad at me, but I really wish she wouldn't treat Joselyn this way.

I watch as Alexandrine wraps a blanket around herself and Charlotte. She looks so much happier than she did before. Charlotte is starting to look more comfortable around her too. A pang of longing runs through me at that moment. Even before Mom's recent betrayal, she was never a loving mother. I wish I had what Charlotte is experiencing right now. I think that's why Rebecca's behavior bothers me so much. She has an opportunity to have a relationship with her daughter, and she's refusing to take it.

After about an hour, Frederick is back with the pot of water. By the looks of him, it was a long journey. The bottom of his shirt, his pants, and his shoes are soaked, and he's staggering under the weight of the pot. Henry comes into view, holding the flashlight as best he can for Frederick. With a grunt, Frederick places the pot on the hot coals and slumps down in an open spot by Matthias.

"What'd ya do? Fall in?" Matthias asks with a hint of amusement.

"It's dark out there. I stumbled over a few sticks and splashed myself. Enjoy your water. I hope you choke," Frederick grumps, staring at the fire with a scowl.

"Thank you for getting the water, Frederick," David says.

"Yeah, thanks." I smile at him.

People around camp take the hint, and soon everyone shows gratitude to Frederick. Even Matthias pats him on the shoulder and says thanks. I watch Frederick's icy demeanor melt, and he's back to the warm, friendly guy we all know.

"Rebecca? You need to come check on Tim," Cass says worriedly.

Tim is leaning against a tree, wrapped up in a thick blanket, shivering, and even though the light from the fire is dim, he looks pale to me. I watch as Rebecca hurries over to him and places her hand on his forehead.

"Someone got a flashlight?" Rebecca asks with an edge to her voice.

Henry brings over David's flashlight. He shines it at Tim as Rebecca removes the blanket. The whole camp is silent as she pulls the bandage off

Tim's wound. I immediately cover my nose as a rank smell hits me. I see that David does the same.

"I was afraid of this," Rebecca says gravely.

23

"What? What is it?" Matthias asks.

I scoot closer to Cass and put my arm around her. She's hugging her knees and rocking back and forth as she cries silently.

"He has an infection," Rebecca says. "If we don't get him the proper treatment, he could get sepsis."

"What's sepsis?" I ask.

"It's something like blood poisoning. If he gets that, he will most likely die," she says matter-of-factly.

Cass starts bawling, and I hold her tighter.

"Well, what does he need?" Henry asks.

"A hospital."

"That's not an option," Matthias says. "Do ya have anything in your medical kit that could help?"

"I have one bag of IV fluids and a small tube of antibiotic cream, but I'm afraid that's not going to be enough."

"Well, we have to try," Matthias says, going to grab the medical kit for her.

"What about plants? Could we find some kingsfoil in the woods and heal him with that?" I ask desperately.

"What's kingsfoil?" Rebecca asks, confused.

"Liv, that's a plant from a movie. It's not real," David says.

I feel my cheeks burn from embarrassment. "Sorry. I watched it so many times, I forget that it's not real."

In this moment of urgency with Tim, Rebecca seems to have forgotten that she's mad at me and smiles. "Your natural remedy idea reminds me of something. I remember seeing a honey bee hive about a quarter mile back."

"Okay?"

"Honey has been used as an antibiotic for centuries. Is there anyone willing to retrace our steps and go get it for me?" she calls out.

"I will," David offers.

"I'll go too," I say, not wanting to stay behind again.

"I'll get you a bag to carry the honeycombs in. It's been getting cooler at night so, I'm not sure if there will be any bees still alive in the nest. Are either of you allergic to bees?" Rebecca asks.

"I don't think I've ever been stung in my entire life," I admit.

"I have. I was fine," David says.

We hear Matthias clear his throat, and we look over to see him looking uncomfortable. "I'm allergic to bees. It's possible that Olivia could be too," he says.

"I never knew that. You should have told me," Rebecca scolds. "As the camp nurse, it's my job to take care of you all. We only have one EpiPen in my kit, and even that is expired."

She shakes her head as she turns back to us. "David, you do most of the bee handling, then. I'll send the EpiPen with you, in case Olivia gets stung and needs it. An expired dose is at least better than nothing."

"How will I know if she needs it?" David asks, holding the EpiPen carefully as though it's a bomb about to explode.

"Difficulty breathing. Hives. Throat or tongue swelling." Rebecca ticks off on her fingers. "Trust me, you'll know."

Rebecca shows him how to use it as I go grab a knife from my bag. My nerves are on edge at the thought of walking off into the darkness, but having David with me helps.

He gets the flashlight from Rebecca and the handgun from Henry. As we get ourselves ready, I hear Joselyn say, "Careful, Olivia. Wouldn't want that pretty face ripped off by any wild beasties!"

"Thanks, Cindy. I'll keep my eyes open."

I'm nervous about leaving Cindy here at camp alone, but Tim needs us to hurry. Let's hope she behaves herself while I'm gone. We take off in the direction we came earlier today.

I follow behind David, watching his feet in the glow of the flashlight. "Do you think this is going to work?" I whisper to David.

"What?"

"The honey."

I hear him sigh. "I hope so."

We walk for a little while more, focusing on keeping our footsteps and breathing as quiet as possible. It's not easy with all the dead leaves covering the ground. David stops abruptly, and I run into his back, grabbing onto his shoulders to catch myself from falling.

"Did you hear that?"

"No, what did you hear?" I ask, looking around at the darkness.

"I heard a small buzz sound, and then it was gone."

We stop and listen, waiting to hear it happen again. The dead leaves rustle as a small breeze blows through the woods. An owl hoots off in the distance, but I don't hear a buzz.

"It's nighttime. If any of the bees are still alive, would they be asleep?" I ask.

"I have no idea. I feel like we're on an impossible search since Rebecca couldn't give me very good directions," David says, frustrated.

We stand quietly, waiting for another buzz. My teeth start to chatter now that we stopped moving. I clench my jaw to keep them quiet.

As I'm about to ask whether we should search the area with a flashlight instead of standing around, I hear a rumbling noise off in the distance. The same noise we heard earlier today.

I look at David, and his eyes are wide. "I heard it," David whispers before I ask anything. "Let's hurry up and find the beehive so we can get back to camp. We should probably tell Matthias about it this time."

I nod, and we start shining the flashlight up in the trees. I grab onto David's arm when a pair of eyes catch the light and shine down at us momentarily.

"Don't worry. It's just a raccoon," David says, slightly out of breath. I think it scared him too. He just wants to seem brave.

I never really cared that much about animals to devote my time to learn about them. I begin to wish I would have paid more attention when they taught us in school. Especially after that run-in with a skunk. It would be really handy to know which animals are dangerous and which ones aren't.

We continue walking for at least a half hour, circling the area David thought he heard the buzzing sound. The rumbling noise we heard doesn't happen again. My curiosity is getting the better of me. I almost want to take off and see what's making the sound, but I've already learned my lesson about leaving camp alone.

After walking another fifteen minutes or so, I hear David whisper-shout, "There!" He points the flashlight at a tree up ahead.

Dangling off a branch is a nest about the size of a basketball covered with bees, but they're hardly moving.

"How are we supposed to get the honeycomb when it's covered in bees?" I ask, exasperated.

David walks around the hive, staring at it with his face scrunched up in thought. "Either we grab the whole thing in the bag, bees and all, or I scrape off as many bees as I can before taking the honeycomb. Either way, you should probably get away from here while I do it."

"We can't take the bees back to camp. Matthias said he's allergic," I whisper, dread filling me at the thought of the other option. "But if you try to scrape the bees off, you're going to get stung."

"If I get stung, I get stung. We need to help Tim. What's a few bee stings if it means saving Tim's life?" David says bravely. "I have on a thick layer of clothes. We'll just hope they don't go for my hands or my face."

"I don't like this, David. How are you going to do this alone with a broken wrist? I have to help you..."

"No, Liv. You could be allergic. I'm not taking the risk. It'll be harder, but I'll figure it out. Now, go stand out there away from me. I need to do this before I lose my nerve."

I give him a worried look before turning around and walking about twenty paces away. I twist back around to watch, and I see David shoo me farther with his hand. I go another twenty paces until I'm just still able to see David.

I watch as David tucks the flashlight in a branch so it's pointing at the nest and then spreads the plastic garbage bag open on the ground beneath the hive. I have a bad feeling about this. But what can we do? Tim needs it.

David takes off one of his extra shirts and ties it around his good hand, using his teeth to pull it tight. He lifts his wrapped hand up slowly toward the hive and carefully scrapes a handful of bees off the nest and bends down to put them on the ground, but by the looks of it, they aren't letting go of his hand. He's bent over, shaking his hand slightly, and that's when I hear it, an angry buzzing sound as the nest of bees start swarming.

David rips the shirt off his hand and jerks upright, swatting at the back of his neck. He spins and looks at the nest for one second and then starts running toward me.

"David!" I yell.

"Run!"

I turn and run as fast as I can. My legs have never moved at this speed before. I feel like I'm flying through the trees. Luckily for us, the clouds broke this evening, and the moon makes it so I can see every tree or branch coming toward me. I dodge them swiftly, never losing speed. I hear the swarm of bees angrily buzz as they chase us. I try to focus on what's ahead of me, hoping I don't trip over a branch and get attacked. Even if I'm not allergic, being stung that many times can't be good.

We run for so long, I'm dripping with sweat. My head is pounding with pain, and I want to stop, but the flight response mixed with adrenaline keeps me moving.

I listen to the sounds behind me; other than David's heavy breathing and footfalls, I don't hear the bees anymore. I duck behind a big tree, crouching into a little ball, with my arms over my head to protect my face. David takes a seat beside me, and we both try to breathe as quietly as we can, listening for the bees.

"I think we lost them," David whispers.

I'm too afraid to lift my head and look to see if he's right, but I'm finding it hard to catch my breath curled up on myself. I finally straighten so I can stretch the cramp out that I'm getting in my ribs. I look around above where we're sitting and don't see any bees. My muscles relax a bit now that the threat is gone.

"Are you okay, Liv?"

"My head is throbbing, but otherwise, I'm fine. How about you? How many stings did you get?"

"I think just the one on my neck. It's a good thing I was wearing so many layers of clothes, or it could have been a lot worse."

We both quiet as we catch our breath. I wish we were back at camp. I look around us and realize I have no idea where we are. We wandered so far away from camp to find that nest and then ran to escape the bees. We might have to wait until morning to find our way back.

"Did you hear that?" David asks, suddenly going still, snapping me out of my thoughts.

"No..." I say, listening hard.

"There! That. It sounded like a popping sound," he whispers.

I turn my head to the side and listen for a moment. Then I hear it. "I think it's a campfire. You don't suppose we ended up making it back to camp, do you? I'm not sure what direction we were even running."

David holds his finger up to his mouth, and I nod as I follow behind him, walking carefully to avoid as many sticks as we can. My concussion makes it difficult to keep steady, but I push through the pain. I can hear the fire popping louder as we get closer.

After taking about fifty slow, meticulous steps, David holds his arm out to stop me. He immediately crouches down, and I match his movements. He holds his finger to his lips again and then points straight ahead.

I move a branch that's blocking my view and see five soldiers camped out around a fire, eating supper.

24

I carefully put the branch back in its place, scared to make any noise at all. David starts crawling backward, and I follow. I want to run out of there as fast as possible, but they'd hear us. We make it behind a tree, and both stand up, facing each other.

"What do we do?" I whisper as quietly as I can.

"We have to find camp and tell Matthias."

I nod as I panic internally. Even if we make it back quickly, there's no way our camp will ever be able to outrun healthy soldiers. We walk away slowly to avoid making any noise, but all this exertion is too much for me with my head injury, and I lose my balance, stepping on a stick with a loud crack.

We both stop moving immediately. I plead in my mind that the soldiers didn't just hear that. A few seconds tick by that feels like hours as we listen.

"Did you hear that?" a deep voice asks from the soldiers' camp.

"Probably just an animal," another voice answers lazily.

"We should check it out. It could be a predatory animal."

"Go for it. But if it's a deer or something, kill it so we can eat it. I'm tired of eating this slop."

David grabs my hand, and we take off running as fast as we can once again. I'm not sure I'll be able to keep it up for long this time. I really need some water. David hangs on tightly as we wind our way through the trees. My legs are starting to give out, but I push on. Footsteps are closing in, and I'm beginning to wonder if David and I should stop and fight. With the two of us, maybe we could take them down.

I'm just about to ask David whether we should when I see a light up ahead. It takes me a moment to realize it's the flashlight David had stuck in the tree to see what he was doing with the bees.

The bees!

I turn my attention toward the nest and see them flying around, agitated. David circles wide around the area, and we make it to the opposite side, where he ducks down behind some brush and pulls me down with him. I watch as he picks up a big rock off the ground and keeps his attention on the bees. I try to stifle my heavy breathing as we watch a single soldier come crashing into the clearing, looking up at the flashlight wedged into the branches. He pulls his rifle up to his shoulder and starts scanning the area through the scope.

When the soldier's back is turned, David throws the heavy stone at the nest, and I gasp as the honeycomb breaks free from the branch and falls to the ground. It's like I'm watching the scene in front of me in slow motion as the swarm of bees flies upwards from the ground in a dark, angry cloud. At the same time, the soldier whips around to see what the noise was. It takes him only a second to register that he's in danger before he starts running away toward his camp. A couple of bees manage to get him on his exposed skin, and we hear him swear loudly as he gets farther and farther away.

David quickly runs over to the honeycomb and stuffs it in the plastic garbage bag, tying the top tightly. He shakes his hand violently to get the bee that's stinging him off. I don't think the honeycomb was clear of all the bees before David tied it up, but we can't stay here any longer.

He grabs the flashlight out of the tree and signals for me to follow. We don't run this time, but we walk at a brisk pace. My balance is still poor, and I keep tripping over sticks, which starts to irritate David. He keeps shushing me every time I make a noise.

"What do you want from me, David? I don't feel well," I mutter.

He stops and looks at me, his face a mix of concern and annoyance. "Do you think you'll be able to make it back? We still have a little way to go."

My head gives a nasty throb that darkens my vision momentarily. I rub my forehead, trying to think, and before I know it, David sets the bag with the honeycomb down and squats to the ground in front of me. "Hop on."

"What?"

"I'll give you a piggyback ride to camp. Hop on. We need to move quickly."

"David, this is ridiculous. You don't need to give me a ride back to camp. You're tired too."

"I'll live. Probably a better chance of survival carrying you than having you stumbling your way through the woods, making such a racket. Now get on my back, or I'll throw you over my shoulder like a fireman."

I hesitate for a moment, but this is probably our best option. I climb on his back and wrap my legs around his waist, hooking my feet together. Then I wrap my arms over his shoulders and hold onto his chest.

"Here. I'll need you to carry the bag. Just hang on tight to this and to me, and I'll get us to camp."

I feel so awkward clinging to him like this. It takes him a moment to get used to my weight, but once he finds his center of balance, he hurries off as though I'm nothing more than a backpack.

My muscles start to ache, and I realize I'm holding on stiffly, trying to take as much pressure off him as possible, which suddenly seems silly, since he's carrying all my weight whether I'm relaxed or not. I loosen up a bit and rest my throbbing head on his shoulder, our cheeks brushing against each other. His stubble feels rough on my skin, but it's not unpleasant. I take a deep breath, and the scent of sweat with a hint of vanilla fills my nostrils. Again, not entirely unpleasant.

The bag of honeycomb grows heavy in my hand. It swings back and forth with every step David takes, making it hard to hold onto with my almost numb fingers. I grip it tighter, trying hard to keep it from bumping into David as he goes.

"Thank you, David," I say in his ear. "For everything."

He nods but stays focused on the task. His pace is slowing down, and I can feel him shaking slightly from fatigue, but he never stops. His transformation from the weak, seizure-ridden boy to this strong, healthy man is incredible. I can't believe how far we've come.

Voices pull me from my thoughts, and I look up to see our camp ahead of us. David crouches down so I can slide off his back. He staggers a bit when he stands back up, and I grab his arm to steady him. We quickly make our way into camp, waving at Stan, who's on watch duty.

I walk over to Rebecca and hand her the bag with the honeycomb.

"It might still have bees on it. You'll probably want to take it out of camp a little way before opening the bag."

"Thanks," she says as she stands up to take the bag out into the woods immediately.

I glance at Tim, who's asleep on the ground. His skin is a sickly gray color and covered in a sheen of sweat even though he's shivering violently. Cass is at his side, looking terrified.

"We need to leave. Now," David announces.

"Why?" Matthias asks.

"Liv and I just stumbled on a camp of soldiers a few miles back."

David has everyone's attention now. Cass starts crying as she looks down at Tim.

"Can we take them on? We have weapons. Maybe we could stand our ground and fight." Alexandrine asks.

"Look around. Half this camp is in no position to even run away, let alone fight," Matthias growls, clearly frustrated. At that moment, the campfire reflects in his good eye, making him look wild and dangerous. "We're gonna have to move."

Just then, Rebecca comes back to camp, carrying the bag of honeycomb. "I got the last few bees off. Someone want to hold the flashlight so I can see what I'm doing with Tim's arm?"

"It'll have to wait. We're leavin'."

"Leaving? If Tim doesn't get treated, he's going to die," Rebecca says, scandalized.

"There's a group of soldiers camped out a few miles from here. If we don't leave now, we're all gonna die!" Matthias barks.

"You don't know that! I have a duty here as a nurse. Tim needs treatment!"

"I have a duty here as well, Rebecca. I'm not gonna let everyone get killed just so you can try to save the kid!"

Both of them are glaring at each other, breathing heavily with anger. Everyone else stays quiet as we wait for a solution to present itself.

Finally, Cindy, of all people, stands up and breaks the silence, "This isn't getting us anywhere. We're running out of time. Let's give Rebecca a chance to treat his infection with the honey and get it redressed. While she does that, how about other people make a stretcher from some wood and a blanket."

"That's a good idea," I pitch in.

"Fine. Ya got an hour. Whoever's not ready by then will be left behind. Move!"

Everyone starts working. It doesn't take long to have the bags and supplies ready since there wasn't enough time to unpack anything.

"I don't know how we're going to do this. The kids need sleep," Caroline complains. "Sonya and Emily are already asleep. I can't carry them all."

"Carry Sonya. The others will have to walk," Alexandrine answers as she helps slide a backpack on Charlotte's back. "Our survival is more important than our comfort."

Caroline grumbles but starts getting the children ready. Rebecca's twin boys, Joey and Isaac, blink heavily as they look around at all the commotion. It's going to take a miracle to get us out of here.

The hour flew by quickly, but everyone is ready to move by the time it's over. Once the fire is put out, we immediately feel the temperature change. I have on every shirt I own, hoping it will be enough to keep me warm. I don't know what Matthias has planned, but I hope we find somewhere safe to camp soon so we can get another fire lit.

A couple of the men place Tim carefully on the stretcher. He looks as sick as ever. They wrapped an extra blanket around him, and it seems like his shivering calms down a bit, but by the look on his sleeping face, he's in a huge amount of pain. Frederick and Stan take opposite ends of the stretcher to carry between them, being extra careful not to tip Tim off it.

Caroline came up with a smart way to keep the children together in the dark. She got a length of rope for the children to hold onto to help them stay in a line. She tied the front end of the rope to her backpack so she can use both arms to carry Sonya, who's still asleep, and Alexandrine is holding the back end of the rope, right behind Charlotte.

It's going to be slow moving since it's not only dark, but everyone is exhausted. Once again, Matthias takes the lead with Saul by his side. Henry is put on the end with a gun to keep watch. I make sure I'm right behind David this time. I feel better knowing I'm following him.

The moon gives barely enough light for those who don't have Rare abilities to see. We're moving almost half as fast as we normally would in the daylight, which is probably a good thing since my head is still aching.

After an hour or so of steady walking, we stop to take a bathroom break and to switch up who carries Tim. Henry swaps places with Frederick, handing Frederick the gun to protect us from behind, while another guy from camp, Leroy, takes the back of the stretcher. Really, Leroy should be the one to take the front, since he's almost twice the size of Henry, but from what I've seen of him around camp, he's rather lazy. He's one of the more recent additions from what I've heard, joining the camp right before David and I got there. You'd think his beer belly would be gone after eating smaller amounts of food and having no access to alcohol, but his gut hangs out over his belt in an unhealthy way.

"Mama, I'm cold," Isaac sniffles to Rebecca just before we're lined back up and ready to move.

She kneels down and gives him and his twin brother, Joey, a big hug. "I know, baby. But we need to keep moving. Moving will help you stay warm."

"He can have one of my extra shirts," Joselyn offers timidly.

Alexandrine must have taken the time to pick up some spare clothes for Charlotte and Joselyn before leaving the city. I don't remember seeing Joselyn wear anything other than pajama pants and an oversized white T-shirt while I was in the hospital with her. That must have been all the hospital was willing to buy her since she was in there for so long.

"That's very—kind—of you, Joselyn," Rebecca says hesitantly.

Isaac looks at his mom, and she nods to let him know it's okay. He grabs the shirt and pulls it on over his jacket. The shirt hangs down to his knees, and it's unlikely that it will actually do anything to help him stay warm, but a smile spreads across both their faces.

We continue on, marching through the night. It doesn't take long before I hear Leroy huffing and puffing up ahead of me. I hope to God he doesn't drop Tim. I think Cass is worried about it too, because I keep hearing little nervous moans coming from behind me.

"You've got to lift him up, Leroy." I hear Henry grunt.

"I can't do it, man! I'm too tired."

"We're all tired, but we need to keep moving. I can't carry Tim by myself. Help me out."

They stop moving, and I almost run into David's back.

"Nah, man. I can't do this anymore."

"Matthias, hold up!" I hear Alexandrine shout from up ahead.

After a minute, everyone gathers around Tim's stretcher. Matthias pushes through the crowd to see what's going on.

"What's the problem?" Matthias asks, irritated.

"I can't do this. I'm sick of it!"

"Sick of what? Carryin' Tim?"

"No. This. All of it," he answers, gesturing around himself. "I just can't do it anymore. At least I had a warm house in the city. And food. It was stupid to leave that all behind to follow you. And for what? Freedom? Is this what you call freedom? What a joke."

"Ya wanna leave? Then get the hell outta here. We don't need ya holdin' us up."

"Fine. Give me a weapon so I can get back."

"No."

"I'll die out there!"

"That's your problem. Ya wanna leave this camp, then leave, but you ain't takin' any of our stuff. You're on your own."

A feeling of danger needles my mind as I see the venomous look take over Leroy's face. I watch in horror as Leroy pounces on Frederick, wrestling the gun out of his hands, and then points it at Matthias. The momentary shock wears off, and I'm about to step in and take Leroy down, but Joselyn's suddenly on him like a crazed cat, clawing at his face and hands. She bites his ear, and Leroy drops the gun with a yowl. Matthias picks it up and points it at Leroy's head.

I glance over at Joselyn to see if she's okay, and she's grinning wide with blood dripping down her chin. Looks like Cindy stepped in again to help.

"You gonna shoot me, Matthias? Hmm?"

"Do it!" Cindy giggles.

"I want everyone outta here. Henry, help your Granddad."

"What are you going to do?" David asks.

"I'm gonna have a little chat with Leroy here, and then I'll catch back up with y'all."

Everyone stands around, looking at one another.

"I said go. Now!" Matthias shouts.

We all obey reluctantly. I have a sick feeling in my stomach at the scene before me. Cass had told me once that he shot people who didn't make it through the reckoning. Is he going to kill Leroy?

"You know the gunshot will be heard by the soldiers if you shoot him," I say, but Matthias ignores me, so I let it go.

I take the back of the stretcher, even though I shouldn't because I'm the one with a concussion, but we need to move. My hands are shaking with adrenaline as I lift him up. David pulls up the back of the line with one of the rifles from camp. I can tell he wants to be the one carrying Tim instead of me doing it, but he can't with a broken wrist.

I hear Frederick mutter from the front of the stretcher, "Goodbye, Leroy," as the group takes off into the darkness once again.

I have to remind myself to breathe as I wait for the gunshot to ring out through the woods. But it never does. I try to relax, but my arms are going numb from carrying Tim. I dig deep inside myself to keep going.

After a while, I hear footsteps coming up quickly behind us, and my heart almost stops. Even though I knew Matthias was coming back, he still scares me half to death, thinking the soldiers caught up to us. Matthias passes by in a blur as he trots toward the head of the line. I couldn't get a good look at him, but I have a sick feeling things didn't end well for Leroy.

What would make Leroy suddenly act out that way? Just because he was tired and miserable? I shake my head in disgust. I really hope Matthias didn't kill him. I hope he just let him go to head back to his life in the city.

I'm starting to get hot from the effort of carrying Tim's weight. My hands are losing their grip on the sticks, but I can't let go. Frederick needs my help. He's got to be getting tired too. He's doing most of the heavy lifting.

I need to focus my mind on something other than the pain in my head and arms, so I start counting our footsteps, but after I reach five thousand, I decide to give up. The tediousness of counting isn't helping.

The kids are whining up ahead again, and I feel like we're not going to make it far enough to avoid getting caught. They're getting tired, and we can't expect them to walk all night.

"Take a break." I hear Matthias call out from up ahead.

Frederick and I carefully lay Tim down on the ground, and I immediately stretch out my hands, arms, and shoulders.

"We can't keep going. We need to find a safe place to sleep, Matthias," Rebecca pleads.

Matthias looks around at everyone and nods tersely. He looks worn-out, but he holds out his hand to David. I look closer at his hand and see that it's covered in dried blood. My stomach gives an uneasy churn. We never heard a gunshot, but Matthias must have killed him some other way. He's a murderer.

"Flashlight," he barks.

David pulls the flashlight out of his pocket and gives it to him.

"Want me to come with you, Pop?" Henry offers.

"Nah. Stay with the rest of 'em. I'll try to be quick."

113

Everyone stays quiet as we rehydrate ourselves and attempt to stay warm. I sit up close to David and whisper, "Does it bother you that Matthias just killed Leroy?"

"A little. But I understand Matthias's position. He couldn't just let the guy go and hope that he doesn't tell anyone about us. Leroy was already proving that he wasn't trustworthy and had a grudge against Matthias."

"But he killed someone. That's not okay," I whisper a little louder than I mean to.

Alexandrine must have heard me. "Matthias has to make decisions for the safety of the camp. He feels responsible for everyone's survival. If our survival is threatened, he does what he feels he must to keep us safe. If that means killing a traitor, so be it."

"'Killing a traitor?' Sounds like Turk," I mutter but realize my mistake immediately.

Alexandrine is on her feet, pointing down at me, her hand shaking with anger. "Don't you ever compare Matthias to Turk."

"You're right. I'm sorry," I say sheepishly. "I'm just not okay with ending someone's life."

"That's not really your call, now is it?"

I blow out a big breath trying to control myself. "No. I guess not."

Everyone is quiet for the moment. The children have all laid down and are now fast asleep.

"Hey, guys? Why is there blood around my mouth?" Joselyn's voice squeaks.

"You attacked Leroy and bit his ear," Cass answers.

"What?" she says, horrified. "Why?"

"To save Matthias from getting shot," Rebecca responds.

"That must have been Cindy," Joselyn mutters in disgust as she scrubs her chin clean.

"Either way, it was very brave," Rebecca says.

This is the first kind thing Rebecca has said to Joselyn since Joselyn got here. Maybe there is hope that they could repair their relationship. I'm not sure they'll be able to if Cindy keeps making an appearance, but she is a part of Joselyn, whether we all like it or not.

The sweat I worked up carrying Tim wears off, and I start to shiver. I try not to think about how miserable I feel, but my stomach gives a loud growl, and I become aware of just how hungry I am. We hardly had anything to eat for supper, and we've been walking for hours. I don't know how much food we have left, but I'm worried that it's getting pretty low.

When we were eating the chickens, someone had commented that the goats might be next, but they have been carrying heavy loads for us, so I'm not sure how we'll get by without them.

My fatigue sets in, and I start to nod off. Before I think about what I'm doing, I lay my head on David's shoulder and immediately start to dream about bees attacking me while being chased through the woods by an army of soldiers. In front of them is Cindy, with blood dripping down her chin.

I wake up with a start and realize David was resting his head on top of mine. He quickly sits up, clearing his throat and shifting away from me a little.

"You okay?" David whispers.

"Yeah. Just a bad dream," I say, slightly embarrassed. "Has Matthias come back yet?"

"Not that I know of. I kind of dozed off there for a bit."

We sit quietly and hear the heavy breathing of sleep around us. I look around and see Frederick and Henry keeping watch, but their heads keep bobbing like they're falling asleep too. Saul snores loudly. We need to find a safer place for us to camp out. Hopefully, Matthias will come back with good news.

Leaves rustle out in the woods, and I watch as a deer plods along past us. I momentarily consider taking Henry's bow and shooting it for a meal, but I know I could never kill it. Not that I couldn't hit it—I'm actually getting pretty good since I've been practicing—but that I could never take its life. I can't help but put myself in its place, and it makes me sad at the thought.

Finally, my ears pick up someone coming toward us. This time, I don't panic, knowing Matthias was bound to return sooner or later.

"Everyone up. I found a spot. It'll be rough goin', but it's safe."

Sounds of moaning and grunts come from all around as people stand up to move again. The kids whine that they don't want to walk anymore, but Caroline bribes them with a pinch of sugar from the small bag she has in the supplies. I secretly wish I could have a pinch of it too.

We switch up positions again. Nathaniel, a guy in his mid-thirties with curly blond hair and light green eyes, who I just recently found out is the father of Rebecca's twin boys, offers to take my spot carrying Tim. Which means I get to take the goats that he was in charge of. They're tired too, but you can usually keep them going with bits of food.

Before too long, a tall wall of rocks stands before us.

"Is there a cave or something?" Alexandrine asks with a yawn.

"There's a secluded area at the top, surrounded by trees and boulders. We can all tuck in there nicely and stay hidden."

I look up, my head tipped back as far as it will go. He expects us to climb to the top?

"How are we going to get up there?" Alexandrine asks what everyone's thinking.

"I told ya it'll be rough goin'. There's a bit of a trail, but at some points, there'll be some climbing to do. We're gonna have to help each other out."

I look around at everyone's expressions of displeasure. Nobody looks happy to be tackling this near-impossible task. It would be hard enough in the daytime, but now we're doing it in the dark while having to carry Tim, push wheelbarrows, lead goats, and help small children. Not to mention, Saul looks pretty worse for wear. But the thought of being able to rest safely once we make it up there pushes us forward.

The sun starts to rise by the time everyone is at the top. We inched our way up by having an able-bodied person climb a little, then stop and reach down to help pull up a child, a wheelbarrow, or Tim. Luckily, the goats took climbing with stride. Even being weighed down with our stuff, they climbed the rocks easier than any of us humans. They were almost pulling me up the rocks at some points.

There were a couple of rough patches. Saul lost his footing and hit his shin hard against a rock. He didn't cut himself, but it has already started to bruise. He had to go even slower after that. And at a particularly steep spot, Nathaniel and Frederick had to tie ropes around Tim and the stretcher, climb up to a safe place, and then pull Tim up to them. Tim had a moment of alertness before they were tying the ropes on. He told them he could climb it himself, but just as he got the words out, he turned and threw up. Frederick told him to lie down and shut up, which Tim did.

As soon as I'm at the top, I find a tree to tie the goats up to, remove the bags off their back, and give them what little water I can find. Everyone is working as quickly as their tired bodies can to lay out their sleeping gear and finally rest. The clearing is a bit small, so we're all tucked up next to one another.

Even though my concussion makes my head throb, I can tell I've gotten through the worst of it. It's not nearly as painful as it was before. I don't think I could have made that climb if I wasn't feeling better. I'm thankful for that.

I lay my bedding down by David's and stretch a little before going to sleep. I can see the sun turning the sky orange as I gaze down at the treetops below us. Many trees have lost their leaves, and now they look like giant sticks stuck in the ground.

As I take one last look before lying down, I spot a small column of smoke in the distance. The soldiers must be awake.

"Matthias," I whisper. He lifts himself up on his elbow to look at me with annoyance.

"What?"

"I just saw smoke coming from out where I think the soldiers' camp is. They're awake."

Matthias sits up, looks around at everyone for a little while, and finally says, "There's nothin' more we can do. We all need to recharge and gain our strength. I suggest ya lay down and put it outta your mind. We should be safe up here."

I nod reluctantly. I lie down on my side, facing David, who's lying on his back with his good arm resting under his head. He has his eyes closed, but I can tell he's not quite asleep yet.

"I'm scared, David," I whisper.

"Don't be. I got you," he whispers back without opening his eyes. He rolls to his side and puts his arm over me protectively. I snuggle in a little closer to let him know I'm okay with this. The weight of his arm feels comforting, and I can immediately relax my mind. Sleep finds me quickly.

■■■■■

I wake up to the sound of distant voices. The sun is now up and shining directly on us. I look around and see that everyone is still asleep. Did I really hear voices, or was I just dreaming?

I slide carefully out from under David's arm. He grunts a little, then rolls over to continue sleeping.

"Their footprints stop here."

"They must have climbed."

"Do we wait down here, or should we climb up and see if they're still there?"

They found us.

I scramble my way through the sleeping bodies to get to Matthias. I make sure I stay down by his feet when I shake him awake to avoid a knife to my neck like last time.

"Matthias!" I whisper.

He snaps awake and sits up in one fluid motion. His green eye locks onto mine, going from kill to confusion in a blink of his eye.

"They found us," I whisper fearfully.

"Where are they?" he asks, seeming to know immediately what I'm talking about.

"On the ground. They haven't climbed up yet."

"Wake everyone up. Be quiet about it. We gotta move."

I nod and start shaking people awake, holding my finger to my lips when their eyes open and they look to see who woke them. Once everyone is up, Matthias fills them in on what's going on.

"The soldiers are comin'. Pack your stuff, and get ready to move. We're gonna head that way and see where it leads," Matthias says, pointing at the trees opposite of the way we came up. The wall of rocks we climbed brought us to this plateau that stretches on through the trees for who knows how long.

"Come on, Matthias. We can't keep running. We have a position of power, let's use it." Alexandrine protests quietly.

"She's right. We could hide everyone out in the woods, have a few of us stay put here, and shoot the soldiers as soon as they make it up," Henry suggests.

Matthias strokes his beard as he looks around at all the eyes watching him. "Fine. David, Henry, and I will stay behind. Everyone else, head out into the woods at least a half-mile, and hide. Olivia, ya listen and wait until ya hear me whistle this." He stops whispering and whistles a three-note tune. "If ya hear that, ya know it's safe to come outta hidin' and that we're on our way. If ya hear gunshots and ya don't hear my whistle, somethin's gone wrong, and the rest of ya will have to take out any soldiers that are left."

"Matthias, do you want me to stay, and you can lead the rest of them?" Frederick offers.

"Nah. I can still shoot usin' my good eye. Ya need to help carry Tim."

I look over at Tim and see that he's still asleep. His skin color looks a little better, but not by much.

I give David a worried look. I wish he wasn't such a good shot. I don't want him to keep being chosen to do dangerous things.

"Matthias!" I hear Rebecca call out in a hushed yell.

I look up to see Rebecca supporting Saul as he tries to take a step but stumbles and falls. Matthias rushes over to him, and I start to panic at how much time we've wasted already. The soldiers could be here at any minute.

"Pop! What's goin' on?"

Matthias helps lay Saul down on his back, and Rebecca lifts his pant leg to look at where Saul had bruised his leg.

119

I gasp when I see it. His calf is swollen to twice its size, the bruise where he hit against the rock is dark purple, and the surrounding skin is an angry shade of red.

"This isn't good," Rebecca says, tenderly poking around the injury. "I think he's got deep vein thrombosis."

"English, please," Matthias grunts.

"It's a blood clot in a vein deep in his leg. I don't have the blood thinners needed to treat this," she says, her voice shaking.

"What's gonna happen if it's left untreated?"

"Well, a piece of the blood clot could dislodge and travel up his bloodstream into his lung, causing a pulmonary embolism." She looks up from Saul's leg to see Matthias giving her a look of annoyance. "In other words," she breathes out heavily, "he could die."

"Uh, guys. I don't mean to interrupt," Nathaniel says, "but we need to get moving before the soldiers get here."

Matthias covers his face with his hands, rubbing his fingers on his forehead, thinking. "You're right. Can you help Saul outta here?" he asks Nathaniel.

Nathaniel nods, as he and Rebecca work together to help Saul up off the ground.

"Get yourselves to a safe place, and find something comfortable for him to rest on. We'll catch up as soon as we can," Matthias says as the hand holding a rifle shakes a bit.

"Be careful," I mouth to David, and he winks at me.

I untie the goats and follow behind everyone as we make our way into the woods, taking one last look at David before I'm too far away. They are placing themselves behind boulders that will allow them to hide while keeping watch for the soldiers to make their appearance.

The goats are being uncooperative this time, and it takes a lot of tugging and treats to make them move. After we walk for about fifteen minutes, Rebecca decides that's as far as Saul's going to make it.

We all scatter out, taking shelter behind trees or rocks that are big enough to conceal us. I find a fallen tree with its roots pulled up out of the ground, making a natural wall to hide the goats with me.

As we all sit there, quietly waiting to hear the gunshots, I shake my head in disgust that we're having to kill people again to assure our safety. Will David really be able to do it? I know I wouldn't. Why are our lives more important than the lives of the soldiers? Even though they've given their allegiance to Turk, does that really mean they deserve to die? What if those men have families back home? What about them and their lives that will be messed up because of us? Anger bubbles up inside my chest at my mother. We wouldn't be in this terrible situation if it hadn't been for her. Now because of her, more people have to die.

My muscles start shaking from the constant tension I'm holding. I hear someone humming "London Bridge" not far from where I'm hiding, and I immediately know Cindy is back.

"Shh! Cindy, be quiet!" I hiss.

"How'd you know it was me?"

"Wild guess," I say. "You have to stay quiet so we can hear what's going on."

"Okalie dokalie."

The minutes tick by, and I start to worry about what's going on. A fleeting spark of hope ignites in my mind that maybe the soldiers decided to turn around and head back to the city.

That's when I hear the distinct sound of a gunshot. I squeeze my eyes shut, praying hard that it wasn't from a soldier's gun. I hear another one, followed closely by another. The goats don't seem fazed by the noise. Meanwhile, I'm barely keeping it together.

Five shots are fired in total, with the last two being a little quieter and spaced farther out than the others. Now the silence feels thick as I listen closely for Matthias's whistle. My muscles are so tense, I feel like they could snap. A crow caws loudly above where I'm hiding, and I just about scream, letting out a weird squeaky noise instead. The goats bleat in response, watching me with their alien eyes. I hold a shaky finger up to my lips at them in vain.

After waiting for what feels like forever, I finally hear Matthias whistle. I collapse on the ground with relief.

I let everyone know I heard his whistle, and we all gather together close to where Saul and Tim are lying. It doesn't take long before the men find us, carrying extra weapons that they must have taken off the soldiers. Matthias heads straight for his dad without a word to anyone else.

David comes over to me with a look of concern.

"What happened? What's wrong?"

"Matthias took them all out himself. I think he was getting revenge for what happened to Saul or something. Only three of the soldiers climbed up, while two stayed on the ground. As soon as he killed the three, he muttered 'know your enemy,' then he climbed halfway down the rocks and sniped the other two. I've never seen him so crazed before. It was kind of scary."

"Apparently, killing people is fun for him or something."

He ignores me and goes on to say, "He took an earpiece out of one of their ears and heard someone on the other end asking if they were okay and whether they knew where we were headed next. He thinks these soldiers weren't hunting us down to kill us, but following us to see where we were going and then reporting back."

"Well, that's good, isn't it?"

"Not exactly. They know where we are right now, and you can just about guarantee they will be sending a larger group out next time. We can't keep this up forever."

At that moment, we hear the rumbling sound again. It's a little louder than before. It's a cloudless day, so there shouldn't be any thunder. I look around to see if anyone else heard it, and Charlotte and Cindy are looking up with confused looks. They heard it too.

"Do either of you know what that was?" I ask.

They shake their heads.

"You hear it too? I thought I was going crazy," Cindy says, tipping her head off to the side and crossing her eyes.

"That's a short trip," Charlotte teases, and Cindy sticks her tongue out at her.

"Let she who hath not been thrown in thine nut house cast thine first stone," Cindy responds in a mock dramatic voice. And they both erupt in a fit of giggles.

I look at David, who's watching them with furrowed eyebrows. He hasn't experienced Cindy's brand of craziness much, and it shows.

"I'm going to go tell Matthias about the noise. Wanna come?" David asks.

The girls start playing a game of thumb war, and I decide to follow him.

Matthias and Rebecca are separated a bit from the group, having an intense conversation. Matthias has a desperate look on his face as he listens to Rebecca telling him that she can't fix Saul.

"There's nothing I can do. I want to. Believe me. I love him too, but this is just out of my hands. I don't have the skill or the equipment to treat him."

"Is there a chance that the blood clot won't break off? That it'll just go away?"

Rebecca looks over at Saul, who's lying on a pile of blankets. His face looks ashen, and his breathing is labored.

"I think it's already happening," she says with a catch in her voice.

Matthias looks at his dad and rushes to his side. He grabs Saul's hand with worry etched on his face.

David and I decide that now is not the time to be bothering him. We quietly back away and have a seat next to Henry, who's sitting against a tree, watching.

"Pop might be a tough and fearless leader, but when it comes to family, he's a big softy. Don't tell him I told you that," Henry whispers to me, then turns back to watch Matthias sadly.

"I'm really glad I found you guys," I say. "I wish I could have known Saul while he could still talk."

"I wish I could have too. But he was able to teach me a lot without having to say a thing. He'll be missed greatly," he says, his voice thick with emotion. "I'm just glad I didn't have to live with Janice. It's a miracle you turned out as decent as you did."

"Thanks, I guess. I often wonder what life would have been like if Matthias had come to rescue me when I was little. Maybe I would be a superpowered Rare by now or something, never having had my abilities suppressed."

"Sorry it didn't work out that way," he apologizes sincerely.

We are quiet for a while, watching Rebecca as she applies fresh honey on Tim's infected stump and then bandages it with a clean cloth. She sorts through her first aid kit with a shake of her head. I have a sinking feeling that her supplies are running dangerously low.

My stomach growls loudly, and David hears it.

"Has anyone figured out what we're doing for a meal yet?"

"I don't think so. I think everyone's still exhausted," I say, feeling tired myself.

"I saw some fresh deer droppings on our way out here," Henry pipes in. "I'll go hunting. I need to clear my head anyway."

■■■■■

The afternoon passes by quickly with people resting and taking much-needed naps. Frederick was able to find a pond of water for us to drink. It has an unpleasant taste even after boiling it, but nobody complains.

Matthias had taken a moment from his dad's side to inform the camp on what's going on. "We got at least two days before we're in any real danger of a new squad of soldiers catchin' up. Everyone needs to take this time to rest and regain your strength. Help out where ya can, and be ready to move when I say it's time."

Henry returns, dragging a deer with him. He looks worn out, so Nathaniel and Frederick offer to prepare it for supper.

Cass has been sitting by Tim's side since his bandage was changed. She's kept herself busy writing in her notebook, but when nature calls, she asks me to stay with him while she's gone.

I agree, and I take a seat next to his good arm. I stare up into the trees, watching a squirrel hop around when I hear Tim make a small noise in his throat. I look down at him, and he has his eyes cracked open. My first instinct is to call out for Cass, but she's in the middle of going to the bathroom.

"Hey, Olivia," Tim grunts.

"Hi, Tim. You okay?"

"I've been better. Why do I feel sticky?" he asks, looking toward the bandage.

"Rebecca is using honey to try to cure your infection."

"Honey?" His brows furrow.

"Yeah, she says that honey has been used as an antibiotic since ancient times."

Tim just nods and blinks his eyes tiredly. "Do you think this is God's way of punishing me for what I was doing? You know, for cutting myself? I was misusing my arms, so he took one away?"

I absentmindedly rub the knot on my head as I try to figure out how to answer his question. "I don't have a lot of knowledge when it comes to God, but I don't think he would take an already broken person and punish them. So, no, I don't think this is a punishment for your cutting. You losing your arm is just a crappy thing that life threw your way."

He nods. "Well, I'm sorry I ever did that in the first place. I would give anything to have my arm back," he says, bowing his head and looking away from me.

We already gave him lectures about cutting, so me saying more negative things about it isn't going to help. I take a different approach. "We all love you, Tim, whether you have one arm or two. Whether you're depressed or annoyingly happy. You're an important part of this camp, and we're all here for you."

Cass comes bounding back and squeals when she sees that Tim's awake. I leave them to have a little sibling time. I go help David with the fire he's building.

"I heard what you were saying to Tim. Those were some important points you should keep in mind next time you're suffering from a bout of depression."

"Yeah, yeah," I say, brushing it off. It's been a while since I've had a struggle with my depression. I don't think I'm completely healed yet, but I think I'm getting better.

"Pop? Pop, please don't go." I hear Matthias plead.

"I'm sorry, Matthias," Rebecca says, and then steps away to give him his privacy. Henry went running as soon as he heard Matthias cry out, but I'm rooted in place.

"You should go over there, Liv. He was your grandpa too. Even though you didn't get to know him for that long, you're still family."

I stand up hesitantly. This feels like an intimate moment, and I haven't been here that long to deserve to intrude on it. I walk up slowly to Matthias and lay my hand on his shoulder. He reaches up and puts his warm, rough hand on top of mine. We all look down at Saul quietly. His mouth is slack, and his eyes are slightly open. His labored breathing has stopped, and now he's lying there motionless. Henry reaches out and gently closes his eyes.

"I'm sorry, Pop," I whisper to Matthias, feeling that the moment calls for sentimentality.

"That's the first time I heard ya call me that." Matthias sniffs.

"I know. I'm sorry about that too. It takes me a while to deal with my feelings."

We're quiet again as we mourn Saul's passing. I can hear sniffles coming from where the rest of our camp is sitting. They are being respectful and giving us our space.

"Guess I should find a place to bury him," Matthias says, standing up abruptly. He rubs his eye quickly as though he hopes nobody knows he's crying.

"Want me to help, Pop?" Henry asks, wiping his tears away with the heels of his hands.

"I need to be alone for a bit. Go help supper get done. I'm hungry," he says quickly, then turns to head out into the woods to find a resting place for Saul.

Matthias insists on burying Saul on his own. It takes him a long time since all he has is a small camp shovel to work with. Once he's done, he comes to get us so we can all say our goodbyes. Then we head back to camp to have dinner.

Frederick starts a toast in honor of Saul, and everyone goes around saying something nice about Saul. Matthias keeps his gaze on the fire but nods with each sentiment.

It comes around to me, and I try hard to find something profound to say. "I didn't get to know Saul for that long, unfortunately. He seemed like a kind man. He always had a twinkle in his eye when he looked at me. I was intrigued by the way he kept carving the same symbols over and over again on sticks. They matched up with a pendant I once found in a box in my old apartment, and that makes me feel somehow connected to him."

Matthias's head snaps up, and he looks at me when I say that. He gets up and walks over to his bag, pulling out his belongings until he finds the pendant he took from me. He walks back, staring at the symbols. He holds it out to me, and I take it gently. The firelight sparkles in the crystal, making the black symbols stand out more.

"Do ya remember what he carved?"

I try hard to think about the sticks I always saw him whittling, but I can't remember the exact sequence. I roll the tumblers around with my thumbs, hoping to land on the right ones, but nothing happens. I can feel everyone's eyes on me, and I don't like it.

I start to shake my head no when I remember the stick Saul gave me. I race to my bag and dig around until I feel the smooth, slender stick with the symbols carved on it. I want to try setting the symbols in order over here, where nobody is watching me, but everyone wants to see what's going on.

I walk back to the fire, holding the stick and the pendant with reverence. Excitement is blooming inside my chest. What's going to happen when I line up the right combination of symbols?

I sit next to David and Cass while everyone continues to watch me. David holds the stick for me to look at while I twist each tumbler into the right place. Holding my breath, I slowly slide the last one into its spot.

Nothing.

I tug on it gently. Nothing happens.

"What's it doin'? Anything?"

I shake my head and hear people letting out disappointed sighs. "I put the symbols in the right order, but it's not doing anything."

"Mind if I try?" Matthias asks.

I hand the stick and the pendant to him, and he sets to work, rolling the tumblers around to reset the combination, then slowly puts them back into order, but once again, nothing happens.

"Maybe it's like a locker combination. Maybe you need to turn them in the right direction too," David suggests.

"David's probably right. Why don't ya fidget with it, Olivia. Let me know when something happens. I'm goin' to sleep." Matthias hands me the pendant and slumps away heavily.

A somber quiet falls over the camp. The chill in the air has us all huddled close to the fire, cocooned in blankets and warm clothes. Rebecca, Caroline, and Alexandrine work on getting the children put to bed, snuggling them up close to one another. Being that close to each other makes it difficult for them to stop goofing around and go to sleep, making bedtime take twice as long as normal.

I offer to take a watch tonight. That way, I can play around with the pendant while listening for danger. As I sit and twist the symbols around, trying multiple combinations, I start to wonder: what if it doesn't open? What if it's a secret code that spells out a word, and I don't know how to decipher it?

After about the fifteenth time of trying and getting frustrated when it doesn't do anything, I hang it back around my neck and take a break. Now that I don't have anything to occupy my mind, I notice just how cold the night is with this constant wind blowing. The chilly temperature seems to go right through me down to my bones. I lay Henry's bow on the ground close by and wrap my blanket tighter around me.

With summer over, the woods are unnervingly quiet. I miss the sounds of crickets chirping at night. A lonely owl hoots off in the distance, but that's the only sound I hear while I keep watch. I guess I'm grateful for that. We don't need any more excitement right now.

I check the wristwatch Frederick gave me and see that my shift was done an hour ago. I wake Alexandrine up to take my post, trying hard to not wake Charlotte too, who's wrapped in Alexandrine's arms. Once again, a wave of longing washes over me. I will never feel that kind of love, and it makes me sad.

She stands up and catches me watching them with a sad expression. "What's wrong with you?"

I don't want to tell her that I'm feeling jealous of her and Charlotte, so I go a different route. "I'm sorry about my mom. For her betraying us all. You were right to not trust her. I was foolish to believe that she could be different. I was blinded by my own longing for a happy family."

"It was foolish," she says bluntly. And just as I'm starting to get angry, she adds, "But I don't blame you. Having Charlotte here with me is everything. You wanted to be with your mom. I get that. Maybe you should focus on getting to know the family you have here with you instead."

I nod as I look at Joselyn lying next to Charlotte.

"Do you think Rebecca will ever believe Joselyn—I mean, Cindy—and forgive her?"

"I hope so. If Cindy was telling the truth about her dad..." she stops as a dark expression crosses her features, making her look like the Alexandrine I first got to know, "then he got what he deserved, and she deserves all the love she can get."

She turns away and stalks over to the lookout spot. I think this topic hit a sore spot with her, and with good reason. I can't even imagine the long-lasting mental anguish a person deals with after going through abuse like she's been through, like Cindy took on for Joselyn. It's no wonder Cindy acts crazy.

I get myself settled next to David and try hard to put those terrible thoughts out of my mind, grateful that I have the option to do that.

■■■■■

When I wake up in the morning, everything is covered in a sparkly layer of frost. I'm one of the last ones to wake up, surprised that I slept so hard. The children giggle as they melt little handprints in the frost on a large boulder.

I run my hand through my hair and realize that it's been a long time since I've washed up. I pull out the collar of my shirt, tuck my nose down in it, and sniff. I almost gag from the stench. What I wouldn't give for a hot shower right about now. I miss the comforts of home, but I know I'm in a better place, even if it means smelling rank and using leaves as toilet paper. Caroline was kind enough to teach me what poison ivy looks like so I don't make a horrible mistake.

I head over to Matthias and take a seat next to him as he tries to build a fire. "How'd you sleep?" I ask kindly.

"'Bout as well as I expected," he answers. "Did ya get anywhere with the pendant?"

"No, but I'll keep trying."

He pokes at the fire with a long stick, causing embers to float up with the smoke. The wood is damp from last night's frost, so there's more smoldering going on than actual fire.

"What are our plans now?"

"We keep movin'. Once I have a fire built, we'll eat lunch, boil up some drinkin' water, and head out."

"Any chance of bathing? I'm filthy."

"You're more than welcome to go with Frederick to the pond. Ya can take a bath after he gets the pot of drinking water out. But it's gonna be cold," he says, slightly amused.

I shiver at the thought. "Can't we just boil up some water, and everyone can take turns washing up?"

"We don't have time for that."

"Don't we want to give Tim more time to heal?" I ask, looking around to see where Tim is.

When I finally see him, I'm shocked. He's sitting up next to Cass, smiling at something she's saying to him. He still looks paler than normal, and his eyes are sunken and dark, but he seems to be a lot better than yesterday.

"I think he'll live," Matthias grunts but then looks away quickly, still upset about Saul's passing.

"What's for lunch?" I ask, changing the subject.

"Goat."

"What? Really? Aren't they carrying our extra supplies?"

"We're runnin' low on food supplies. The goats slow us down. We'll have to distribute the supplies amongst ourselves to carry and get some new animals once we find a place to settle."

Just then, I hear the rumbling sound once more. I look up at Matthias, but he doesn't give any indication that he heard it. "Did you hear that rumbling?"

Matthias looks up at the sky and then back at me, shaking his head. "What rumblin'?"

"David and I have been hearing a rumbling sound a couple times a day for a few days now. We haven't had the chance to mention it to you. It's weird because it sounds a little like thunder off in the distance, but there never seem to be clouds in the sky when it happens."

"Ya hear it twice a day?"

"Yeah."

"Is it around the same time of day?"

I scratch at my lump, which has shrunk down to about half its size, and think. "Now that you mention it, yeah, I think so. Usually once in the morning and once in the evening."

"It's a train." He stands up and starts pacing. "Which direction is it comin' from?"

I think about it for a second and point to my right.

"West. Good," Matthias mutters almost more to himself than to me.

"If I can hear it, does that mean we're getting too close? Will they see our smoke?"

"Nah. We're not that close. Plus, they're fast trains, so by the time they spot our smoke, they'll be speedin' away."

I nod, relieved that there isn't something else we need to worry about.

After lunch, we all get packed up and ready to move. I get in line behind David, both of us weighed down with some extra supplies the goats were carrying. I'm sad about the goats, but I think we'll move a lot faster without them.

We all wait as Matthias and Henry stop by Saul's grave one last time before we take off. I hold the pendant tightly in my hand while they're gone. I hope I can figure this thing out soon. I had a moment of frustration earlier and thought about smashing it open with a rock but decided that wouldn't be a good idea. Not only is it sentimental, but what if there's something valuable inside?

Once the men return, we finally set off again.

"Matthias thinks the sound we've been hearing might be a train," I say to David as we plod along.

"Really?"

"Yeah, but he said not to worry about it. That we're a safe enough distance away."

David's quiet a moment then turns his head to say, "Too bad we can't hop on the train and make our trip quicker."

"I don't think the train would lead to the Haven."

David shrugs and continues following the line of people.

Tim is a little ahead of him, walking on his own now, but Cass is at his side in case he needs help. We make good progress today. The plateau we were on eventually comes to an end, and we climb our way back down. It's not as steep as going up, so it doesn't take too long, especially since the kids seem to think it's fun climbing on the rocks. They get way ahead of their moms and find themselves in trouble once they reach the bottom. Much to everyone's surprise, Matthias tells the women to lighten up, smirking at the children's antics.

Once we're all on the ground, we walk about a mile before we reach an abandoned road. I knew we couldn't stay in the wilderness forever before finding remnants of civilization. The pavement is all broken up where plants have pushed through, making it look less like a road and more like a strange stony garden.

There are a few cars on the side of the road that are nothing but shells. All the engine parts have been stripped, leaving just the body of the car. Even the wheels are gone. The gas tanks are open, and Matthias says that's because the gas was siphoned out. Too bad we couldn't hop into the cars and drive. I would love to crank the heater on full blast and fall asleep.

We walk by the road, keeping ourselves hidden in the woods just in case, until the sun starts to go down. Matthias finally leads us away from the road, and we come to a house that's half standing. The left side of the two-story house has been destroyed by something, leaving a giant pile of debris, while the right side is still in relatively good shape. The paint is chipping away, and a few of the windows are broken, but the rest of it seems intact.

"Everyone, wait here. I'll go check it out," Matthias says.

As we watch Matthias walk stealthily to the abandoned house, I hear the rumbling again. This time, it's loud enough for everyone to hear.

"Sounds like a storm's coming. I hope we can sleep inside tonight," Caroline comments, looking at the cloudless sky.

"It's not thunder. Matthias thinks it's a train," I say.

"Well, let's hope he's right. I'm not feeling like getting soaked through with these cold temperatures. I'd never be warm again."

I watch as a flashlight beam passes by an upper window, then disappears again. The wind picks up and seems to blow through every layer of clothing I have on. I shiver, hoping along with Caroline that we can sleep inside tonight.

Finally, Matthias is back out, walking toward us. "Looks safe enough for the night."

A few cheers erupt, and the kids go racing toward the house. Their happy giggles mimic what I'm feeling inside. I wonder if the plumbing still works.

30

We walk into the house, and by the light of the flashlight, we see that we're not the first ones to have been here. The living room walls are graffitied with all sorts of anti-government propaganda: Turk's name crossed off inside a circle; the words "The Coalition are liars!" and "Long live the Rare!" in giant red letters as well as other assorted phrases. I hope the kids can't read or at least don't recognize the swear words painted up there.

I look around at the rest of the room and see that the furniture is moldy and moth-eaten. The carpet isn't any better. It's filthy and full of dead bugs, which is probably not unrelated to half the house missing. We keep walking, and I spot a torn coalition flag lying in a heap in the corner. Whoever was here better hope they don't get caught doing this stuff. They'll more than likely be killed for it.

"It's a dump, but it's shelter. The rooms upstairs aren't as bad as this."

"Anything in the kitchen?" Rebecca asks as we walk through the doorway leading to a ransacked kitchen. The cupboard doors are all open, and some of them are hanging by one hinge. The white refrigerator is rusty and has more swear words scratched on the surface. I walk to the sink and pull up the faucet handle. It gives a few sputters, and then rusty brown water trickles out slowly.

"The plumbing still works. Maybe there's a bathroom," I say hopefully.

Stan heads through a door, and we hear him say, "Bathroom's in here, but I don't think this toilet's working. Yuck!"

"Hey, I found some canned food. They're expired, but maybe we could open them and see if they're still good," Rebecca says. She has climbed onto the counter and searched the top cupboards for anything that might have been left behind.

Matthias hands her a knife, and she cuts the tops open. "They look fine," she says while Matthias shines the flashlight at the food. "Smells fine too."

"Everyone, grab one and dig in," Matthias says.

I end up with green beans that taste like the can they're in.

David takes something I've never seen before.

"What is that?" I ask, slightly disgusted.

133

"I don't know. It says 'Spam,' but I have no idea what it is. I think it might be meat." He digs a chunk out with his fingers and sniffs it before putting it in his mouth. He chews a few times, then nods a little. "Not bad, actually. Want some?"

"No, thanks. I'm good." I wrinkle my nose at him.

We all pile our empty cans on the table and head up the stairs to see what other wonders await us. The stairs creak under everyone's weight, and I start to worry whether the second floor will support us all. I reach the landing and see the hallway end abruptly with a tarp covering the hole where the other half of the house collapsed. The wind blows, making a howling sound that sets my nerves on edge. I've only ever seen a couple of horror movies in my life, but this is definitely how one would begin. Matthias points out the two bedrooms, and we split up into groups.

"Which room do you want to sleep in?" David asks me.

"Well, Joselyn is in with the kids, which means Rebecca is in there too. Maybe I should stay close by to support Joselyn if she needs it."

"Lead the way."

I step through the door and see that this must have once been a little girl's room. The pink walls are now dirty, but the vibrant hue peaks out beneath the grime in various spots. Lacy curtains are hanging in front of a window seat lined with dolls, a zoo of stuffed animals, and fluffy pink pillows, all covered in a thick layer of dust. The four-poster queen bed is a mess, but the mattress looks intact.

Caroline and Rebecca get busy stripping the dust encrusted bedding off the mattress and throw it into the closet. They lay out the children's blankets and have them sleep across the width of the bed so they can all fit. Once they're settled, Caroline and Rebecca take opposite sides of the bed on the floor. Charlotte, Joselyn, and Alexandrine settle in by Rebecca, leaving a space at the foot of the bed where David and I can lie. Cass and Tim tuck themselves on the other side of David, against the wall. It must be hard for Tim to get comfortable with his injury, but luckily, the infection is almost gone. Rebecca has been treating it every day with honey, and surprisingly, it's working.

"No kissy facing, you two," Joselyn says, and Charlotte giggles.

"Oh, knock it off, Cindy," I say.

"No, it's me. Joselyn. I was just kidding, Olivia."

I'm taken aback slightly. That seemed like something Cindy would say. "Sorry. I just assumed. Goodnight, Joselyn."

I lay out my bedding and get comfortable next to David. It's still chilly, but it's a definite improvement to sleeping outside. I fall asleep with thoughts of how glorious a shower would feel on my sore, aching muscles.

We're running with all our might. The broken-down buildings and destroyed roads pass by in a blur as we run to our only hope of survival. The kids can't run as fast as we can, so I scoop Emily up into my arms, her weight making me slow down more than I care to. The sense of impending doom keeps my legs going, though, so I push through.

I look behind me and see the soldiers coming up quick in a military truck. We're far enough ahead of them that they can't use their weapons yet, but it won't be long.

"Matthias!" I shout with what little breath I have left in my lungs. "We need to get off the road! They're getting too close!"

"We're almost there! Follow me!"

We turn off the road and start running through the woods. I hear the truck come to a stop. I chance a look behind me and see at least ten soldiers hop out and start chasing us on foot.

"There it is! It's starting to move. Hurry up!"

I look up and through the trees and see a rectangular metal box moving slowly forward. Then another right behind it. And more after that.

A train!

We reach the train, and Matthias pulls the door open. He jumps into one of the boxes and then leans out the edge to grab our hands. We all have to run next to the moving box to get in. Once the children have been pushed up into it, the adults start climbing on. David gives Tim a hard shove, making him faceplant on the floor, but there's no time for apologies.

I look behind me, and the soldiers are just coming to the tracks. They're close enough to use their guns now, and a loud gunshot rings out behind me as a bullet hits the track next to me with a spark. I jump up and catch the edge of the platform. Hands immediately grab onto my arms and shirt and pull me to safety.

I lean my head out and see David has fallen behind a bit. He's holding his arm as blood seeps through his fingers. He puts on as much speed as he can, barely able to keep up with the train that's moving twice as fast as before. With a giant leap, he belly flops into the car, and Frederick drags him in just in time. A soldier comes into view outside of the box we're on, and Matthias shoots him in the face without hesitation.

The train has worked up its momentum, and we speed off, leaving the rest of the soldiers behind.

■■■■■

I'm awakened by a loud voice shouting from below us: "You ate all my food! You kids better hope to God you're not still here, or I'll kill you!"

Everyone is sitting up, looking wide-eyed at each other. The sun is just starting to come up, making the room bright with the early rays of sunshine. Rebecca holds her twins tightly as we hear heavy footsteps on the stairs. David gets up, grabs the lamp by the bed, and stands next to the door.

"Hey, mister," I hear Matthias's gruff voice say outside the bedroom. "We don't want any trouble. We just needed a place to sleep for the night."

"Who're you?" the stranger asks. His voice sounds a bit wavery, like an old man.

"The name's Tom," Matthias lies. "My friends and I are travelin', and we found your house. We thought it was abandoned. Sorry for intrudin'."

"You ate my food," he accuses.

"I'm sorry, sir. We helped ourselves, and we shouldn't have. I'll have my group pack up, and we'll be out of your hair."

Silence follows, and I hold my breath as I wonder if the guy is going to make trouble or not.

"Eh, stay as long as you like. I could use the company," the old man says tiredly, and then we hear him stomp back down the stairs.

Everyone in the room lets out the breaths we were all holding. David puts the lamp back on the table and then opens the door slowly.

"It's safe to come out," Matthias says. "Let's all head downstairs so we can thank him for lettin' us stay here."

David swings open the door, and we all shuffle our way downstairs.

"I thought you were the damn hooligans who destroyed what was left of my house. I leave for a few days to see if I can find some food, and I come back to this," the old man calls from the living room as we all troop downstairs.

"No, sir. We're just passin' through."

The old man whistles as we pile into his living room. "There sure is a lotta you. Where are you all headed?"

I step in behind Cass and get a good look at the old man. He's bald on the crown of his head but has long gray hair on the back and sides pulled into a ponytail. He's thin and fragile-looking; however, his eyes hold a fire that lets us know he's not one to be messed with. He's wearing a red flannel shirt with brown patches on the elbows and a pair of well-worn jeans. His boots look like soldiers' boots, which make me suddenly worried that maybe he's hiding something.

"West. We outstayed our welcome at the last place."

"You friends of Turk?" he asks, picking at a hole in the couch.

"No, sir," Matthias answers.

The old man squints at him, waiting for him to continue, but when he doesn't, the gentleman looks around the room at each and every one of us. His eyes linger on me and then David for longer than I like.

"Well, Tom. I know I said you can stay as long as you like, but I can't be found housing a bunch of Rares, so you're going to have to keep your visit short."

"How do you know some of us are Rare?" Alexandrine asks, glancing at Charlotte with a look of concern.

"Just putting two and two together, darling," he says with a wink.

"Don't...call me darling," Alexandrine growls, balling her fists up.

I watch as Matthias lays his hand on her shoulder, and she pulls away from his hand, giving him a glare.

"Sorry, Margarite's a little feisty," Matthias says, trying to defuse the tension. "We're just curious how ya could know just by lookin' at us?"

The man's eyes sparkle a bit as he looks around at us again. His gaze lands on Joselyn, and his eyes widen slightly. "I can sense it. It's one of my gifts. This girl here is powerful. You'll want to keep an eye on her," he says, pointing at Joselyn.

We all look over at Joselyn, whose cheeks are turning bright red.

"One of your gifts? Are ya Rare too?" Matthias asks.

"You got that right. Though I'm not as strong as I once was, I'm still sharp as a tack," he says, tapping the side of his head.

"What do you mean by 'one of your gifts'? Rare people only have heightened senses and reflexes..." I begin to say.

"Ah, I can see they brainwashed you too," he says, clicking his tongue, "Do you really think people having good eyesight or hearing was the cause of the war? Think! The Rare are more powerful than you can imagine. Especially untainted ones."

We all stand there staring at him in stunned silence.

"Haven't there been things you've done that you can't explain?" he asks impatiently. "That would be your Rare abilities shining through. 'Course if you've been unlucky enough to be living in the city, then your abilities were most likely tampered with."

"Could that be what the vitamins do?" David asks.

"I don't know, Son. I'm just going off what I've heard. I've never set foot in any of the cities, and I don't intend to either. I like my freedom, and I'm keeping it that way."

"You sound like Matthias," Alexandrine mumbles.

"Who's Matthias?" the old man asks.

Matthias gives Alexandrine a quick look of annoyance but lies for her. "Her ex-husband." He quickly changes the subject. "Once again, I'm sorry we ate all your food. Is there anything we can do to repay ya?"

"Don't worry too much about it. I was beginning to wonder if that food was good anyway. Hope none of you got sick from it."

We all look around at each other and shrug.

"We have some good hunters here. We'll get some meat, and I'll show ya how to dry it out so ya can have better eatin' than outdated canned food."

"Much appreciated."

"Mind if we use your shower, sir?" I ask with some slight desperation.

"Sorry, you can't. The septic's backed up since there's nobody around to pump it out. I just heat up buckets of water I pull up from the well and use that to clean. You're welcome to it if you like."

I slump my shoulders a bit but remember to say thank you.

"Well, I reckon I better get to my chores. I could use some help around here if anyone's willing. Oh, and a word of advice to you hunters: don't go off that way," he says, pointing to the west. "Train's that way. Wouldn't want you to be killed or, worse, caught."

31

By the time evening rolls around, we're all exhausted. We helped the old man with numerous chores as a way of saying thank you for letting us stay. I didn't envy Caroline as she scooped the backed-up toilet's nasty contents out with a big empty can and took it to his makeshift outhouse. I gagged a little just at the thought of doing it. The old man said the mess was from those hooligans who wrecked his house and that he was going to get to it someday, but he just didn't have the stomach for it. How he could live with the stench of it in his house, I have no idea.

The dream I had last night has been running through my mind all day. What if what the old man said was true? What if Rares have more gifts than just reflexes and better senses? What if I'm dreaming about the future? Before I even set foot in the woods, I had that dream about Matthias and Henry finding me and killing the Havoc. Reality didn't play out exactly as the dream had, but it was close enough. What if this dream is the same? I see Matthias outside chopping wood with the old man's ax in the evening's fading light. I decide to tell him about it.

"So, ya had a dream that we hopped on the train?"

"Yeah, because the soldiers were chasing us."

"And from your dream, it sounds like we got on a boxcar, which is made for carryin' cargo, not people."

"So?" I say stupidly. I don't know much about our modern-day rail systems.

"The trains have been revamped since the war, made to reach high speeds to travel faster between the cities. The front of the train has enclosed cars, fit for carryin' passengers, while the back of the train has boxcars for supplies. Ya get on one of those goin' up to speed, it would be one helluva ride."

"Why?"

"They just took the old boxcars, modified the running gears, and threw on airfoils for aerodynamics. They're either lazy or cheap. Most likely, both."

I want to ask what airfoils are, but I already look like a moron, so I don't bother. "I think we could handle it," I say stubbornly.

Matthias lets out a breathy laugh, shaking his head slightly. "Well, did ya happen to see why the train was stopped?" Matthias continues on skeptically.

"No, just that it was starting to move by the time we got to it."

"Well, trains don't stop in between cities, so I'm not sure how much weight ya should be putting into this."

"But the old guy said Rares have special gifts..."

"If ya ask me, the old coot is a little off his rocker. He's talkin' about people havin' superpowers, Olivia," he says, shaking his head in disbelief as he picks up his ax to continue chopping. "And hoppin' on a train would be foolish and dangerous."

"But it would also get us to the Haven faster," I say, getting frustrated with him. How can he be dismissing the idea of the Rare being more powerful than what we previously thought?

"We're headed to the next city over, which ain't the Haven."

"Well, if my dream is right, the train stops at some point, and we could get on it!" I shout, letting my anger get the better of me.

He stops chopping and points the ax at me, "If ya figure out some way to make the train stop, let me know. In the meantime, we keep doin' what we're doin'."

"What? Continuously walking and hoping we don't all die?" I mumble as I turn and storm back into the house. I head over to the old man, who's sitting on his couch reading in the candlelight. "Excuse me, sir," I say meekly and wait until he looks up from his book. "Has the train nearby ever stopped for any reason?"

He puts a strip of paper in his book to mark his place and sets it down beside him. "There have been a few times. There's a cliffside nearby that crumbles from time to time and leaves a mess on the rails. They usually slow down through here because of it. Wouldn't want another derailment like they had about ten years ago," he answers and then furrows his eyebrows. "Why do you want to know?"

"Oh, just wondering. I want to make sure my friends are safe in case the train does stop. We'll want to steer clear of it," I lie on the spot.

"That'd be wise," he says. "Now, you got anything else to ask? I'm getting to a good part in my book."

"No. That's all."

I head off to find David. Maybe he'll see things my way. I don't know why boarding a government train seems like such a good idea to me. It's really not. We could get caught and thrown in jail or killed. But after that dream, I can't seem to let it go. I find David out back, building a fire.

"You know he's got a wood-burning stove inside the house, right?"

"I prefer campfires now," he says and then adds quietly, "Plus, his house gives me the creeps."

I nod as I take a seat next to him on the cold ground. "David, do you think he was telling the truth? That Rares have more power than what we thought?"

David stares down at his hands and clenches his jaws a few times as he thinks. I take notice of the facial hair that's starting to fill in on his face. His hair is black, but his facial hair has highlights of light brown and red. It looks good on him.

"I think I do. Bartholomew saved my life, Liv. I'm not sure who Bartholomew is or what he is or how he showed up when he did, but I can't stop thinking about him. I would have died if he hadn't saved me."

"You think Bartholomew and your Rare abilities are connected?" I ask, confused.

"Maybe? I haven't figured out how yet, but I'm leaning that way."

"I think I might be able to dream of the future," I say, wanting to impress him.

"What makes you think that?"

"Well, I had that dream while I was in the hospital about Henry and Matthias saving me from a Havoc, and then it came true. And last night, I had a dream that felt real, like the one in the hospital. We were running for our lives and got on a train that had stopped nearby. We all made it, but you got shot in the arm," I say, giving him an apologetic look.

"Why would we get on a train?"

"So we can travel faster? I don't know. We were being chased by soldiers, and it seemed like the best way to escape," I say, annoyed.

"But wouldn't the soldiers chasing us just radio in that we got on the train? Then we'd be caught."

Anger bubbles up inside of me. "I don't have all the answers, okay? All I know is what I dreamed."

"Calm down, Liv. I'm sorry. I was just trying to understand," David says, bumping his shoulder into mine.

We sit quietly next to each other, and I think about what he said. He's right. My dream was probably nothing more than just a dream. There are so many bad consequences that could happen if we boarded a government train. But then something clicks.

"What if my dream is just one possible outcome? What if my dream shows what could happen unless we change things?" I say excitedly. "What if we somehow made the rocks crumble onto the tracks on purpose, and while they cleaned it up, we got on the train? You know, before we're chased by any soldiers. Then we're getting on the train on our own terms."

David stares at the firepit, thinking. Then he finally says, "But how would we make rocks fall onto the tracks? You would need some dynamite or something, and the last I checked, we aren't carrying any of that around with us."

I instantly deflate when he points that out. "You're right. I'm an idiot."

"No, Liv. You're not. I'll mull it around in my mind for a while and see if a solution comes to me," he says supportively.

We go back to sitting in silence for a little while. The cold evening air makes me shiver, and David notices. He puts his arm around me, rubbing my shoulder to help warm me up. I lean into him, resting my head on his chest, and I feel him sniff my hair. I close my eyes, relishing the touch.

What am I doing? I shouldn't be toying with him like this. I told him no to a relationship, yet I can't deny that I like this. Maybe it's time I give him a chance. But just not yet.

■■■■■

A few days pass, and I'm starting to get the itch to keep moving. I hate to admit it since he's been kind enough to let us stay in his house, but Mr. Wick gives off a vibe I don't like. I can't really put my finger on why, but I don't like being around him. Maybe it's the way he seems to watch me whenever we're in a room together. He watches Joselyn and Charlotte that way too. He's sneaky about it. You can't usually catch him doing it, but you can feel his eyes on you when you're around him. Maybe he doesn't trust other Rares? Either way, I make sure I'm never alone with him.

I talk David into ducking out of doing chores today, and we venture our way over to look at the rocks. We wait until after the morning train goes through so we know we'll be safe to search around for a while.

The rock face is steep, but we manage to climb it. David has to be careful since he can only use one hand, but I stay close behind him and offer help where I can. Once we reach the top, we're able to see the surrounding area better. With the leaves gone off the trees, we can spot about a hundred houses that have either been destroyed completely and are being reclaimed by nature or are in far worse shape than Mr. Wick's house. By the looks of things, I think this area used to be a small town before the war. Once again, those feelings of gratitude toward the people willing to stand up and fight for the Rare overwhelms me. So many lives lost or ruined because people had to be bigots and try to get rid of other people who are different from them. And even though the war is over, the government is still trying to control the Rares and make our lives miserable.

"Liv, look over there," David says, snapping me out of my thoughts.

I look to where he's pointing and see a giant boulder about the size of a car, sitting ten feet away from the edge. "What about it?"

"Maybe we could push that boulder onto the train tracks," David says with hope in his voice.

"I know we're stronger than we once were, David, but you and I can't possibly move that thing ourselves..."

"We'll get Frederick and others to come here with us and push the boulder onto the tracks after the evening train goes through. Then we wait until the morning train has stopped. While they're busy cleaning it up, we can sneak everyone onto the train and make our way to the next city."

"Let's go run it by Matthias," I say, high-fiving David.

32

"I suppose it could work," Matthias says, stroking his beard. "At least the boulder part, but I just don't know if it's worth the risk of bein' caught."

"I'm ready to leave this place. I don't like it here."

Matthias takes a deep breath and blows it out slowly. "Let me talk to Alexandrine about it first."

•••••

Alexandrine is on board with the train idea. I think everyone is getting tired of staying here.

Mr. Wick has been getting crankier since we arrived. It doesn't help when the children complain about being bored and make a ruckus with the volleyball by dribbling it upstairs over the top of him as he's trying to read. He doesn't say anything, but you can see it on his face.

A heavy frost set in overnight while we were sleeping. I wake up to Emily squealing with delight when she looks outside from the upstairs window. I get up and take a peek too. The morning sun is shining brightly on the frost, making it sparkle like diamonds. It's quite beautiful.

Today, David and I are taking a group of able-bodied people up to see the boulder and get a better plan on how to do this. By the time everyone is up and ready to go, the morning train has already gone through, and the frost is almost completely melted. Only the frost in the shady areas remains, making parts of the climb a bit slippery.

"That's a big rock," Frederick says, walking around it. "You guys really think we have enough man-power to push that thing over?"

"Accuracy of getting it on the tracks would be nearly impossible," Alexandrine says, peering over the cliff's side.

My shoulders drop as they make these observations. I had my hopes up that this would work, but now I realize it's probably not going to. I look over at David, and he's got a stony expression.

"We're going to at least try, right?" David says.

"I think it'd be a waste of time," Nathaniel says. "A boulder this size doesn't just tumble off a cliff. The conductors would catch on that this wasn't a natural occurrence, and they'd send someone to look for whoever did it."

"So, what's your solution, then?" David asks, getting worked up.

"Calm down, David," Matthias growls. "Nathaniel is right. I say we find some hammers and chisels and hack this boulder into smaller rocks. Then we can toss 'em onto the tracks, make it look like a rockslide."

"Let's get started then," David says.

"Hold on. We didn't agree to it yet," Nathaniel says. "Tell me how this isn't a really bad idea again."

"In my dream, we were being chased by soldiers and got on the train. I think we should take matters into our own hands and not wait for the soldiers to be chasing us before we hop on the train to get to the next city. Winter's coming, and we are dangerously low on supplies. We need to get there fast."

"So now we're following dreams? Last night I dreamed I could fly. Think I should throw myself off this cliff?" Nathaniel goads.

"Go ahead. Rid us of your stupidity," Matthias snaps, wiping the smirk off Nathaniel's face. "Since ya don't have Rare abilities, keep your mouth shut."

Nathaniel gives Matthias a threatening glare but then drops his gaze, surrendering.

"You think the old man has the tools we need?" Frederick asks.

"If he doesn't, one of the surrounding houses might."

▪▪▪▪▪

To nobody's surprise, the old man does not have the tools we need. Matthias doesn't divulge why we need them, and I think it's because he doesn't trust Mr. Wick much either. It's not hard to miss the way Mr. Wick watches us Rares like a hawk. I don't understand why, though. He has Rare abilities too, so why would he act as though we're untrustworthy?

We pair up and start searching houses in the area. David and I head up a side street that's more vegetation than pavement now. The bare tree branches reach overhead, entangling with each other from opposite sides of the road. A breeze blows, causing the branches to click together eerily, setting my nerves on edge. I've come to notice that there aren't as many birds singing anymore. The sounds of summer are gone, leaving just crow caws and the calls of a few hardy birds that stay for the winter.

We come to a small house that's still standing. The paint is faded and peeling, and all the windows are broken, but it seems to be in okay shape otherwise.

We walk to the garage and see that the door is slightly ajar. David pushes the door open slowly while staying outside. His muscles are tense as he prepares himself for whatever might be hiding inside. He shines his flashlight in every direction, and I can see his muscles relax as he rules out any threats. I peek my head inside and see that whoever lived here was a neat freak. Every tool is hung on the wall in a perfectly organized manner. David hands me the flashlight and walks into the garage.

As David steps over the threshold, we hear a strange whiny buzzing sound. I look around the rafters for bees, even though it sounded different than bees buzzing, but I don't spot any. I follow David over to a hammer that's bigger than I have ever seen before. Its wooden handle is almost as long as my leg, and the head is a black barrel shape that's bigger than my hand.

David picks it up with a grunt. "This thing is heavy!"

He hands it to me, and I almost drop it. It has to weigh at least twenty pounds. I carry it up against my shoulder, balancing the weight so it's easier to hold.

We look at the rest of the tools, but none of them look like they would help us break apart a rock, so we leave them. As we walk back to the door, we hear that buzzing sound again.

I look up and see something black and round mounted up in the corner of the wall. "David? What's that?"

David looks up to where I'm pointing and swears loudly as he grabs my free hand and pulls me outside quickly. "That was a camera, Liv. We have to warn the others," David says worriedly. He keeps a hold of my hand as we trot back to the house.

"A sledgehammer? Nice," Frederick says, giving us a thumbs-up as we hurry past him to find Matthias.

We find him out by the firepit, arranging some tools he must have found.

"We need to leave now," David says as we get closer to him.

"What's goin' on?"

"The house we went to had a surveillance camera in the garage."

Matthias scratches at his beard. "So?"

"It was still working!" David says urgently.

"Ya sure?" Matthias asks seriously.

David nods.

"Couldn't it just be an old camera the owners put there to protect their stuff?" I ask.

"We can't take the chance. It could be a government camera watchin' for traitors," Matthias answers while gathering up the hammers and chisels from the ground. "Let's get this plan into motion and get outta here."

■■■■■

We spend the night hacking away at the boulder. By morning, Matthias, Henry, Frederick, Nathaniel, and I have a pile of sizable rocks tossed down on the tracks, and sore, tired arms to show for it. I pushed it a bit too hard, and now my head throbs, but I keep that to myself, not wanting to seem weak. David won't let me hear the end of it if I push myself too hard. He was reluctant to let me go without him, but with a broken wrist, he wasn't able to help.

We told everyone else to have our stuff gathered up and to be ready to go when the train comes through. Now I'm hoping we have enough time to get back down off the cliff before it gets here. I hope David packed my stuff for me.

We are almost back to the house when I hear the familiar rumbling sound off in the distance. A jolt of nervous energy courses through me as I think about what we are about to do. Is this even going to work? Horrible images run through my mind of us being caught, tortured, or killed and how it would be all my fault. I'm already starting to feel guilty, and nothing has happened yet.

As we walk down the driveway, I see everyone waiting for us outside, but something seems off.

"Where's Joselyn?" I ask Charlotte.

"Mr. Wick wanted to show her something. I asked to go too, but he wouldn't let me," she says sadly.

"She's alone with him?" I ask frantically.

People nearby us glance around at each other, shrugging as though this was news to them. David gives me a worried look.

I race into the house, heart pounding. She should not have been left alone with him. I run upstairs, hoping she's still packing or something, but a terrible feeling is needling at me.

I punch the wall in frustration when I see the empty rooms. Where could she be? I hurry back downstairs, almost running into David. He grabs ahold of my shoulders, steadying me, and I hear a faint scream come from the woods. David's eyes widen, and I know he heard it too.

We rush out of the house and sprint in the direction we heard the scream. I hear footsteps behind us and glance back to see Matthias and Henry are tailing us with weapons drawn.

I frantically scan around the area, looking for any sign of where Joselyn could be. Some of the wet leaves have been disturbed, as though something was dragged across them. They turn off to the right, through a thick tangle of underbrush. We follow the drag marks that come to a weather-worn shack up ahead. The boards are grayish brown and covered in splotchy moss. The roof's shingles are curling up on the edges with an even thicker layer of moss.

Anger courses through my veins, and I can feel heat radiating up my neck from beneath my sweatshirt. As I start to step toward the shack, David holds out his arm to stop me. I give him a glare, wondering why he isn't charging in there himself, but he holds up a finger to his mouth to warn me to be quiet.

"Wait for Henry and Matthias. They're the ones with the weapons," David says smartly.

After a few moments, Henry and Matthias come charging in behind us, and David waves at them to be silent. We all creep up to the building, listening for any signs of life. I hear muffled yelling, and my fists ball up at my sides. Joselyn doesn't deserve this. Mr. Wick better not have hurt her, or he's going to regret it.

"I know you're out there. I can sense Rare abilities, remember?" We hear Mr. Wick's voice call out.

Matthias marches over to the door and tugs it open with a creak from the hinges. I follow right behind him and see Joselyn tied to a rickety wooden chair with a gag in her mouth, eyes wild. Cindy's come back to save Joselyn from the trauma again.

"Let her go!" I shout.

"Why would I do that? I told you she was a powerful one. She's going to fetch me a pretty price," he says, running the back of a blade down her cheek. "I'm going to be set for a while once I turn her in."

"Turn her in? I thought you were a Rare, a traitor just like the rest of us," Henry says.

Mr. Wick laughs coldly. "My Rare power benefits both the government and myself. I made a deal. I'm allowed to live on my own, and I'm rewarded with things I need if I turn in any other Rares I find. I think I'm going to ask for double what they usually give me for this one." His eyes shine greedily.

Matthias points the gun at him. "How're ya gonna do that with a bullet in your brain?"

The old man's smugness falters a bit at the sight of the gun. He ducks down behind Cindy, and all we see of him is his arm holding the knife against her neck. "Shoot me, and I'll make sure the last thing I do is slit her throat."

Cindy rolls her eyes and yells angrily into her gag. She doesn't even look afraid. She looks annoyed.

"Ya don't need to do this," Matthias says calmly, nodding slightly at Henry. "We're gettin' ready to leave. Just let her go, and we'll pretend none of this ever happened."

"Why? The soldiers are almost here. I called them as soon as you fools showed up."

As the men talk, I watch Henry nock an arrow and take aim at the old man's exposed elbow. I want to yell at him to stop, that it's too close to her face, but he pulls back the string and lets the arrow fly, hitting his target with perfect accuracy. Mr. Wick yells out in pain, dropping the knife. Matthias marches up to the old man and shoots him through the temple without a second thought.

33
. . .

After I untie Cindy, I see the wildness in her eyes disappear, replaced by a look of terror and confusion. That's the first time I've seen Cindy give control back to Joselyn so quickly. I want to ask about it, but we don't have time. I grab on to Joselyn's hand, and we all head back to the house, where everyone is nervously watching the direction we ran.

To my surprise, Rebecca is the first one to come rushing toward us. "Are you okay?" she asks, stopping a few feet in front of us. Her eyes are misty and full of concern.

"Yeah, I think so," Joselyn replies shyly.

"Good." Rebecca reaches out and rubs Joselyn's arm tentatively.

Joselyn starts weeping and steps forward, wrapping her arms around Rebecca. She looks uncomfortable at first, but after a few seconds of Joselyn sobbing into her shirt, Rebecca wraps her arms around Joselyn and holds her close.

"We need to go. Soldiers are on their way," Matthias says, stomping past them.

"They're almost here!" David shouts. "I can hear them. They're about a half a mile that way," he says, pointing to the east.

Everyone scrambles to collect their things, and we take off running toward the train tracks. Let's hope they're almost done cleaning up the rock mess we made.

The small children are falling behind, so I scoop Emily up in my arms and run with her. Her weight slows me down more than I like. I chance a look behind me, and I can see the soldiers approaching in their vehicle with remarkable speed. They're still too far away to shoot at us, but fear of being hunted makes me dig deeper for the strength to run faster.

I suddenly realize that things from my dream are playing out. I look ahead for the train, and sure enough, there it is, and it's just starting to move. We run alongside the train car as Matthias hops up, grabbing onto the lever, which he pulls up, sliding the door open. I pass Emily to Caroline, and she hands her up to Matthias, then climbs on. The other adults do the same, passing the children up to the train and then climbing on themselves. It takes a few tries for some to make it as the train steadily speeds up. David gives Tim a push to help him, and Tim ends up face planting, just like in the dream. All that's left is David and me. I look behind us, and there are the soldiers coming up to the train now.

"Hurry, David!" I scream, just as a bullet ricochets off the track. I shove off the ground with my right foot and just barely flop into the train, the edge of the platform bruising my rib cage. Hands immediately pull me in, and I turn right around, reaching my arm out toward David, hoping I can be quick enough to stop what's coming next.

But I'm not. David is already holding onto his arm, and I groan as I see the blood seeping between his fingers. He's fallen behind too much, and I worry he's not going to catch back up. I'm just about to hop back off the train to help him when he pushes himself harder and jumps onto the car just as a soldier comes into view. I grab ahold of David and drag him inside, then cover my ears. Matthias shoots the soldier directly in the face.

The train speeds off, leaving the rest of the soldiers behind. The wind howls in the open door of the train car, setting my teeth chattering. I pull David to the back of the car and help him sit up against the wall. Matthias calls Henry over to help him slide the door back shut. The speed of the wind makes it nearly impossible to push the door forward, but they finally do. The sound of the wind continues howling through the crack in the door. Matthias was right about how uncomfortable this ride will be.

"Rebecca! David's been shot!" I yell over the racket of the train and the wind combined.

She crawls her way back to us with her medical kit. "Help me by getting his shirt off," she says as she digs in her bag for supplies.

He's been shot in the same arm as his broken wrist, making it difficult to get his arm out of the sleeve. I fumble around, trying to pull the sleeve out straight so he can slip his arm down out of it. When that doesn't work, I grab the bottom of his shirt and start sliding it up.

"You know," he says, a mischievous glint in his eye, "I've had dreams that started like this."

I laugh. "What? Being shot in the arm and bleeding all over?"

"No, you pulling my shirt off..." he says just loud enough for me to hear, and my cheeks grow hot.

Rebecca shuffles up to me, startling me out of the moment. "What are you doing? I need to see his arm. Here, let me." She pulls out a pair of scissors out and carefully makes a cut in the shirt over the wound. "Good. This is what I hoped for," she says, poking around on his arm, making David wince in pain. "The bullet went clean through your muscle. I won't have to dig the bullet out. It's going to hurt, but it should heal up nicely."

She gets to work bandaging his arm up, and I look around at the rest of the group. Matthias is standing closest to the door, keeping watch out a window. His shoulders are slumped, and his face is sullen as he watches the landscape pass by in a blur. I wonder if he's thinking about Saul. He hasn't talked about him since it happened, but I've seen him lost in thought from time to time, always with a sad expression on his face.

Everyone else is tucked up against the walls, silent and alert. We still don't know whether this is going to work or not. If one of the soldiers radios in that we hopped on a train, we're doomed.

Rebecca finishes up and turns her attention on Tim, whose nose is bleeding from smacking it on the floor.

I wedge myself in between David and Cass, grateful for the body heat. "Sorry about your arm."

"Eh, it's just a flesh wound," he says in a terrible British accent. We both laugh at the quote.

The vibration of the train starts to lull me to sleep. I lay my head on David's shoulder and close my eyes, grateful to finally rest after staying awake all night. The heaviness of slumber starts tugging at me, but then my mind becomes alert again when I hear Cass ask over my head, "Are you two boyfriend and girlfriend now?"

She must think I'm asleep, so I keep my eyes closed and my breathing steady, wanting to hear what David has to say.

"No. She said she's not interested."

"Could've fooled me." Her voice sounded playful.

"I don't know what this is, but I'm not going to spoil it. If she wants to hold my hand or lay her head on my shoulder, I'll let her. I'll take what I can get."

"I hope she comes around. You two would make a cute couple."

They both go quiet, and David rests his cheek against the top of my head. Their conversation makes me feel awkward, like I'm using him or something, but before I start to feel too bad, I fall asleep.

■■■■■

"Wake up! The trains slowin' down," Matthias calls out.

My eyes pop open as what he says registers through the fog of sleep. I scramble to my feet and help David up. Everyone else straps on their bags and looks around with worry.

"Are we at the next city?" I ask, looking out the door at the passing trees and fields no longer blurry from speed.

"It feels like it's been long enough," Matthias answers, peering out the window. "But we're not. It's just trees outside."

"What are we going to do?" Alexandrine asks, holding Charlotte close.

"We're gonna have to fight," Matthias says, opening the bag of weapons he carries.

"Can't we just hop off the train and run?"

"As soon as this train stops, there's gonna be soldiers on top of us. Our best bet for survival is to kill every last soldier we come across," he says with hatred in his voice.

He hands out the weapons, giving me a sword. I've practiced with it enough times that the weight of it is familiar in my hand, but the heaviness of what he's asking from me turns my arm into lead. I know we need to fight for our survival, but my stomach turns sour at the thought of killing someone. Maybe I can just wound them without taking their life.

Matthias instructs the women and children to get up against the wall, as far out of the way as possible. Alexandrine looks torn between wanting to help Matthias fight and wanting to join the women in protecting the children. In the end, she swallows her pride and stands in front of Charlotte, shielding her from the train car opening.

"Everyone, stay quiet, and wait for my signal," Matthias says.

I take a deep breath to gain my courage. I look over at David, wondering if this will be the last time I see him. He has a handgun in his good hand, and when he catches me looking at him, he winks at me as though this is just a minor setback. I wish I could have some of his bravery.

The train slowly stops. Without all the noise from the train moving, it seems eerily quiet. Matthias gets into position, wearing a look of murder, and I start to wonder if he actually likes killing people. He doesn't seem at all bothered by it, and that bothers me. His intentions may be good, but his actions are not.

The seconds turn into minutes as we wait for the soldiers. Maybe we're overreacting. Maybe the train just stopped for maintenance. But just as I'm about to let my guard down, I hear the crunch of boots on gravel about five train cars ahead.

They're coming. My muscles turn rigid, and I grip my sword handle harder.

"Get ready," Matthias says deadpan.

Henry is next to Matthias, an arrow nocked on his bow. "How long do you want to wait before we start taking them out?"

"We'll wait for 'em to come to us."

Everyone stays as quiet as they can, but little Sonya, unaware of the dire situation, starts squirming away from Caroline, screeching to be let go.

Caroline grabs her around the waist and covers her mouth with her hand, but it's too late.

"Got 'em. They're in the last car," a soldier calls out.

The older children cling to their moms in fear. Everyone waits with bated breath, listening to the footsteps coming closer and then stopping right outside the train car.

This is it. Time to fight for our freedom.

The latch starts to turn, and Matthias holds his rifle up to his shoulder, ready to shoot, but the door never makes it open. Instead, we hear gunshots and shouts as though a fight has broken out between the soldiers. What is going on?

After about a minute, it's quiet, and we all look around at each other in confusion. We wait, listening for any noise. When we don't hear anything, Matthias holds his finger to his mouth and slowly slides the door.

The scene before us is ghastly. A dozen soldiers lie on the ground in pools of blood. Some have their heads turned at impossible angles, necks obviously broken. Standing by the tree line is a group of men, easily outnumbering us two to one. They're wearing black ski masks and leather jackets with various scraps of metal strapped on as makeshift armor over their chests, arms, and legs. They are each armed with guns, some with two, and they're pointing them directly at us.

3|4

"Off the train," one of them barks.

We look to Matthias for our next move. He grabs his bags and hops off the train. Everyone follows. The adults try to shield the kids from the grizzly surroundings, but there's nowhere to turn without seeing it, and I hear Emily whimper.

Once we're all down, they order us to hand over our weapons, shoving them in Matthias's weapon bag as we do.

"Who are you?" Alexandrine asks as they start pulling out lengths of rope.

"We call ourselves the Metal Militia," an enthusiastic voice answers from a scrawnier looking rebel. At least, I presume they're rebels since they willingly killed the soldiers.

"Shut up!" another one shouts at him. The scrawny guy hangs his head from the scolding. "There'll be no more talking from anyone."

The militia members get to work tying everyone's wrists together, even David's, causing him to wince in pain. I look around to see if anyone dares to resist, but Matthias stands tall, with a look of annoyance on his face. He doesn't seem fazed by their antics. In fact, he looks at them as though they're a bunch of amateurs.

"What do I do with this one?" someone who's standing in front of Tim asks.

"Uh, tie his wrist down to his thigh," another answers, improvising.

"Please, I have to carry her. You can't tie my wrists together," Caroline says, holding Sonya.

A husky militant looks at her, stroking his chin through his ski mask, thinking. "Our orders were to tie everyone up," he says uncertainly, looking at Sonya, who's wiggling in Caroline's arms to get down. "I'll carry her."

He takes Sonya from Caroline. Holding her in one arm, he starts playing peek-a-boo with his free hand. After a few times, she giggles. Whoever these people are, they don't seem overly threatening.

"Who's the leader?" asks a man with two handguns strapped to his side and a belt full of bullets slung across his body like a sash.

Another one scoffs, "Isn't it obvious?" while holding his hand outward toward Matthias.

"Orders are to blindfold and gag you," he says, taking out two strips of black cloth from his pocket.

"You can't..." Henry starts to say, but Matthias lifts his bound hands up to stop him, and Henry backs down.

It's rather odd that Matthias seems to be going along with these people. Maybe it's because they just killed the soldiers, so he trusts them. It almost seems as though he knows these people.

"All right, let's move!" the guy who blindfolded Matthias shouts as he grabs Matthias's upper arm, leading him toward the woods.

Apparently, the orders to blindfold and gag were only for Matthias. I'm grateful that I can still see.

We all stay quiet as the Militia escorts us through leafless forests and open fields. There doesn't seem to be a rhyme or reason behind any of the twists and turns these men take us on, and I start to hope that they know where they're going.

Hours slip by as we march out of the woods and through what used to be suburbs. I worry that we'll be spotted, but the militia people just keep guiding us along as though it's no big thing.

I look around and shake my head at the aftermath of the war that happened so many years ago. Abandoned cars are parked in driveways, slowly rusting away, never to be driven again. The houses look like they were once nice places, but since they've been deserted, the elements have had their way with them, leaving them to rot. Trees have overtaken yards, turning them into forests.

We continue on through various neighborhoods, sometimes passing under huge roads lifted up into the air. I've never seen this before, and it kind of scares me at the thought of being in a vehicle so high in the air, especially since sections of the roads have now collapsed. We walk by large forsaken stores and restaurants, some with their brick walls crumbling, leaving gaping holes that allow anyone or anything to enter with ease. I hate to think of what kind of animals could be calling them home now.

The last neighborhood we pass through has an old elementary school in its midst. I have to say, the long-forgotten playground kind of creeps me out. The wind's blowing just enough to make the swings move back and forth on squeaky chains, and the merry-go-round seems to be spinning on its own accord. My brain starts imagining ghosts of the children who died during the war playing on this equipment, forever stuck between worlds. I don't like it.

The sun hangs low in the sky as we leave the remnants of humanity and come to a vast forest of towering pine trees. I'm staring up at the impossibly full branches of these green giants when everyone stops walking abruptly, and I run into David, who's right ahead of me. I peek my head around him and see that we've come to a large encampment. Shelters with mismatched siding and different colored roofing tiles are built just inside a perimeter of a barbed wire fence that seems to encircle the entire area. In the center is a big barn with a rusting silver roof and a patchwork of multicolored wood. It looks like they replace the boards as they rot out with whatever wood they can find. The barn's windows are still intact but dirty, leaving them more brown than clear. A brick building is behind the barn, and in the very back of the encampment is a large greenhouse. I've never seen one this close before. They had greenhouses in the city to help grow our food, but they were in a part of town I never visited.

People of all kinds mill around inside the encampment, some going about their business, completely oblivious to our arrival, while others stop to watch as we are all ushered through the narrow gate into their territory.

The men lead us straight into the barn. At the end of the building is a massive fireplace built with smooth rocks with a cheery fire roaring in its depths, giving the building a warm stuffy feel. Two lines of various dining room sets are placed along the sides of the structure, leaving an open aisle down the center of the room.

A man wearing jeans and a tight gray wool sweater stands facing the fire with his hands clasped behind his back. After everyone has been brought into the barn, our escorts close the doors once again, making the already dim light even darker. With the sun almost gone and the pine trees blocking any of the feeble light it's still giving off, our only source of light is the blaze coming from the fireplace. The flickering flames send shadows dancing on the walls, which keep catching my eye, making me think someone's there.

"Here they are, boss," says the man holding Matthias's arm.

I watch as the guy rocks up and down from toes to heels a few times, then slowly turns to face us. He almost looks like Matthias, but it's hard to tell because this guy's beard and hair are shorter and better groomed.

"Well, well. Look what the cat dragged in. What do you have to say for yourself?" the man goads Matthias by turning his head and putting his hand up to his ear as though trying to hear Matthias's answer.

Matthias grumbles something through his gag, and I'm pretty sure it wasn't a nice word.

The man nods at the militant, who takes his cue to free Matthias.

"Still one for the dramatic flair, huh, Eli?" Matthias says as soon as he's free.

The man named Eli smiles big and pulls Matthias into a bear hug. They both slap each other's backs hard, almost as though they are trying to hurt one another.

The rest of the men untie us all, and I watch in confusion at the scene playing out before my eyes.

"What are you doing all the way up here, Matt?" Eli asks as he lets go of Matthias.

"Matthias," he growls. "Ya know I don't like bein' called Matt."

"I could call you Fury." Eli laughs, pointing to Matthias's eye patch.

"Ya haven't changed one damn bit, have ya?" Matthias shakes his head.

"What would be the fun in that? If I lost my sense of humor, I would become you, and that's just terrifying," he says with a mock shiver.

"Care to explain to us what's going on?" Alexandrine asks.

"This is my brother, Elijah," Matthias answers.

"You can call me Eli." He holds out his hand for a handshake.

Alexandrine stays put, looking him up and down with an expression of distaste.

Eli holds his hand out for a few awkward seconds, then lets it drop, taking a look around at the rest of us. "Henry, my boy!" Eli says warmly, stepping up to Henry for an embrace.

"Hey, Uncle Eli." Henry returns the hug.

"Let me have a look at you!" Eli steps back with his hands up on Henry's shoulders. "I see you've been blessed with the same handsome gene I have. Too bad your father missed out on that one." He winks.

"We're twins, ya idiot," Matthias grunts, not appreciating being the butt of his brother's jokes.

"Shh! Don't tell people that. I have a reputation to uphold." Eli pretends to be scandalized.

"Cut the crap," Matthias huffs. "How'd ya'll know where we were gonna be?"

"Nice southern accent you got there." A playful smile tugs at Eli's lips.

"Ya know I lived in the south for years. Ya pick up on it after a while. Now answer my question."

"We found a few government radios, and we leave them running so we can know our enemy and what they're up to."

Know our enemy? He sounds just like Matthias. They look similar, but their personalities are like night and day. I wonder what the story is between them.

"We've been tracking you for a little while now. They've given a description of you a few times. I hear you blew up a military weapons cache. I didn't realize you'd be dumb enough to try to start a war. You're being called a terrorist now," Eli accuses. "What were you thinking?"

"We didn't blow it up," Matthias growls. "I wasn't tryin' to start anything. We were given a tip that it was there, and it ended up bein' rigged."

"Uh-huh." He pauses, giving Matthias a look, then moves on. "Then we heard that a group of rebels hopped on a train headed west. I knew right away it was you, so we decided to come get you."

"Thanks," Matthias mumbles while clearing his throat. "Did ya really need to tie us up, though?"

"No. That I did just to annoy you." He guffaws. "I gave them orders not to tie up Dad, though. Where is the old man?" He searches our group for Saul.

"He's gone," Matthias answers, voice thick, unable to look Eli in the eyes.

"What'd you do?" Eli asks seriously, his jocular demeanor changing so quickly, it's like he's a different person. Now the resemblance to Matthias is uncanny.

"It wasn't my fault," Matthias says, getting defensive.

"Everyone out!" Eli yells. "Horace. Benjamin. Take the rest of them to their shelters," Eli says, staring daggers at Matthias while he addresses his men.

Why is he so angry with Matthias? What happened to Saul was an accident. I want to stay and hear what his problem is, but David grabs my hand, leading me out of the barn and back into the chilly, pine-scented air.

3|5

The men take us to a few empty shelters with cots for us to sleep on. We hear some muffled shouts coming from the barn, but neither David nor I can distinguish what is being said. After a while, I stop trying and fall asleep easily.

I'm the first one awake in the morning. I sit up and look around at the building we're in, impressed by its quality. There's a small wood-burning stove on the back wall that keeps out the chill, there aren't any gaping holes between the wood plank walls, there's an actual floor instead of just dirt, and they even put in a door and windows. It's like a little house instead of a crude shelter. If they put so much work into it, that must mean they don't have to move as often as our group. I'm looking forward to hearing more about Eli and his camp and what makes their camp different from ours.

Once everyone is awake, we head outside to find the rest of our group and see what's expected of us. We're handed plates of steaming eggs and fried potatoes for breakfast. It's the best food I've had in a long time. Is that salt I taste? I haven't had food with salt since I lived in the city.

As I eat, I observe the people who live here and notice that they are all clean and well-dressed. Their clothes are washed and hole-free. Their hair isn't greasy and matted down. I start to feel self-conscious about the way I must look and smell. I anxiously run my fingers through my hair and then take a whiff down my shirt to see how bad it is. I cough at the stench of BO and sweaty clothes. I'm suddenly worried that David has smelled me and hasn't said anything just to be nice. I'm so embarrassed.

I turn my thoughts away from myself and realize I don't see Matthias. I wonder what happened between him and Eli last night. As I'm about to ask David what he thinks, Matthias steps out of the other shelter, his bottom lip fat and bloody.

Someone hands him a plate of food, which he takes with a grunt; then he plops down next to Henry.

"What happened to you?" Henry asks.

"Eli and I worked out a problem."

"Men," Alexandrine mumbles.

"What was the problem?" I ask, swallowing my last bite of potato.

"Pop was in my care, and I was supposed to protect him," he answers, stabbing at his eggs.

"But you were. We were getting away from the soldiers. What happened was an accident," I say, confused at what the problem was.

"He sees things my way now." Matthias looks up from his plate at Eli, who's approaching us. "With one eye anyway."

Eli steps up to our group, his right eye swollen shut and bruised.

"Mornin'!" Eli says brightly. "My people and I had a discussion this AM, and before we ask you to pitch in around here, we're going to give you a day to rest and to wash up. We'll show you how to fill the cistern atop the wash house, and you'll have showers and sinks available for you to use."

"Really?" I jump to my feet.

"Yes, really," Eli laughs. "We have a wood-burning stove to heat up the water too, so you can have hot showers."

Tears, real tears, spring to my eyes at the thought of a hot shower. Everyone around me mutters happily.

"We have two shower stalls and two sinks, but since it takes a while for the stove to heat up the cistern of water, you'll want to be conservative with how much you use. You won't want to just stand with the shower running constantly, or you're going to run out of hot water quick."

I nod, not really listening to what he's saying as I daydream about how good it's going to feel.

"I don't suppose you have working toilets too?" David asks.

"No, sorry. We have a few outhouses, though."

"Toilet paper?" Caroline asks hopefully.

"Yes, ma'am."

Everyone seems to be cheerful at the thought of having some real creature comforts.

"You look familiar," Eli says to me as everyone stands up to get started on laundry and showers.

"I'm Olivia, Matthias's daughter."

"Ah, yes. The spitting image of Janice. You anything like your mother?" His features darken a bit as he mentions Janice's name.

"No, sir. Not at all."

"Good." He pats my shoulder. "Welcome to the camp and the family, Olivia."

■■■■■

We spend the majority of the day taking turns with showers and washing the laundry. We're shown how to get water from a spigot that has to be pumped by hand, collecting it in buckets that we carry up a ladder to the cistern on the second story. I didn't know what a cistern was until this day. It's a big metal tub placed high in the building with a pipe to let the water flow out by gravity to the first floor. I'm tempted to hop in it and take a bath in the hot water, but that would be terrible of me.

We work at keeping the woodburning stove fueled as well. It's a long day of tedious work, but everyone stays in chipper moods as we all clean up. When it's finally my turn in the shower, I let out a moan as soon as the warm water hits my body. It's so hard to make myself shut the water off while soaping up, but I remember what Eli said and try to conserve the water for other people. I scrub myself until my skin turns pink and slightly raw. I feel like a whole new person by the time I'm done. I had chosen an outfit that was the least smelly to put on after my shower, but after getting all scrubbed up and smelling nice, these clothes feel dirty now. I hate doing laundry, but I'm excited to have clean clothes again.

I eventually get my turn to wash laundry sometime after lunch. Eli has ropes tied up for us to hang our wet clothes on. I don't like the idea of my underwear being out where everyone can see, but this is survival mode. The day is just warm enough that our clothes don't freeze, but it will take them a while to dry. As I'm hanging up the last of my laundry, I see a girl with shoulder-length dark brown hair, wearing a black leather jacket and jeans ripped at the knees, approach David. She has a big smile, which David returns easily. I hurry up, throwing my last two shirts on the line haphazardly, and fast-walk over to them.

"I could show you around, handsome," the girl says as I get closer. She links her arm with his just as I step up to David's other side.

"Hi," I interrupt. "What'd I miss?"

"She was just going to show me around camp," David says.

"Is this your girlfriend?" The girl looks me up and down.

"No," David answers quickly. "We're just friends."

Ouch. A pang of jealousy tears through me as I see the girl tighten her grip on David's arm. "Who're you?" I ask, keeping my tone in check.

"You can call me Angel."

"Angel?" I give an involuntary small, breathy laugh.

"Well, my real name is Angelina Maria Raquel Consueala Tomasine Yolanda Esperanza Lola Martinez," she responds with attitude.

"Angel it is," I say.

"Do you mind if Olivia comes with us?" David asks.

"I guess she can tag along." Angel winks at him.

They turn and start walking arm in arm, and I follow behind, biting my tongue. I see David glance over his shoulder at me a couple of times, but he lets her lead him around the camp. She shows him where she stays first, much to my annoyance. Is this chick for real? She's coming on a little strong.

"So, Angel," I interrupt her story about how she once got caught skinny dipping in the nearby lake. "How old are you?"

"I just turned eighteen. How about you, handsome?" she asks David.

"I'll be eighteen in a few months."

"Sweet! Legally an adult. That means you can do whatever you like," she says flirtatiously. "I'm a bit of a troublemaker around here."

"You got that right." A man with the same colored hair and skin ruffles her hair as he passes by.

"Hey! Watch the hair!" she yells, her cheeks turning red as she smooths it back out.

"Who was that?" David asks.

"That's my big brother, Jesús."

"I have a big brother too. Of course, I didn't know that until recently," I say lamely, trying to remind them I'm still here.

Angel raises an eyebrow at me, then links arms with David again and leads him on. I reluctantly follow. She points out different cabins and who sleeps where, listing off names I only half hear. I'm not really paying attention to what she's saying. I'm more concerned about how cozy she seems to be getting with David. Now not only is her arm linked with his, but she has her other hand resting on David's forearm. I want to force my way in between them, but I would look like an idiot, so I stay behind, repeating to myself, *You told him you were just friends. It's okay for him to like other people. You told him you were just friends. It's okay for him to like other people...*

"And this is the kitchen." She stops in front of the large brick building behind the barn. "We do all our food prep and cooking here. No one's allowed in there unless you're helping with the meals, but I like to sneak in and snitch food when nobody's looking."

David peeks his head inside the building. "Wow, you guys have a lot of food."

"Yeah, well, we have a lot of people." She laughs at David's shocked expression. "I'm guessing your camp never had this much?"

I peek my head inside and see shelves full of canned goods, baskets of seasonal produce, bags of rice and beans, fresh bread laid out on a counter, boxes of snack foods... "Holy crap! Is that soda?" I ask, my mouth watering at the thought of drinking a can of it.

"Yeah, that's for special occasions, or when Eli gets a migraine."

I look closer, and what I thought was Mountain Dew actually says "Mello Yello."

"What's Mello Yello? Don't you guys have any Mountain Dew?" I ask.

"What's Mountain Dew?"

"You don't know what Mountain Dew is?" I ask incredulously.

"Isn't that what I just said?" Angel snaps.

"Sor-ry," I mutter childishly.

"How do you guys have so much good stuff here?" David interjects, trying to calm the tension.

"We get it from the city. Eli's got some good connections," she answers David with her sultry tone once again. "Basically, once a week, we send some guys in to get the stuff they've collected for us."

"What does Eli have to offer them in return for all that?" David asks the same question that has come to my mind.

Angel looks around conspiratorially and then leans over to whisper, her lips almost touching his ear lobe. She doesn't keep her volume down enough, and I hear her say, "Eli grows weed in our greenhouse and trades it for supplies."

"Why would he grow weeds? And why would anyone want them?" David asks, confused.

Angel laughs loudly. "Oh, aren't you cute! Don't you know what weed is?"

We both shake our heads no, but she only has eyes for him.

"Weed, as in marijuana," she says quietly, still laughing.

David looks at her blankly.

"Have you two been living under a rock?" She looks at us, her brown eyes wide in surprise. "Marijuana is a drug. It's illegal to possess any in the city, so it's highly valuable."

"What if the guards find out?" I ask, horrified.

Angel laughs again. "Some of the guards are his biggest customers. As long as we keep a low profile, we can basically come and go as we please in the city."

I shake my head in disgust.

"What?" Angel asks.

"I can't believe my uncle is a druggie," I say.

"He's not a druggie; he's a dealer," she says with a temper. "And it's how we're able to have so much."

"Great. Your leader's a criminal."

"Nobody asked you for your approval. If you don't like the way we do things around here, you can leave," Angel says, taking a threatening step toward me.

David reaches out and grabs her shoulders to stop her. "Whoa, whoa, whoa. Settle down," David says to Angel and then turns to me. "Liv, Matthias's ways weren't exactly innocent either. We stole things from the city, which is also a crime. In survival situations, sometimes you gotta do what you gotta do."

"So you're taking her side?"

David looks at me uncomfortably but doesn't respond. Angel glances at him and then back at me with a smug smirk on her face.

"Fine." I turn around and storm away from them.

"Liv!" I hear him plead.

But then Angel says, "Let her go. C'mon, I'll show you my favorite spot to hide when I want to be alone."

I stomp my way back to the shelter I slept in last night and see Cass doodling in her notebook again. I flop down on the cot, wiping away angry tears.

"What's up?" Cass asks.

"Angel." I put as much disdain in my voice as possible.

"Who's Angel?"

"She's a stupid girl who has the hots for David."

"Uh-oh. Is someone jealous?" she asks playfully.

"Ha! Hardly." I avoid making eye contact. "It's just sick that she's all over him, and she doesn't even know him. And he doesn't seem to mind. We don't know these people. She could be a Coalition spy or a mass murderer, and he's letting her hang all over him!"

"Uh-huh," Cass says. "I don't get you. You have a cute boy who's madly in love with you, and you keep friend-zoning him. Of course he's going to be interested in a girl who's giving him attention. Maybe you should just go out with him already!"

"She also told me how Eli can get all this good stuff," I say, changing the subject quickly. "He grows marijuana and trades it."

"Marijuana?" Cass asks, just as confused as David and I were.

"Apparently, it's a drug."

Cass looks up at the ceiling for a moment in thought, then back at me. "Smart."

"What?" I ask, shocked.

"Well, the drug part isn't great, but growing something that's valuable and making trades is smart. Matthias was able to steal us stuff, but nothing like what these people have. Plus, Eli seems to be..." She pauses, snapping her fingers as she thinks. "What's the word? Charismatic? Yeah, that's it. He's more charismatic than Matthias."

"I got a tiny glimpse of another side of Eli that made him more like Matthias. He asked me if I was anything like my mother, and he suddenly seemed dangerous. Like someone you wouldn't want to mess with."

"That must be how he's the leader. Friendly but tough."

I nod, thinking about the nut job family I belong to. My mom's a liar, a traitor, and a murderer. Matthias is a murderer and a thief. And my uncle is a drug dealer. It's no wonder I'm messed up.

Speaking of messed up: "Where's Tim?"

"Some geeky-looking guy started asking him about his missing arm and took him off somewhere. I don't know what they're doing now."

She goes back to her notebook, so I lie down facing the wall, wondering what Angel and David are doing. I get more and more agitated as I think about how cozy she was getting with him, but once I picture them kissing, I can't take it anymore. I get up off the cot and pace around the room.

"Why don't you go find him and tell him how you feel?" Cass thrusts her hand out toward the door.

"No. I already made a mess of things."

"Fine, but could you at least do your angry pacing outside? You're distracting me."

I head outside, the temperature shocking me slightly after being inside the warm shelter. I decide to check on my clothes, knowing they're still going to be wet, but I don't know what else to do with myself. As I'm checking them, Matthias steps up next to me with his laundry.

"I've been meanin' to ask ya if ya've cracked the code on the pendant yet?"

"No. I kind of forgot about it with everything that's been going on," I admit sheepishly.

"Keep workin' on it. I'd like to know what Pop thought was so important."

I nod and start to walk away, but I turn back toward him and say, "I found out today how Eli has so much stuff. He grows drugs and trades it for things."

"I know," Matthias says.

I wait to see if he's going to say more, but he just keeps hanging up his clothes. "You knew? Are you okay with it?"

"Of course not. That's why I'm not part of his camp. When I first found out what he was planning to do, we got in a fight, and I told him to leave."

"That must have been hard, fighting with your twin brother."

"It hurt him more than me. Pop refused to go with him because he disapproved of Eli's choices too. Eli was crushed but too stubborn to give up on his plan, so he'd send a guy to check in now and again to see how Pop was doing."

"Is that why he was so mad when he found out the news about Saul?"

Matthias stops hanging his clothes for a moment, his jaw flexing as he stares at the flannel shirt in his hands. I recognize it as one Saul used to wear.

"Yeah," Matthias says distantly.

"It wasn't your fault," I remind him.

"I made some bad choices. The injury was an accident, but the reason he got the injury was my fault."

"But you shouldn't blame yourself," I say, trying to help.

"When ya make a mistake, ya own up to it, then ya get over it. Something you should keep in mind." He gives me a significant look. He turns back to his laundry and hangs the last few things on the line. Once he's done, he pats me on the shoulder. "Let me know if ya crack the code, hmm?"

I nod and watch him leave toward the barn where Eli hangs out. Now that he mentioned the pendant again, I decide that I want to work on it some more. I'm desperate to get my mind on something other than what David is doing, but as I get closer to the shelter, I spot Angel and David standing right outside the door. She's holding onto his hoodie strings, looking up into his eyes with a smile.

"Thanks for showing me around," David says politely.

"Anytime, handsome."

I watch as she pushes up onto her tippy toes and plants a kiss right on David's lips. My face turns hot as my stomach does a flip from the sight of them. I immediately spin around and walk the other direction, not sure where I'm going to go, just knowing I don't want to be here.

I can't leave the compound, so I find a building by the fence and hide behind it. Hot tears burn my eyes, but I force myself to not cry. I slide my back down the wall until I'm sitting on the ground with my knees to my chest. I wrap my arms around my legs and stare out at the woods, seething.

Why am I so angry? I should be happy for him. He's finally found a girl who's showing interest in him. Am I mad at the thought of him spending more time with her, which means less time with me? Maybe I'm afraid that I'm going to lose him as a friend.

Geez. I'm lying to myself now.

I'm so lost in my thoughts, I don't hear someone approaching.

"What are you doing back here, Olive-uh?" someone says, getting my name wrong on purpose.

I jump a little at the voice, but when I see it's Cindy, I go back to staring at the woods. "Leave me alone."

"Sheesh. What's got your knickers in a twist?"

"Nothing," I snarl.

"Liar." She matches my tone.

"I'm not in the mood right now." I glare. "Why are you even around? Did something happen to Joselyn?"

"I don't have to have a reason to come out and play. I can be here if I want."

"Whatever," I say. "So, are you on your way somewhere?" I ask, hoping she'll keep moving along.

"As a matter of fact, I am. But I saw you sitting here like a lump and thought I would come see why."

"Well, that's very—thoughtful—of you," I say as evenly as possible, hoping she doesn't pick up on my sarcasm. My head still hurts at times from when she hit me, making me highly skeptical of her "concern."

"Yes, well, I am known for my rational thoughts and empathy," she says airily.

I start chuckling, and she joins in. Soon we're both holding our stomachs as a wave of laughter washes over us. Am I having a moment with Cindy?

Once we both settle down, Cindy grows serious. "Sorry I tried to kill you."

"No, you're not." I wipe the laughter tears off with the heels of my hands.

"I am."

I look up at her and see that this is the most sincere I've ever seen her. "Where is this coming from? I thought you hated me."

"I did, but I don't anymore."

I lift an eyebrow at her. All those death threats, then she actually tried to kill me, and now she's saying she doesn't hate me?

She sighs dramatically. "You believed me when nobody else did. Then you gave me a hug without knowing whether it was Joselyn or me. I always knew we were going to be best friends!" Her face splits in a creepy smile.

"I wouldn't go that far." I give an unsettled laugh. "But I'd be willing to be your friend as long as you're done hitting me with sticks."

"Promises, promises." She puts her fists on her hips. "Fine. Just don't piss me off."

I nod. I think that's about as good of a deal as I'm going to get.

Just as she's about to leave, I say, "I hope you don't mind me asking, but what did Mr. Wick mean when he said you're a powerful one?"

"He must have been talking about Joselyn." She shrugs, then skips away.

"Thanks for clearing that up," I mumble. The talk with Cindy distracted me enough that I'm ready to go work on the pendant now, even if it means facing David.

3|7

David isn't in the shelter when I get back, and Cass is gone too, which I'm grateful for. I just want to be left alone. I retrieve the pendant and Saul's stick out of my bag and set myself up against the wall, trying to get comfortable. I spin the tumblers around randomly as a way of resetting it. I'm not really sure if that's how it works, but I do it anyway out of habit from when I had a locker.

I try to mentally keep track of the different combinations I use, but after a while, I just can't anymore. I need a piece of paper, but the only paper around is in Cass's notebook. I know she would be outraged if she caught me messing with it, but desperate times call for desperate measures.

I slide off the cot and look out the window, checking to see if she's back yet. I don't see her, so I quickly open her bag and pull the notebook out. All I need is a clean piece of paper, so I flip to the back of her notebook, expecting to find an empty one there. Instead, I find a tear-stained letter addressed to her mom. I hear my conscience screaming, *Put it away! Don't look!* but I can't seem to stop myself from reading it.

> Mom,
>
> I know you won't ever see this, but I need to write it. It's been 7 years since you sent us with Matthias. You told us you'd come find us as soon as you could. LIAR! I was only 6 when you sent us away. Tim told me why, and I hate you for it. How could you do this to your own kids? How could you choose that loser of a boyfriend over us? You wanted to start a new family with that jerk, so you got rid of us?
>
> Now that I think about it, I guess I'm glad you gave up on us. I'm glad you're not my mom anymore. The people in this camp are better parents than you ever were. They taught us how to survive, how to look out for ourselves, how to be good people, things you never would have been able to teach us. The women in camp have been teaching Tim and me the important stuff we've missed since leaving school, like reading and writing. I'm glad about that too because now I can

*write this letter to tell you how much I hate you and
that I hope I never see you again.*

Poor Cass! I quickly flip through her notebook, trying not to pay
attention to anything else until I find a clear page. I rip one out and stuff
her notebook back in her bag. I take the blank page and pen back to my
cot, still shaken by her letter. I guess I never really thought about where
their parents were. I just assumed they had died or something. That would
have been easier than abandonment. I know that from experience.

I try to put the letter out of my mind as I work on the pendant. I
write *L* or *R* in a column to signify which tumbler I turned left or right.
After about twenty columns, I start to wonder again if this thing actually
opens or if these symbols are a kind of code instead.

I decide to give it one more try before putting it away for the day. I
haven't spun them all in the same direction yet, so I reset it and spin them
to the right until the correct symbols line up. I hear the tiniest click as the
last tumbler is set into place. My hands are trembling as I grab the very top
and the bottom of the cylinder and pull gently. It slides apart, revealing a
USB stick at the top of the pendant. I'm not sure what I was expecting it to
be, but this wasn't it. I tip the bottom part of the pendant over, shaking it
to see if maybe there's a secret note or something stuck inside. Nothing.
We're going to need a computer. Let's hope Eli has one.

I hop off the cot and race toward the barn to find Matthias. I see him
lounging at the head of the table with Eli next to the fireplace.

"I got it!" I shout as I run up the aisle. "I finally got it open!"

Matthias pushes up out of his chair so quickly, he almost knocks it
over. I've never seen him excited about something, and the sparkle in his eye
reminds me of Saul for a moment. I hold it out by the chain, and he takes it
gently into his palm.

"It's a USB stick. Do you have a computer, Uncle Eli?" I ask.

"No, sorry," he says.

My shoulders slump, and I hear Matthias make a frustrated noise.

"But I know where we can get to one."

"Then let's go," Matthias says eagerly.

"Hold on. It's not that easy. It's inside the city," Eli says. "You can't
just run in, guns blazing, like some sort of cowboy."

"Fine, O mighty wise one, then how do we get in?"

They glare at each other, and I almost chuckle when I realize Eli's
black eye is the same as the one Matthias lost.

"We're going to need to put together a team—"

"I'll go," I interrupt. "I should get to go since I figured out how to open it. It's kind of been my project this whole time." I'm desperate to get away from David and Angel. If this mission turns out to be dangerous, all the better.

"Sure," Eli says. "We're going to need to collect supplies."

"Ya mean drugs?" Matthias says testily.

"How else do you think I get into the city?" Eli's voice is dangerously low. It's clearly not the first time they've had this argument.

"Criminal," Matthias grumbles.

"Idiot," Eli responds.

"Guys! Let's get back on topic. When can we go?"

"Give me a couple of days, and I think I'll have the stuff we need by then."

"So, where is this computer?" Matthias asks.

"It's in one of the towers. There are four of them on the outskirts of the city, and one of them is close by. I can get us inside easily, but getting our hands on a computer is going to be a challenge."

"We'll figure it out," Matthias says with hope in his voice.

We're interrupted by someone knocking on the door to be let in. The doors open, and a procession of people enter, bringing in steaming bowls of food and dishes. Supper time. Eli slaps Matthias on the back, and they move their chairs up to the table.

I watch as David walks in with Angel still hanging on his arm. He makes eye contact for a split second, and I see guilt written all over him. I turn away and find that the seats are filling up quickly. I don't want to be stuck next to them, so I pick a spot between Stan and Cass.

Cass and I sit on tall padded chairs where my feet can't even touch the ground. The table is a tall dark brown wooden square that only seats four people. I have to look down to see Stan, who's sitting at a formal oak table made to seat six. It has beveled edges and decorative chairs with cream-colored upholstery that look like they belong to someone with lots of money.

The barn grows loud as everyone from the camp comes in to have a meal together at the mishmash of tables. The noise is a little overwhelming, but I remind myself that I can't run off and be alone every time I'm sick of the noise. I watch as Angel pulls David over to the other row of tables to sit next to her brother.

"I figured out the pendant," I say to Cass, turning my attention away from them.

"Really? What happened?" she asks excitedly.

"It opened up, and there was a USB stick inside." I beam.

"A what?"

"A USB stick. It's something that holds information that you plug into a computer. Eli said he knows where we can use a computer to find out what's on it. It's inside the city, and I told him I'm going."

"Cool! So, how did you figure out the code?" She reaches for the bowl of green beans. Someone sets a plate of grilled chicken breasts on the table in front of us.

My face flushes as I try to decide whether I should be honest about the notebook or not. I dish up some food as I work up the courage to spill my guts, but just as I'm about to say something, Tim and the geeky guy Cass told me about show up and take the seats across from us. I do a double-take when I see a strange metal hook sticking out from Tim's sleeve.

"What's that?" Cass asks, dumbfounded.

Tim's face lights up. "Denis made this and gave it to me to wear. It's a prosthetic arm. Here, watch this."

Tim sets the forearm down on the edge of the table and screws up his face as he makes the hooks open and close a little. Denis strokes his goatee deep in thought as he watches Tim intently. He wouldn't look that geeky except for his clothes. He had removed an olive-green tweed jacket with brown suede patches on the elbows so he could eat. Now he sits at the table with black suspenders, a black and green striped bow tie, and a white dress shirt with a pocket filled with small screwdrivers and pens.

"It's going to take me some time to figure out how to work it," Tim says.

"That's so cool!" Cass says. "You made that?"

"It was quite simple, really," Denis starts to say. "Finding the right materials was the difficult part."

"Denis is a genius," Tim gushes.

Denis beams a bit from the compliment, nudging Tim with his elbow. "I wouldn't say genius, but it's definitely a passion of mine. I had a best friend who was missing an arm, and his family couldn't afford to buy him a prosthetic, so I learned all about them and vowed to make him one."

"I bet he was grateful." I take a bite of chicken breast.

"I'll never know. He was killed before he got a chance to try it out." Denis rakes his fingers through his brown curly hair.

"I'm so sorry." Cass's eyes grow misty.

"Yeah, well, it turns out he and his brother had been plotting to kill President Sawyer. They were caught with blueprints of the Coalition headquarters and a gun."

"Wait...did you just say, 'President Sawyer'? Don't you mean Turk?" I ask, confused.

"No. President Sawyer is the leader of our city. Each remaining city has its own leader. Didn't you know that?" He stuffs a forkful of green beans into his mouth.

Tim, Cass, and I all shake our heads.

Denis looks at us, surprised. "There's so much distance between the cities, they appointed a president for each one. Honestly, the term president is a bit pompous if you ask me. It's more logical to call them 'mayors' like what city leaders used to be called back before the war. I guess they want to feel more important."

"So, what's President Sawyer like?" Tim asks.

"Well, he's somewhere in his fifties, balding, fat, and he's about as smart as a bag of rocks. It's his wife you need to watch out for. She's a conniving, cold-hearted witch. I'm almost certain she's the one who ordered John and his brother to be killed." His blue eyes fill with hate.

"I'm sorry about your friend, Denis," Tim says.

"Yeah, well, that was a long time ago. C'est la vie." He sighs. "Anyway, the prosthetic Tim's got on is the one I was going to give to John. I saw Tim and knew the fit would be a close match. He's just about the same size as John and everything. There's more tweaking we're going to have to do to get it just right."

"It hurts a bit to wear right now since I still have some healing to do, but I'm excited for when I can use it regularly. Thank you, Denis."

"Of course." He waves Tim off.

We all finish eating and help clear the table. Denis tells us to stack the dirty plates at the end table by the door, where the people on dish duty can grab them easily.

We follow him into his shelter. It's stacked high with tools, metal parts, and books. Loose papers with drawings and notes are scattered everywhere. There is only one bed in the room, and it's piled high with more notes and schematics. He grabs it all and stacks it into a pile on the floor next to a red wingback leather chair. He motions for us to sit on the bed as he throws a fresh log in his wood-burning stove. He then takes a seat and pulls a pipe out of his jacket pocket. I've never seen one in real life. I

175

recognize the pipe from watching a movie about a detective who used one. He pulls out a little cloth pouch and stuffs something inside the end.

"That's not weed, is it?" I use the term I heard Angel use.

Denis shakes his head. "Nah, I don't go near that stuff. This is just some dried up flowers and herbs. I find it calming to puff on a pipe. I hope you don't mind."

I shake my head. "So, what's it like around here? What's your city like?" I make conversation.

"I imagine the city's like all the other cities. It's only about a quarter of the size it used to be."

"Is there fog?" I ask.

"Sometimes it's fog. Sometimes it's radioactive dust clouds." He puffs out a smoke ring.

"What?" Tim watches the ring drift upwards with fascination.

"It's pretty windy in the city for the most part. Fog will be present some of the time, but it gets blown away by the wind and isn't a big deal. However, the land to the west of here was decimated by nuclear bombs. When the wind blows from the west, clouds of dust come swirling in carrying radioactive particles. So, as a precaution, mandatory shots are given to the citizens to keep people from getting radiation poisoning. If you guys plan on staying here for long, we're going to have to use our stock of shots we keep around for new members and babies."

"Holy crap," Tim says quietly.

"I don't know if we're staying that long. I really don't know what the plan is. We're headed to a place called 'The Haven.'" I watch to see how he responds.

He just nods, taking a puff of his pipe.

"So, you've heard of it?" I ask.

"Heard of it? Yes. Do I know where it is? No."

"Well, if it's a wasteland to the west of here, it probably isn't that way. Could it be north?" Cass asks.

"You don't want to be going north," Denis says seriously. "There are rumors of terrible creatures up there."

"Really? What kind of creatures?" Tim asks.

"They say it has large claws, a long tail with spears at the end, huge fangs, and two horns sprouting from its temples. It supposedly breathes fire and smoke, and smells terrible, like a combination of buzzard meat and skunk perfume."

"Sounds fake, but then again, we had beasts called Havocs outside of our city. Do you have any of those around here?" I ask with a yawn.

"No, can't say that we do." He puffs on his pipe again.

The shelter is filling up with hazy smoke. That, combined with a full stomach and the stove's cozy warmth, makes my eyelids grow heavy.

I shuffle behind Matthias down a narrow alleyway. The smell of rotting garbage and stale urine assaults my nose, making me pull my shirt up over my face so I don't lose the contents in my stomach.

We come out to a street that's identical to the one we left: tall buildings still mostly intact, shop signs promising low prices, office buildings with windows glinting in the fading sunlight. I never got to see the buildings in my city this well because of the never-ceasing fog. But just as Denis said, there's a breeze blowing here from the east that clears the fog away. When the wind isn't blowing, the streets fill up with fog again, only to have it blow away once more. Clearly, it's not a natural fog.

The street is empty of people, except for one old man standing on the corner, holding a cardboard sign with a word written in black marker. The sign reads: "BELIEVE!"

Eli turns right, heading down the street toward the tower. As we pass by the old man, he starts preaching: "The world is actually on our side! If we would just go to them, they would accept us. Listen to the voices from above. They tell me encouraging words."

I grab Joselyn's hand and drag her faster past the crazy guy.

FLASH!

I'm inside a room, surrounded by guards with guns, but they're not pointing them at us. They have their hands gripping the sides of their heads, and their faces are twisted in pain. The overhead lights and computer screens are flashing on and off like strobe lights as the sirens blare from the tower's security system. I see Joselyn screaming at the top of her lungs just before I feel an unbearable squeezing pressure inside my brain. My hands fly up to my head too in some sort of lame attempt to stop the agony that's going on inside my skull. It feels as though someone has my brain in their hand, and they're squeezing it like they would a wet sponge that they're trying to get every last drop of water out of. I succumb to the pain and pass out.

FLASH!

I'm being dragged outside the tower by my arms. My shoulders are on the verge of dislocation, but the pain in my head seems to have lessened. I look to see who's pulling me, and it's Joselyn.

"Ugh. Why are you so heavy, Olive-uh?" she grunts when she sees me looking at her.

"Cindy? What are you doing?" I start coughing.

"Saving everyone's asses," she says as she stops and lets go of my arms.

I look over and see Matthias, Eli, and Charlotte lying in the grass. Alexandrine's sitting next to Charlotte, stroking her hair.

"Saving us from what? What happened in there?"

"From Joselyn's drama and the fire she caused. I told you not to let her go on this mission. I warned you this would happen, but did you listen to me? No. Crazy Cindy doesn't know what she's talking about," Cindy scolds.

I look back at the building, and sure enough, there's smoke coming from the ground floor window. "You dragged everyone outside all by yourself? Do you have super-strength too?" I ask, confused.

"No." She looks at me like I'm a moron. "I got the fire under control long enough to start pulling Charlotte out. Alexandrine woke up before any of you did and helped me with the guys. I left you in there for last," she says with a hint of amusement. "Sorry. Old habits."

I start coughing again as a response.

"I can't remember what happened in there. Did we find out what was on the USB stick?" Matthias asks.

"No. We didn't have time before the guards showed up and Joselyn went berserk." Cindy wipes sweat off her forehead.

"Then this was all for nothing." Eli groans as he sits up.

"Hold your horses, Mr. Mary Jane. I might have swiped something that could be useful," she says, picking something up off the ground. She turns around and has a laptop in her hands.

"A laptop! Smart girl." Eli holds his hands out for her to give him the computer.

"Tut, tut, tut. Back off there, grabby. I just saved your lives. What's in it for me?"

"Let's talk about this back at camp, shall we?" Alexandrine looks around.

The sky has turned a pale orange on the horizon as the sun lets off its final rays. I notice that all the surrounding buildings are dark. Even the streetlights are void of their usual golden pools of light. I look back at the tower, and the only light I see is from the fire Cindy saved us from. Whatever knocked us out knocked the power out too.

"Wake up!" Cass yells, shaking me awake.

I sit up with a jolt when I realize I have fallen asleep, and now Tim, Denis, and Cass are all staring at me.

"Oh, thank God! You had me scared!" Cass's hand is on her heart.

"I'm sorry. I must have fallen asleep." I sit up, rubbing my eyes.

"You weren't sleeping. It's like you were in a trance. You looked like you were in pain, with your hands to your head, and you kept opening your eyes looking at us...but not looking at us," Cass tries to explain, looking spooked.

"I think I had one of my dreams again. I better go talk to Matthias."

3|8

"Why would Joselyn even be there with us?" Matthias asks.

I found Eli and Matthias still in the barn, sitting by a roaring fire. They have a couple of chairs pulled over to the fireplace, one for sitting and one to rest their feet on. They each have a glass of wine in one hand and a chunk of chocolate in the other. Unfortunately, neither one of them offers me any chocolate. Rude.

"I have no idea. I'm just telling you what I saw. This dream was different. It was longer, and it kept skipping ahead. Just showing me pieces of events."

"So, ya didn't get to see what was on the USB stick?" Matthias asks once more.

"No, like I already told you," I say, getting annoyed.

"It would have been convenient if you had. Then we wouldn't need to track down a computer," Eli chimes in airily, taking a sip from his glass.

"When should we have a meeting about this mission?" I'm anxious to get started.

"The sooner, the better," Matthias answers at the same time as Eli says, "No need to rush into anything."

They both look at each other with their eyes narrowed and lips tight.

"I'm with Matthias on this," I say. "Especially after what Denis said about radiation poisoning."

"What about it?" Matthias asks.

"Denis told us that if we don't leave here soon enough, we'll all need to get shots to stop us from getting radiation sickness."

"Denis is a bit of a drama queen." Eli waves me off. "I'm not sure I buy into this radiation nonsense. I think it's just the government using scare tactics."

"So, ya haven't taken one of the shots then?" Matthias challenges him.

"No. I did," he says, taking a bite of chocolate. "Better safe than sorry."

"You're so full of crap. Maybe ya should step out to your garden. I'm sure the plants would love the BS that's constantly spewin' outta your mouth."

"What?" Eli gives a confused laugh.

"Ya talk big, but when it comes to actually standin' up for your beliefs, ya fall right in with the rest of the sheep."

Eli gives Matthias a hard punch on the arm, which Matthias is about to return, but I clear my throat loudly, and they stop.

"I think we should have a meeting soon to get this computer plan hashed out," I say, interrupting yet another squabble between these two.

"Fine. We'll set up a meeting for tomorrow at noon. I don't think we'll need that many people for the mission, though. I know a few guys who're willing to look the other way for us to do what we need to get done."

Matthias heaves a big sigh.

"Knock it all you want, Brother. At least I get results." Eli raises his glass toward Matthias, who doesn't return the gesture.

"Okay, tomorrow at noon. In here?" I ask. I'm getting antsy to get out of here and head to bed.

"Sure. After lunch." Eli says.

I head back outside and see David leaning against the side of the barn alone. "Liv. I want to talk to you." He pushes off the wall toward me.

"Go talk to your girlfriend." I start walking quickly toward the shelter.

"She's not my girlfriend," he says defensively. "C'mon. I've only known her for a day."

I laugh mirthlessly. "I saw you guys kissing."

He grabs my wrist to stop me from walking away from him. "No, you saw her kiss me. I never asked for it. In fact, if you had been watching closer, you would have seen me push her away. And what difference does it make if I kiss someone else or not? You shouldn't care, remember?" he says angrily.

"You're right. I don't. Go ahead and kiss whoever you want." I twist to get out of his grip.

"Why are you so mad at me?" he asks with pain in his voice.

I stop trying to get away and face him. He has a desperate look in his eyes, and I realize I have the power to hurt him with how I respond at this moment. I stare into his eyes, seeing the boy I've come to rely on, the boy who's always been there for me whenever I needed him, the boy who has proclaimed his love to me, and it finally hits me.

I love him too.

The thought terrifies me, and I suddenly don't want to be here. I feel vulnerable and confused standing in front of him, feeling how I'm feeling. "Can we talk about this tomorrow?" I ask quietly. "I need some time to think about things."

"Sure," he says, releasing his grip on my wrist. As I slide my wrist out of his grasp, I grab onto his hand momentarily, giving him a light squeeze before walking away to the shelter.

The next couple of days pass, and David doesn't hold me to the talk I promised him. It almost seems as though he read my thoughts that night, because he's been even sweeter than normal, if that's possible. He asked Angel to cool it and told her that he's more than happy to be her friend. She bristled a bit at first but backed off. She still calls him handsome, which annoys me, but I try my best to ignore it.

The meeting we had about the computer mission didn't go over too well. Some of Eli's group seems to think it's an unnecessary risk and use of their resources. In the end, we took a vote and got enough people to agree to it. Finding people to volunteer for the mission was a different story, though. I already knew who would be in the group, so I wasn't surprised by the lack of volunteers.

It did surprise me, though, when Alexandrine suggested Charlotte go with us. It didn't make sense to me that she was there in my dream, but apparently, Charlotte has the ability to make people fall asleep by singing. Alexandrine prompted her to show us while plugging her own ears. It took Charlotte a while to get brave enough to sing, but once she did, the effect was immediate. My entire body went slack, and I started dreaming within moments of my eyes closing. When I woke up, I had no idea what time it was or how long I was out. Alexandrine told us it had only been ten seconds. I was dumbfounded.

Charlotte agreed to go, but only if Joselyn could go too. We tried to talk her out of it, but she folded her arms over her chest and refused to speak to anyone until Alexandrine finally caved. David looked like he was going to raise his hand, but I shook my head at him to remind him of the conversation we'd had earlier in the day:

"It's a dangerous mission, David."

"Exactly why I want to go. I want to be there to protect you."

"I'll be fine. I saw what happened in my dream, and you weren't there with us. It was Cindy who saved everyone, if you can believe it."

"Liv, I—" David starts to protest, but at that moment, I grab his face gently and kiss him to stop him from talking. I'm just as surprised at what I was doing as he is.

"As you wish." He leans his forehead against mine, and I smile at the quote. "But don't get it in your pretty little head that you can kiss me to get me to do what you want."

"Of course not." I give him a flirty wink.

He wraps his arms around me, pulling me in for a hug. I could feel him turn his face toward my neck and breathe in deep, sighing as he let it out.

An unspoken change is happening between us, and I think I'm finally okay with it.

■■■■■

"Everything's ready for the mission," Eli announces at supper a couple days after the meeting. "We'll be leaving tomorrow after lunch."

"Are you sure you don't want the Metal Militia to escort you?" a young man asks eagerly.

"I appreciate your enthusiasm, Edward, but I'm afraid that would draw too much attention."

I see Edward's shoulders slump in disappointment.

"I still don't get why this is so important," an angry-faced old woman asks.

"What's on the USB stick seemed important to my dad, so it's important to me. It's not for you to question my decisions," Eli says with utmost authority. His casual attire of a soft dark blue sweater and brown skinny jeans seems to clash with the powerful tone in his voice and the threatening way he's holding his body. A vision of him welcoming someone in for an embrace only to snap their neck once they get close pops in my head and makes me shiver.

"You guys shouldn't be letting Joselyn go. You have no idea what kind of power she has when she gets scared," Cindy says.

"She's going because it's what Charlotte wants," Alexandrine says firmly.

"Do you always give your kid everything she wants?" Cindy asks in a bratty tone.

"When we're asking her to do something special for us, yes." Alexandrine glares.

Cindy puts her hands on her hips and says to Charlotte, "That was a stupid use of a favor. Why didn't you ask for your own shelter? Or a unicorn or something cool?

Both the girls giggle, and everyone directs their attention back on Eli.

"We'll make sure everything is under control while you're gone," someone says reassuringly.

"I appreciate that." Eli nods and dismisses everyone to go about their business.

I head back to the shelter to check over my bag again. I had it packed up yesterday, but I just want to triple check that I'm not missing anything.

"Are you absolutely sure I can't talk you out of this?" David asks again.

I sigh and grab his hand. He lifts my hand up to his lips and presses them against my knuckles.

"I need to do it. The pendant was obviously important to my grandpa," I say, stumbling a bit over the word "grandpa." I feel sadness settle in a bit when I think about Saul and how I wish I could have been his granddaughter for longer.

"Just promise me you won't get yourself into trouble like you always do when I'm not around." He nudges me with his elbow.

"I can't promise anything, but I'll try my hardest," I say.

He raises his eyebrow and gives me a look of frustration.

"Hey! Things just kind of happen to me. It's not my fault."

David rests his hand on the back of my neck and rubs my cheek with his thumb, sending goosebumps down my body. Just then, Cass comes barging in the shelter. I quickly move away from David, uncertain whether I want people to know we're becoming something more than friends, but the smile that spreads across Cass's face makes me relax a bit.

"It's about time!" she squeals. "Sorry to interrupt. I'll just go find somewhere else to be."

"No, Cass. It's okay..." I try to say, but she gives me a wave and closes the door behind her.

I can't quite meet David in the eye when I realize what Cass thinks we're doing. She's acting more mature about all this than I feel, and she's three years younger. I'm just so far out of the loop with what couples are supposed to do that I think my maturity is more like a ten-year-old.

"Tell me again what happens after you get the computer," David says, knowing full well I don't know.

"We skip our merry way back out of the city with the laptop in hand. The guards happily open the gate for us, saluting us as we pass by, and once we get back here, we plug the USB stick in to find that it's a map leading us to a buried treasure." I laugh.

"Very funny," David says with a half smile. "What if something bad happens after Cindy saves you? What if you guys get caught and are thrown into jail? Or worse?"

"I'll be with Matthias and Eli. They wouldn't let something like that happen." I rub his arm.

"You're right. They'd probably shoot you and themselves to avoid being captured," David says darkly. He looks so concerned that my resolve wavers for a moment.

"What if the information on the USB is the location of The Haven?" I challenge. "Don't you think that's worth finding out?"

David chews on his inner cheek a moment and finally agrees. "Fine. You're right. Just don't lose the pendant while you're in there. It would be bad if the Coalition got their hands on that information."

I nod. His concerns have me a little worried now. I didn't think much about what happened right after Cindy saved us from the tower. I hope what's on the USB stick is worth the risk.

[40

After a secret farewell with David, I found it hard to leave, but now that I'm outside the compound, the excitement of adventure draws me forward.

Eli leads the way, while Matthias takes up the rear. We wind our way for hours through empty streets and eerie subdivisions. The vacant houses seem to peer at us with dark windows, giving me the unsettling feeling of being watched. I focus my attention on Charlotte and Joselyn, who walk ahead of me with their arms linked, whispering secrets to each other. It gives me a pang of longing for David to be here with me.

"We're almost there," Eli announces.

I look up and see a city encompassed by a fence. There's a thin cloud of fog, but you can still see the buildings for the most part. There are houses on the outskirts surrounding the tall skyscrapers that are still standing. As we get to be about a hundred yards from the fence, Eli tells us to wait in the wreck of a building, out of sight.

"Ya sure about this?" Matthias asks uncertainly.

"Of course. Just stay put. They can get a little suspicious if a group of people is standing outside the gate."

I listen to his boots crunch on the gravel as he approaches the city gates. His footsteps stop, and when I don't hear anything else, I go to peek my head around the corner, but Matthias grabs my arm and shakes his head. He mouths, "wait," and I hold my breath as I try to listen to what's going on.

"Hey, hey! Bryce, my man!" Eli's voice calls out.

After a beat, I hear some hand slapping and a deep voice answer, "Yo, Eli. You looking to get in?"

"That I am, my friend. Got a small group of people looking to gather supplies."

"Small group?" Bryce asks.

"They're back there. I didn't know whether Godzilla was working this afternoon or not. You know how he is."

"Sure do," Bryce answers knowingly. "Coop's got the day off, though. You're safe. So," —Bryce pauses, lowering his voice to where I can just barely make out what he's saying— "you got the goods?

"Of course," Eli says. There's another pause and I assume he's handing off the drugs.

I can hear Bryce take a deep breath and say, "Ahh! That's some good stuff."

Matthias looks like he wants to murder his brother and this Bryce person. His disdain for the way his brother conducts business is clearly showing as he curls his lip and balls his hands into fists. If it weren't for the laptop, I wouldn't be going along with this either.

"Pleasure doing business with you, Bryce," Eli says. Then we hear a whistle signaling it's safe to come out.

As we walk through the gate, Bryce nods to each of us but does a little double-take when Matthias steps past. Even though Matthias keeps the hair on his head and face vastly different from Eli's, their similarities are still noticeable. Bryce locks up the gates behind us and gets back to his post. We continue to follow Eli as he leads us toward the tower, trying to blend in as much as we can, but I notice the few people on the streets watch us walk past, and I don't like it.

We make it through the residential area and come to roads lined with businesses. I take a deep breath and almost shout in jubilation when I recognize the smell. I keep sniffing until I'm lightheaded, and my mouth waters.

Tacos!

"Eli, please tell me you have some money or something to buy tacos," I plead.

"We don't have time for that," Alexandrine answers, and I whip my head toward her and give her a shocked look.

"There's always time for tacos! C'mon, Uncle Eli. Please," I beg. "Please, please, please!"

Eli laughs a little. "Yeah. I have a pouch of Coalition coins. We'll get you some tacos."

I jump while clapping my hands. I haven't been this excited in a long time. Everyone's looking at me strangely, so I stop and try to control myself. We look up and down the road and spot a truck parked on the street with a big window open on the side and a menu posted next to the window.

"Why is there a truck selling tacos?" I ask.

"You didn't have food trucks in your city?" Eli asks, surprised.

"No. This is weird. Can you trust it?"

"Honestly, some of the best food I've ever had came from a food truck. It must be a city ordinance thing. Maybe your president didn't allow it."

I shrug, and we walk closer to the truck, the scent getting stronger until it's the only thing I can smell. "Street tacos?" I read. "I've never had these before, but if they taste as good as they smell, I'll try them."

They have ground beef, chicken, and steak. I order one of each and an extra ground beef one to take to Henry. We'll have to reheat it, but since he's never had a taco before, he won't notice it's not quite as good as when it's fresh. I suspect he'll like it anyway. Everyone else only orders one, making me look like a pig, but you know what, I don't care. These tacos are so much smaller than the ones I'm used to, and they don't have salsa, but as soon as I bite into the chicken one, I close my eyes and moan. I try to make them last as long as I can, but it's a struggle. I'm tempted to eat the one I got for Henry too, but with a huge amount of willpower, I wrap it up in the foil they came in and stuff it in my bag, sighing.

Once everyone is done, we walk down the sidewalk until I recognize the area from my dream. Sure enough, Eli leads us down an alleyway connecting the streets. The smell of rotting garbage and stale urine causes my stomach to churn. I quickly pull my shirt over my nose so I don't have to taste the tacos again.

We come out to a street like the one we were just on. I look around with a feeling of déjà vu as I see the tall buildings still intact, a store selling clothes with a sign in the window promising "Low Prices!" and office buildings with windows glinting in the fading sunlight.

I take notice of the fog—or rather, the momentary lapses of fog—just like in my dream. Then I remember the old guy on the corner. I check the direction where I remember seeing him, and I spot him holding the cardboard sign that reads, "*BELIEVE!*"

His appearance is off-putting: ratty clothes, hair matted with dirt, and crooked black teeth. He sees us coming and turns his sign toward us. "The world is actually on our side! If we would just go to them, they would accept us. Listen to the voices from above. They tell us encouraging words."

"Nut job," Eli mutters so only we can hear.

We stay on the opposite side of the street, trying to ignore him as we make our way toward the tower that's straight ahead.

Out of the blue, a voice rings in my head as clear as someone speaking directly to me. *Please, listen to me. They want to find us. We'd be set free. I hear their voices at my home. Come with me. You can hear them too.*

I peer in the guy's direction and see that he's staring straight at me with a curious look. I purposefully look away and pick up my pace, blowing past Eli in an effort to get away from his unsettling stare.

Carl. My name's Carl. You don't have to be afraid, girl. I won't hurt you, the voice says inside my head.

"Hey. Slow down, Olivia. We need to keep it cool, or people will take notice of us, and we don't want that." Eli grabs my arm to slow me down.

"Sorry. I just wanted to get away from that guy. Anyone else hear him talking inside their head?" I say quietly.

"Oh! That was him? I just thought I was hearing voices again," Joselyn says with a nervous laugh.

"What are you girls talking about?" Alexandrine asks.

"I think that guy's a Rare, but he's insane. He told me to come to his home to hear the voices. That the voices tell him the world is on our side," I say.

"Ignore him. Keep walkin'," Matthias grunts.

The guy stops trying to talk to me, and I'm relieved, but I'm also kind of interested in what he was talking about. What if he's not completely crazy? Clearly, he's a Rare, but what happened to him? He must have telepathic abilities, so who's he talking to? Voices from above?

I'm so lost in thought, I don't notice we're about half a block away from the tower until Eli shows us where we should keep out of sight again.

"Are you ready, Charlotte?" Alexandrine asks.

Charlotte nods slightly.

"Sing loud!" Joselyn gives Charlotte a hug.

"I'll be watchin' the whole time," Matthias reassures Alexandrine. "If anything seems to be goin' wrong, we'll come get ya."

"Make it convincing," Eli throws in.

We watch as Alexandrine and Charlotte move toward the tall gray cone-shaped building with metal poles that stick up into the sky. As they get closer to the entrance, Charlotte puts her hands between her knees and crosses her legs, bouncing up and down as though she has to go to the bathroom. She says something to Alexandrine, who does a show of looking around for somewhere to go, just like they rehearsed. They need to make it convincing, in case there are cameras or someone watching from the narrow windows.

She grabs Charlotte's arm and pulls her toward the entrance. Charlotte continues to dance around as Alexandrine knocks on the door. The door stays closed, but Alexandrine leans toward the wall.

"I'll bet they use intercoms," Eli comments.

The door suddenly pops open, and a Coalition guard steps into the doorway, holding a rifle in his arm. I see Alexandrine lift her hands up to her ears and stick in the earplugs she was carrying.

Within a few seconds, the guard drops to the ground like a marionette whose strings were just cut. I can hear a faint melody, and even from this far away, I begin to feel the effects. Alexandrine sways a little on her feet, but she manages to stay standing.

"All right. Put your earplugs in, and let's go get this over with," Eli says.

I take the squishy earplugs out of my pocket, roll the tip of it between my fingers until it's thin just like I was shown, and then stuff them in my ears. The ambient sounds of the city are instantly muted.

We walk to where Charlotte is still singing. The earplugs work but just barely. I'm finding it hard to keep my eyelids from closing. We step past the sleeping guard and into the tower, where the polished tiled floors reflect the fluorescent lights, and the scent of cleaning solution burns my nose. There's a desk by the wall where several monitors show what's outside the tower, but unfortunately, there's no computer here.

We walk along the corridor as quietly as we can, while Charlotte continues to sing. We're getting far enough away from the sleeping guard that I'm worried Charlotte's singing won't affect him anymore. If he wakes up now, he'll probably find us.

Finally, Eli peers into a window on one of the doors and motions for us to stop. He holds his finger up to his lips at Charlotte so she'll stop singing. He takes an earplug out and gestures for us to do the same.

"There are computers in there, but there's also about five guards sitting around those computers. So here's what I'm thinking. We'll crack the door open just enough for Charlotte's voice to get in. Then, once they're all asleep, we'll go in and use the computers."

"I already told you we never get a chance to use one. Cindy steals a laptop."

"It'll have to be one of us who takes the laptop," Joselyn says quietly.

"Why's that?" I whisper.

"I made Cindy promise to leave me alone on this mission," Joselyn says. "I wrote her a note and told her I wanted to try to handle things myself. That I'll never be strong if I don't try. She promised, 'crosses her heart and hopes to die.'"

This bit of information helps me to understand my dream now. I couldn't figure out why Cindy would allow Joselyn to stick around long enough to freak out.

"Let's not even bother with pluggin' in the USB stick here. Someone should grab the laptop, and we'll take off," Matthias says, and everyone nods.

"Earplugs back in. Charlotte, are you ready?" Eli asks.

Charlotte looks frightened, but she whimpers a yes.

After everyone replaces their earplugs, Eli puts his hand on the door handle, ready to start our plan, but at that moment, a guard comes marching around the corner and catches us. "Stop right there! Hands up where I can see them!" the guard yells.

"Sing!" Eli shouts, but Charlotte seems too scared. Her voice cracks, and she starts bawling instead.

Eli puts his hands up in the air, stepping in front of us. "We're so sorry. My friend here needed to use the facilities. The nice guard at the front door let us in, but we got lost trying to find the bathroom," Eli lies as the guard moves in closer, pointing his gun at us.

Charlotte continues to cry, unable to use her abilities.

"Put your hands behind your head, and turn around," the guard barks, obviously not believing the lie.

The guard is now right behind Eli, pushing him up against the wall. He grabs ahold of his radio to call in backup, but Matthias takes this moment of distraction to pull out the handgun he had tucked in his belt and shoot the guard. Sirens start blaring throughout the building, and I look back toward the entrance and see the guy who opened the front door awake and talking on his radio as he walks toward us.

Alexandrine is trying to soothe Charlotte to get her to sing again, but Charlotte just looks at her in terror. We push our way into the room with the computers, desperate to get it and go. The five guards who are in the room are grabbing their guns to respond to the alarm system going off. Matthias has his gun drawn, but he never gets a shot fired.

Joselyn starts screaming at the top of her lungs, and everyone in the room immediately grabs hold of their heads. The lights flicker as though someone is playing with the light switch. The computer screens are flashing too. The pressure inside my head is unbearable. I feel like my brain is about to pop. Everyone around me drops to the floor like flies, and right before I pass out too, I see sparks shooting out of the wall sockets, catching the desks and nearby wastebasket full of paper on fire.

[4|1

I wake up to my wrists and shoulders feeling like they are about to dislocate. My shirt has pulled up a bit, and my back is getting scratched from sharp rocks and rough concrete that I'm being dragged over. My head is still throbbing from whatever happened in there. I take notice that the sounds of the siren have stopped, and it's ominously quiet, except for Cindy's grunting.

"Ugh! Why are you so heavy, Olive-uh?" she says, pulling me up next to Matthias.

"Cindy? What are you doing here?" I ask groggily, forgetting my dream for a moment. I start coughing and can't seem to stop.

"Saving everyone's asses." She lets go of my arms.

"Saving us from what? What happened in there?" Eli asks.

"From Joselyn's drama and the fire she caused. I told you not to let her go on this mission. I warned you this would happen, but did you listen to me? No. Crazy Cindy doesn't know what she's talking about," Cindy scolds.

I look back at the building to watch the smoke coming from a ground floor window. "You're the one who promised Joselyn that you'd leave her alone. You could have jumped in to stop her from freaking out," I challenge.

"A promise is a promise is a promise. I at least had the sense to take over right before everyone's heads exploded and you all burned to a crisp."

"Seriously? Is that what would have happened? Our heads would have exploded?" I ask, horrified.

"Did you get the laptop?" Eli interrupts.

"Yes, indeedly doo, Mr. Mary Jane," Cindy says, picking the black computer up off the ground.

Eli reaches out to grab it, but she pulls it away from him. "Tut, tut, tut. Back off there, grabby. I just saved your lives. Well, me and Alexandrine. What's in it for moi?"

"Let's talk about this back at camp, shall we?" Alexandrine looks around.

The sky has turned a pale orange on the horizon as the sun lets off its final rays. I notice that all the surrounding buildings are dark, just like in my dream. The streetlights aren't working either, leaving us in the convenient veil of darkness. I look back at the tower, and the only light I see is from the fire Cindy saved us from. Joselyn's ability not only knocked us out, she knocked out the power too.

Now that every part of my dream has played out, I'm suddenly nervous. I don't know what's going to happen, and I don't like it.

"Is Charlotte okay?" I ask Alexandrine, who's on her knees, holding Charlotte.

"She feels guilty."

"I'm s-so, so s-sorry guys," Charlotte squeaks.

"Shh. It's okay," Alexandrine shushes Charlotte, then says to us, "Let's get moving."

Eli leads us as fast as he can to an alleyway out of sight of the tower. The guards will be waking up soon—that is, if they haven't died in the fire. A pang of guilt washes through me at the thought. We should have tried to save them, but then again, that would mean our capture. I feel like Matthias making the choice to kill someone just for our sakes. I feel dirty.

Once we're safely out of sight, we slow down a little since it's dark and hard for those without Rare abilities to see. I can hear people on the streets murmuring about the power outage and making wild guesses about what's going on. Some are worried that the city has been attacked, while others blame the president for using too much power for his estate.

We quietly work our way up and down sidewalks and alleyways, trying hard to stay unseen. As we're coming out of an alley, Eli peeks his head around the corner and throws his arm out to stop us. He guides us back behind a dumpster. We squat down to keep out of sight. I peek my head out to see what we're hiding from, and a guard steps into view, shining a flashlight down the alleyway. I whip my head back just as the beam of light scans back and forth a few times. He must not have seen me, because the light disappears, and the guard's footsteps move on. I blow out the breath I was holding in, willing my heart to settle down.

Where are you going? a voice echoes inside my head. *Come hide at my place. Then you, too, can hear the words of comfort.*

That weirdo is trying to communicate with me again.

I don't know you. Leave me alone, I think as clearly as I can. I don't know whether he can read my thoughts or how his abilities work.

If you ever want to listen, remember: QRP 14.060. You're not alone.

I try to ignore what he's saying and focus on following behind Cindy. The man doesn't say anything more, and as we get to the subdivisions again, I can feel myself breathe. I just want to be back at camp with David.

The houses in this part of town still have their electricity. It appears that Joselyn's abilities only work in a certain radius. We have to be more careful to stay in the shadows now. I don't know if the residents know what's happening downtown, but we can't take any risks.

Eli must have taken a wrong turn and struggles to remember his way back to the gate. We stop a few times as he spins around in circles, trying hard to spot something that will spark his memory. I offer to climb up on the roof of a dark house to see if I can spot our exit. He refuses at first, but after walking in circles a couple of times, I get fed up with him and pick out a tall tree instead.

I almost yell in frustration once I'm high enough to see the gate. It's lit up with floodlights. There's no way we're going to be able to leave without being caught. Even if the same guard is still manning the post, he's going to know we caused the trouble, and I doubt he's going to just let us go scot-free.

I climb back down and give them the bad news.

"What do we do?" Alexandrine asks.

Eli strokes his beard, a lot like Matthias does while thinking. "Well, we have two girls with us who have some serious powers. I hate to ask you to use them again, but it might be the only way."

Cindy lets out a laugh. "You really want to unleash Joselyn's power again?"

"Like I said, it might be the only way."

"Whatever. It's your funeral," Cindy mumbles.

"Do ya have a better plan?" Matthias barks.

"How did you and Loverboy escape the city?" Cindy asks me.

I frown at her. "*David* cut a hole in the chain-link fence, and we climbed under it. We were skinny back then, so we didn't need to cut much."

"That's not going to work here. The fence has hot wires," Eli says. He looks at our confused faces and explains. "They're wired with electricity."

"Really? That seems extreme," I say.

"That's why I had to work so hard to make connections with some of the guards. The only way into the city is through the gate or across the lake, but even that is monitored pretty heavily."

"Charlotte, do you think you could sing our way out?" I ask.

Charlotte looks at me uncertainly, shaking her head slightly. "I can't. I'm too scared."

"Baby, there's nothing to be scared of. You have a wonderful gift!" Alexandrine throws in.

"I know, Mama. But it makes my throat hurt."

"Oh, for Pete's sake! You're gonna have to sing, or we're stuck in here," Matthias says callously.

"Don't talk to my daughter that way, Matthias."

"Then ya better explain to her she can't chicken out now." He and Alexandrine stand almost toe to toe.

"You all better calm down, or we're bound to be heard." Eli looks around nervously.

"While you idiots were arguing, I hashed out a plan." Cindy picks at her teeth. We all watch her as she impolitely finishes picking out whatever it was stuck in her teeth and sucks it off her fingernail.

"Care to share your plan?" Eli says impatiently.

"Huh?" She glances around at us, confused.

"The plan! The plan you said you hashed out to get us out of the city!" Eli says loudly but then bites his lips together.

"Oh, right. That," she says as though she suddenly remembers.

The adults throw their hands up in exasperation.

"It's simple. You people will stay put out of range while Jossy does her power surge thing and knocks the electric fence offline. Bada bing, bada boom! We cut the fence and escape."

"I don't know. What if the guards hear her screaming and come check it out while we're trying to cut the fence?" I interject.

"She doesn't have to scream to use her powers. She just keeps them buried deep down until she has a freak-out and loses control of them."

"Well, what do we use to cut it?" Alexandrine asks.

"I don't have all the answers here, people," Cindy replies. "If you don't like my idea, come up with one of your own."

"It's not a bad plan, Cindy. We just need to figure out the details," Eli says.

I watch as Cindy gets her twisted smile again, the one she uses when she wants us to be "best friends." Looks like Eli made her best friend list.

"I don't suppose anyone has a tool for cuttin'?" Matthias asks.

"I have a multipurpose tool, but there's no way it's going to cut through a fence," Eli says.

We stop talking for a moment when we hear a strange siren. The sound is coming closer, and I see flashing red and blue lights down the street. We all duck down quickly behind a bush and watch as it turns onto a different road.

"What was that?" I ask.

"An old police car that the guards use from time to time," Eli answers.

"Police?" Cindy asks.

"Back before the Coalition was put into place, police officers used to keep the peace. Law and order," Eli explains.

Cindy nods as though she understands, but her expression reads otherwise.

"If your multitool has pliers, then I have an idea of how we can get out," Alexandrine says, getting back on topic. "Joselyn will knock the power out, and as soon as she does, we'll use the pliers to untwist the top and bottom connections and then unweave the fence. I've done it before at our old city."

"That fence is at least twelve feet tall. How are you going to reach the top?" Eli asks skeptically.

"I'm a good climber. I'll climb up there and do it," I offer.

"Fine. Let's go. We've been standin' here yackin' for too long," Matthias says.

42

We head off to a part of town far enough away from the gate that we should be safe. It's mostly rundown buildings over here, making me think of the bad part of my home city. Let's hope it's empty and not full of criminals.

Matthias picks a building that still has all four walls, and we tuck ourselves inside it while Cindy reassures us she's got this. I don't like relying on Cindy with something this important, but we need Joselyn.

"I'll make Jossy come out, and then you guys will have to explain what to do."

"Should we plug our ears or something?" Eli asks.

"Her powers don't have anything to do with sound," Cindy answers condescendingly, as though it were obvious. Then she turns and walks a few paces away. "Jossy. We need you to do this thing for us. Pretty please, come out and use your 'knock out' power to cut the electricity. The peeps need you."

Quiet.

"Don't be such a baby! You could actually help people this time."

Silence.

"If you don't come out now, I'll punch you in the face!" Cindy threatens.

It is so strange seeing Cindy talking to herself. Her face darkens as she stands around, waiting for Joselyn to show up. Without warning, Cindy punches herself right across the chin, hard.

"Ow!" she says, tears forming in her eyes as she holds her face. "What just happened to me?"

"Joselyn?" I ask.

"Yeah. What's going on?"

We explain the plan to her, and she seems reluctant to help.

Charlotte steps up to her and gives her a hug. "It's okay to be scared about your power, but if you don't do this, Joselyn, we aren't going to make it out of here."

Joselyn seems to understand what Charlotte's saying but still looks unsettled.

"This is the last time we'll ask you to do this," I say. "You're not hurting anyone anyway. Just knocking out the power so we can get out of here."

Joselyn looks around at us for a moment and then seems to make up her mind. "Okay. I'll do it," she says, voice quivering a bit.

We watch from the doorway as she works her way to the chain-link fence. Matthias keeps the gun out and ready in case she needs help. Joselyn holds her hands out in front of her, standing with her legs shoulder-width apart. Her back is turned to us, so I can't see what she's doing, but suddenly, the fence starts sparking and making loud snapping noises. Then it stops just as quickly as it started. I could feel the pressure inside my head while she was using her ability, but it was more like a bad headache than intense squeezing.

We race over to the fence to get started before anyone notices. Charlotte gives Joselyn a high five once we get to her, and I rub her arm a little, giving her a thumbs up.

"You did great!" I whisper, and she smiles proudly.

Alexandrine holds a flashlight for Matthias to see, keeping her hand over the end to conceal most of the beam. Matthias pulls a long weed out of the ground and holds it against the fence to check if it's still live. He seems satisfied.

"Hand the tool here, Elijah," Matthias says.

Eli pulls the multitool out of a pouch that's hooked on his belt and slaps it onto Matthias's outstretched hand. Working quickly, Matthias undoes a couple of wires that hold the fence to the metal frame at the base. Then he untwists two wires of the fence that are twined together at the bottom.

"How will I know what ones to untwist at the top?"

Matthias strokes his beard a moment as he thinks of a plan. "Anyone have a length of rope?"

I pull the bag off my shoulders and dig out the paracord roll I have and hand it to Matthias. He crouches down and ties the cord to the fence where he just untwisted it.

"Now, climb up to the top, pull the cord straight, and ya should have the right spot to untwist." Matthias hands the tool to me.

I slip it into my front pocket, feeling nervous about this. Everyone is relying on me, and I'm afraid to mess this up. Matthias gives me a gentle pat on the shoulder. I throw the cord over my shoulder before grabbing on to the fence to start my climb. The toes of my shoes are too round to fit in the links, so I do the bulk of the climb with my arms while pushing my feet hard against the fence. By the time I reach the top, my hands are so sore, I can barely hold on any longer. Climbing trees is far easier than this.

199

I make it to the metal bar at the top and wrap my arm over it to hold myself up. The twisted sections of the fence dig into my armpit, making me work as quickly as I can to get this over with. I pull the cord straight until I find the connection I need to untwist. Fumbling around, I try to dig the tool out of my right pocket with my left hand since my right arm is holding me up. My hand is so slick, I almost drop it. My pulse is racing, and my hands are trembling so bad, I can barely manipulate the tool to do what needs to be done. I recognize these as the symptoms of a panic attack, and that makes me freak out just a little bit more. I really can't have one right now. I close my eyes, trying to focus my mind. After a few breaths, I've calmed down enough to get back to what I was doing.

With a lot of effort, I untwist the top part of the chain and put the tool back into my pocket, where it's safe. I glance down at the faces looking at me and give them an okay gesture. I decide I can't climb back down because my hands are still sore, so I drop and do a roll once I hit the ground. Joselyn and Charlotte clap enthusiastically until Alexandrine shushes them, and they do a silent clap instead.

I put my bag back on as the two men get to work, twisting a piece of the fence like it's a screw. It looks like a loose spring as it comes unlinked with the rest of the fence. I watch as the top parts fall open now that they're no longer being held together. Excitement courses through me until I hear light footsteps coming toward us.

I look to the right and see guards wearing night-vision goggles headed our way. They've got their guns pointed at us, and I put my hands up to show them I'm unarmed.

"They found us!" I alert everyone.

Matthias immediately stops what he's doing and goes to pull his gun out.

"Hands where we can see them!" a guard yells, training his gun on Matthias.

It looks like Matthias doesn't want to comply, but he seems to think better of trying to take on that many guards and puts his hands up slowly.

The guards march over to where we're standing, and I hear Joselyn whisper, "You got this."

Charlotte lets out a little whimper, but then Joselyn takes her hand and squeezes. That seems to give her courage.

"Ears!" Joselyn shouts, and we all cover our ears.

As the guards try to understand what's going on, Charlotte starts singing, and they crumple to the ground. All except one guard. Why didn't he fall like the rest of them? As he turns his head, I notice the hearing aid stuck in his ear. He turns his gun toward Charlotte, and in the time it takes me to register what's happening, Joselyn steps in front of Charlotte just as the guard pulls the trigger.

I let out a scream, but surprisingly, Joselyn seems unharmed. The guard hesitates too long, confused by why Joselyn is still standing, and Matthias takes that pause to shoot the guard, showing no mercy once again. Charlotte is still singing quietly, but her voice is wavering. If she can't keep it up, the other guards will wake up and catch us.

I desperately want to ask Joselyn if she has bulletproof abilities too, but we need to get out of here. The men work even faster at untwisting the fence until it finally falls open. Alexandrine guides the girls through the fence, and I jump when I hear sirens coming our direction.

"Hurry!" I shout as I climb through the fence. Once we're all through, we take off at a fast run through the city ruins.

Eli leads us down roads I don't remember walking on when coming to the city, but I trust he knows his way back to his compound. We take breaks to catch our breath, hidden in copses of leafless trees that used to be manicured parks or large yards, now overgrown and wild. I listen for sirens or footsteps, but from what I can tell, there's nobody following us.

Hours pass by as we hurry our way back to the compound, my fingers frozen from the chilly air. With temperatures like this, it feels like it won't be long before the first snowfall happens. I wonder where we will be when winter finally comes. Does Matthias have a plan?

It seems like we've been running all night, and just when I start to worry that maybe we're lost, the towering pine trees that hide Eli's compound come into view. I almost cry in relief at the sight. He leads us through the fence and guides us to the barn, promising a roaring fire and hot chocolate to drink. I'd like to wake up David, but it's only a couple more hours until sunrise. I'll just let him sleep.

We all wait around patiently as Eli sets to work building a fire. I take this moment to ask Joselyn the question that has been burning the back of my mind. "Joselyn, are you bulletproof?"

"What?"

"You stepped in front of Charlotte just as the guard shot at her, and nothing happened to you."

"I did?" she asks, confused.

"Yeah! It was really cool of you," Charlotte says.

"Very brave," Alexandrine says, not unkindly. "Thank you for that, by the way."

"I have no idea what you guys are talking about. I was shot?"

I watch her to see if she's pulling our legs, but she seems sincere. "You black out when someone takes over. Maybe it's Cindy who's bulletproof," I suggest.

"I think each of my personalities have a different ability, but only one each," Joselyn says thoughtfully.

"Well, let's go through them then. You have knock-out power that affects both people and electrical things," I begin, listing them off with my fingers. "Cindy can handle trauma and shields you. Jack can talk to the dead..."

Joselyn nods.

"But there's one more. Who am I missing? I feel like I'm missing someone."

Joselyn scratches at her head as she tries to remember who I'm talking about. She runs her hand over her hair and feels the fly-aways from her ponytail. She pulls the hair tie out and shakes her head, finger combing the snarls out. Her long black hair momentarily falls over her face, covering half of it. Then it hits me.

"Landon! What about Landon?" I ask. "Maybe he's the one who can dodge bullets," I say excitedly.

"What do you mean 'dodge'?" Alexandrine asks. "She was standing still when they shot."

"You're right," I say, absentmindedly rubbing the still-present lump on my head.

"Maybe," Charlotte begins meekly, "he's not dodging them but making them move through the air to avoid hitting their target?"

"You know what? You could be right," I say, thinking about what I had seen earlier. The guard shot right at Joselyn, but the bullet never hit her. "That would be so cool!"

Eli has the fire lit, and I can feel the warmth radiating from it, taking the chill out of the air. "All right, let's see what's on the USB stick."

Cindy sets the laptop on the table, and everyone gathers around as Eli pushes the power button. The screen lights up, and we watch as it goes through its power-up process. Finally, a picture of the coalition flag shows up on the login screen with a spot in the center to type in the password.

"Crap! Anyone have any idea what the password could be?" I ask.

"The battery isn't going to last forever, so we can't spend too much time trying to figure it out," Eli says wisely. "I may have to see if I can do a factory reset, but let me just try something first." We watch as he types something into the box. He hits enter, and the screen changes to the desktop screen. "Idiots," Eli says, shaking his head.

"How did you do that?" I ask. "What did you type in?"

"'adminadmin.' It's a default password that, apparently, these morons were too lazy to change. Or too cocky, thinking nobody would ever get ahold of their computer."

"How do ya know so much about computers?" Matthias asks.

"I meet people inside the city, Brother. Some of those people are beautiful women who take me back to their place and teach me a thing or two." Eli smiles slyly.

Alexandrine curls her lips at him in disgust.

I pull the USB stick out from under my shirt and unhook the chain. I hand it over to Eli, who plugs it into the computer. A little alert shows up in the bottom corner, prompting us to click it to open. Eli clicks it, and we watch as a screen comes up with a list of files. Some of the files have names, while others are just gibberish.

"What the heck are those?" I point to the files that make no sense.

"Those are encrypted files. We're not going to be able to look at those right now," he says, clicking on a file that reads "Entry1."

I try to read it, but I don't quite understand what it says.

"You've got to be kiddin' me," Matthias mutters in shock. He's up on his feet, shoulder to shoulder with Eli as they click on another file.

"What?" I ask.

"You gonna tell us what's going on?" Alexandrine snarls.

"The Haven isn't a city," Matthias starts to say, and I fall back into my chair, disappointed at the news. Matthias continues, "The Haven is the United States. The US still exists out there."

At that moment, Matthias is interrupted by someone slamming the barn door open. "Someone's here to talk to you, Eli."

"Who could it be at this hour?" Eli says, frustrated at being pulled away from what he was doing.

Two of Eli's men walk in, leading someone who has their hands up in surrender. The two men move to the side, revealing who it is. I let out a gasp.

"I'm alone and unarmed. I've just come to talk," Janice says sincerely.

As Eli is about to respond, Matthias turns from the laptop, pulls out his gun, and shoots her.

SUICIDE PREVENTION

If you are feeling suicidal or an urge to harm yourself,
please, find someone to talk to.

You are not alone.

If you can't talk to a family member or a friend, reach out to
the National Suicide Prevention Lifeline:

1-800-273-8255

or

www.suicidepreventionlifeline.org

You have a purpose.
Don't ever give up.

ACKNOWLEDGMENTS

Thank you to my Maker for all he has done for me.

Thank you, Sage, for being the best husband ever. You have never stopped supporting me in my writing endeavors, and that has meant the world to me.

Thank you to my fans who encourage me to keep writing. Your enthusiasm helps me to not give up, even when my self-doubt rears its ugly head!

Thank you to the ladies at Authors 4 Authors for helping me get my book out into the world, making my writing dream come true.

I want to give a special thank you to Kari Donald, who went through my manuscript with a fine-toothed comb and got all my timing problems fixed up. I appreciate it.

ABOUT THE AUTHOR

Diane lives in central Wisconsin with her husband and three boys. When not reading or writing, she likes to go hiking as often as she can. Her favorite trail—so far—is the Ice Age Trail with Skunk Foster Lake being her favorite section of it.

Diane's fascination with superheroes sparked the idea for her first novel, *Supernova*, taking some inspiration from X-Men.

Diane can also be found serving as an Awana leader at her local church. She has been serving there for ten years.

Follow her online:

www.dianeanthony.info
Twitter: @DianeMAnthony
Facebook: @DianeMAnthony

Also by Diane Anthony
SUPERNOVA

When librarian Madeline Hayes wakes up in the front yard with no
memory of why she's there, her simple life in a small town becomes
more complicated than she ever imagined. Strange things start
happening: her father heals an injury with a touch, her elderly
neighbor seems to become younger, and everyone starts getting this
strange blue light in their eyes—and in their veins.

And then people start dying.

Can Madeline unravel this mystery and stop the strange
transformations before it's too late?

books2read.com/supernova

Authors 4 Authors Publishing

A publishing company for authors, run by authors, blending the best of traditional and independent publishing

We specialize in speculative fiction: science fiction, fantasy, paranormal, and romance. Get lost in another world!

Check out our collection at https://books2read.com/rl/a4a or visit Authors4AuthorsPublishing.com/books

For updates, scan the QR code or visit our website to join our semi-monthly newsletter!

Want more YA Science-Fiction? We recommend:

Hard as Stone
by Beatrice B. Morgan

Seventeen-year-old Raven Thane wants an adventure...and she's going to get one. Just not the way that she expected. Bored and disinterested with a routine life in her remote underground community, she fails to notice a thief during her turn at guard duty. Zander, a charming sharpshooter, tasks her with helping him retrieve the mysterious stolen item. Can Raven fix her mistake and prove herself more than a simple country girl? Or will she create even more chaos?

books2read.com/hardstone

www.ingramcontent.com/pod-product-compliance
Lightning Source LLC
Chambersburg PA
CBHW010735100726
47899CB00009B/3061